Quarter *life* Crisis

Anshuk Attri

Quarter *life* Crisis

Anshuk Attri

pblishing.com
write • share • connect • publish

Quarter Life Crisis by Anshuk Attri

Published by www.pblishing.com

pblishing.com
write • share • connect • publish

Marketed by

Maple Press Private Limited
sales office A 63, Sector 58, Noida 201 301, U.P., India
phone +91 120 455 3581, 455 3583
email info@maplepress.co.in
website www.maplepress.co.in

ISBN: 978-81-93324-82-0

Printed in India at Yash Printographics, Noida

10 9 8 7 6 5 4 3 2 1

Table of Contents

Prologue 9
Chapter I 13
Chapter II 20
Chapter III 34
Chapter IV 50
Chapter V 59
Chapter VI 64
Chapter VII 71
Chapter VIII 85
Chapter IX 95
Chapter X 105
Chapter XI 117
Chapter XII 126
Chapter XIII 136
Chapter XIV 147
Chapter XV 156

Chapter XVI 165
Chapter XVII 170
Chapter XVIII 177
Chapter XIX 187
Chapter XX 195
Chapter XXI 207
Chapter XXII 218
Chapter XXIII 226
Chapter XXIV 235
Chapter XXV 243
Chapter XXVI 250
Chapter XXVII 258
Chapter XXVIII 266
Chapter XXIX 274
Chapter XXX 281
Chapter XXXI 297
Acknowledgements 301
About the author 303

Prologue

"Work hard son; make something of your life." Those were words I had been hearing ever since I was a child. But *why* must I do so? That was never told to me. Maybe it was because my parents themselves had no clear answer to this question, except that the current economic system forces everyone to engage in a vocation. "Work or perish of hunger" - brilliantly motivating words for our kind!

Finding their son aimless and without a purpose, my parents took it upon themselves to plan my life for me. I did not resist; after all, they were older than me and I felt they knew a thing or two about existence.

Like an obedient child, I followed the path set before me, and worked towards *their* goal of having an engineer for a son. I performed above average, class after class, year after year. It was not all bad I must admit. I discovered that science was a field hardly anyone could resist falling in love with. By the time I finished high school, I willingly accepted the turf of applied sciences.

Sadly, the euphoria was short lived. During my first engineering class, I realised that I had lost the motivation to learn.

Why must I endure a lesson about differential equations? Why should I not go and have a nap in my room instead? I would keep asking myself. Learning is pointless without the will.

Anyhow, like every other student in India, I managed to slog for a bachelor's degree. I was not ready for life in the 'real world'. Not surprisingly, when reality was shoved down my throat, I choked.

What followed was a journey that pushed me towards adulthood. Who wants to grow up? I resisted too; but in spite of everything I did, I was handed responsibilities that I did not sign up for.

Thinking back, I feel that it all started with meeting Neera at school. Her father had been transferred from Una, a district in the serene state of Himachal Pradesh, to Shimla. As luck would have it, they settled in the same locality as my family. We grew up together, becoming close friends, and, finally, joining the same university.

She had brown eyes, jet black curly hair, and a smile radiant enough to solve India's energy crisis. Her aura was enchanting, and her lively nature endearing. One might doubt the words I write in praise of this maiden after I mention that she and I started dating in the ninth grade, but believe you me, any beholder, whether old or young, man, woman, or someone of the third sex, would have described her as stupefyingly beautiful.

A hard working girl, she was clear about her goal to become an officer in the Indian Allied Services. On the other hand, I was, to put it delicately, a little lost. Even though she and I were different people, we managed to form a strong relationship based on trust and honesty. Having her in my life made me want a purpose, made me want to make something of myself.

I always felt lucky to have her. She was definitely 'out of my league', and I never understood why she loved me the way she did. With every passing day, our bond became stronger. Eventually, as we were about to complete graduation, she started discussing our engagement with me.

Neera and I were meant to end up with each other. We knew it since we started dating. Our families knew it, so did our relatives. All my teenage years, I had known no other future, but even then,

I never understood why I did not want things to change between us. It was not that I lacked the will to commit to spending a lifetime with her, but that I wanted to wait to see what lay ahead of me.

Amidst all this disarray, God or chance, who I know not, intervened and inevitably bound me to her.

CHAPTER I

On a blistering June afternoon, I was walking through the campus, occasionally wiping my forehead with a handkerchief. The class on Rocket Propulsion 407 had just concluded and my hostel room seemed miles away.

A screech of tyres made me swivel around only to be greeted by a round-faced boy, with short, trimmed hair, wearing square-framed glasses and a wide grin. He was a little overweight, which was not a big problem for the old Pulsar motorcycle he rode.

"Yo, Prachur," he said. "Do you want a lift to the hostel?"

I nodded and climbed onto the back seat of his bike. "Can we go and get some cigarettes first, please?"

Mudit and I were batchmates at the State College of Engineering, Chandigarh - a decent campus spread out in the entire Sector 13. The streets were clean and lined with trees. No building was more than three storeys tall and most of them were brick red in colour. There was a certain gloom over the premises, a pall of mediocrity, which I guess is common in most government institutions. All things considered, this campus probably would not find a place in the *Architectural Digest,* but to me, it was my second home.

Our journey to Ram Ji, the infamous cigarette vendor, located barely a hundred metres from the college gate, was quick.

"Two Marlboro Golds, Ram Ji," I said, alighting from the bike.

We lit the cigarettes and sat on a low black metal fence that separated the road and a well-maintained park.

"I hear that you won't be appearing for the interviews tomorrow?" Mudit enquired.

We were to graduate by the end of July. It was a slow time for us; our final examinations were due next month and nearly every student had received an offer for a job.

"Yeah, I won't," I replied.

"Why, may I ask?"

"I don't want to take up a job yet. No other reason," I replied, apathetically.

"Bro, you need to just show up there looking decent. It's a mass recruiter. The job is yours if you want it."

I did not answer.

When you know someone for a long time, you know the meaning of their small gestures. He sensed my silence meant that I did not want to pursue the topic anymore, and he did not push it. On finishing our cigarettes, we rode back to the college gates. Once inside the campus, instead of driving us straight back to the hostel, he took a detour through the section with the academic buildings to — as he loved to put it — "check out the local flora and fauna".

We drove past the Civil Engineering Department, and turned towards a crowded road.

"Really?" I asked him. "You want to do this now? Can't we just go to our hostel? I'm tired."

"You have a girlfriend. I don't. I need to find one, and for that I need to see what's out there. Only two minutes, OK? After that, we go."

I must say that he was quite a skilled rider — he could drive fixating on the girls we passed, without even glancing at the road.

"Oye, Neera's there. Let me get off, please," I said, pointing at a tall girl sitting under a flight of stairs leading up to the college canteen.

I jumped off the bike and told him that I would find my way back to the hostel. After he drove away, I waved at Neera and walked towards her.

Looking gorgeous in a dark brown shirt and blue denim jeans, she shaded her face with her hand, and squinted at me. She wore an earring only in her left ear, not because she did not have a pair, but as a conscious fashion choice.

"You look breathtaking," I said, helping her stand up. "What're you doing here?"

"I have a class in twenty minutes," she answered, in her angelic voice. "Yukti and Yashika have gone up to the canteen to buy something. I'm waiting for them."

She and I were not in the same course. I was pursuing Aerospace Engineering, while she was studying Electronics Engineering. She had got admission in a college of a much higher reputation than ours, but had chosen to study with me.

"How was your day?" she enquired, beaming.

"Boring. I've already attended three classes since morning. I'm done. I am going back to my room to sleep."

"Don't you have your lab this afternoon?"

"I do. I'll skip it."

She shook her head and asked, "Anyway, did you talk to your family about us?"

"Not yet. I'll do it soon, though."

"Prachur, you promised you'll do it by this morning," she sulked.

"I forgot. Sorry."

"Don't you want to?"

Obviously, I could not tell her that I dreaded talking to my parents about us for reasons that I did not quite understand. So I said, "Of course, I want to, baby. Why wouldn't I? I will talk to them soon. You need to give me some time. I'm just a bit shy, I guess. Anyway, you haven't told your parents either. Why don't you do it first? There's no way they'll agree!"

"I did, yesterday. My mother said that it's better for us to get engaged. She thinks it'll give our relationship a name. What's your excuse?"

Having no answer, I reiterated that I would do it soon, but she was not happy.

"You're impossible," she said. "Sometimes I feel you have no intention of being with me after college."

I was saved by the arrival of Yukti and Yashika.

Yukti, a slightly chubby girl with broad shoulders, was dressed in a checked tee and blue denims. Her nose was a little crooked because a kid had punched her 'accidentally' when she was six. Her habit of correcting people's grammar in her nasal voice often invited offers to restore her nose to its former glory, but I, personally, found her genial.

Yashika was a tall, thin girl with hungry looks and a sharp chin. She had black hair, which she wore in a bun.

"Hi," I said to both of them.

"Hello, Prachur," Yukti replied, cheerfully.

"Why does Neera look sad?" Yashika asked me. "What did you do, Prachur?"

I shrugged and she rolled up her eyes. I knew she despised me, and the feeling was mutual.

"Let's go," she said, tugging Neera's arm.

Neera gave me a defeated look, following which, they all left, with only Yukti bidding me goodbye.

Drearily, I walked back to my hostel room.

+++

After spending the evening with Mudit, working on a few assignments that I was supposed to submit the next day, we decided to go out for a drink. With this intent, he and I rode his bike to Sector 17.

The centre of life in Chandigarh City, Sector 17 has heavily lit shops, always brimming with people; the bars are fancy but surprisingly cheap; and you can buy pretty much anything, maybe not babies or planes, but a plethora of other useful items.

We had some trouble finding a parking spot, and after securing our helmets to the bike, we walked to Leo's - my favourite place to drink in the city.

Drinks kept pouring and hours passed. At about half past ten, Mudit suggested that we ride back to our college, to our friend Sanchit's room, and continue the festivities.

Mudit proudly claimed to be an exemplary drunk driver, which, when I think with a little maturity, is not a skill to take pride in. Thankfully, when we finally jumped off the bike outside Sanchit's hostel, our limbs were intact and my phone and wallet were safely in my pockets.

Sanchit was a fresher living in the first year hostel, where no seniors were allowed since ragging was a concern. We scaled the wall on the back side of the building and walked to his room through a garden with knee-high grass.

The wooden door of the room opened, and a thin boy peeped outside. His orange t-shirt was stained with food, and his eyes were red.

"Hi, brother," Mudit said, hugging him. They were distantly related.

"Hi, guys!" he replied. "Care for some *Maal?*"

I smiled and entered his room. We spent the next hour or two smoking and ranting about the terrible times he was going to have during the rest of his stint in college; and how he should value his time as a fresher, after which Mudit and I took our leave and walked out of his room.

"Don't you miss our time here?" Mudit asked.

"I do," I murmured, as I bent down to take a sip from a water cooler.

"Remember we used to drink up there," he said, pointing to the top floor of one of the buildings.

I nodded and reminisced about the past. Barely four years ago, I had first visited this hostel. Getting old is something no one desires, but apparently, time does not care.

We walked through a dark corridor, occasionally stopping to greet a few other friends. Soon, we reached the wall behind which stood Mudit's bike, and we were trying to scale it, when we heard someone shout, "Hey! Stop there!"

We turned around and saw four people standing behind us, flashing a torch light.

"Is it you Thakur?" a deep voice said to me.

Instantly, I recognised the voice. It belonged to our professor, Dr Kumar. From what I could make out, he was standing with three security guards.

"Yes, Sir. It is," I replied. "Is there a problem?"

"Yes, there is a problem," he snapped. "You're trying to scale a wall out of a place that you're not allowed into. Both you and Mudit Garg, come with me. Don't you dare try anything stupid!"

We glanced at each other, and quietly followed him. The sky was clear and the wind pleasant. What a beautiful night to be incriminated!

He led us to the mess hall of the hostel, and ordered us to sit at one of the tables.

I should have realised the severity of the situation we were in, but a brain stewed in alcohol and marijuana does not care much for the future. The only emotion I felt was anger, at Prof. Kumar for ruining our night.

"Do you know that you're not allowed into the first year hostel?" asked he, standing beside me.

We nodded, reluctantly. I was staring at the table, so I could not look at him, but I could imagine him rubbing his bald head, as was his habit, while he searched for the right words.

"This is why I conduct these random searches," he said, pompously. "If you are the warden of a hostel you must care about the students living in it." Maybe he was expecting us to applaud, and when we did not react, he enquired, "Were you here to rag your juniors?"

"No, Sir," we answered, in chorus.

"I can smell alcohol on this one," one of the security guards with a stubble, stated, sniffing Mudit. His manner of conduct made me suspect that he was drunk himself.

"Both of you are drunk and in the first year hostel so late into the night!" Prof. Kumar said. "How dare you?"

We said nothing and looked at each other.

"What is wrong with you?" he continued his rhetorical enquiries. "Don't you know how big an offence ragging is? You can be expelled for this."

"We were only here to meet our friend, Sir, nothing else," I slurred.

"And where is this friend?"

"He's sleeping, Sir," Mudit droned, in an effort to keep Sanchit out of the controversy.

Prof. Kumar shook his head and a look of disgust and anger streaked his face. He took out a small notepad from his front pocket, and proceeded to scribble something on one of the pages. Following this, he stared at us and said, "Now I want you two to go back directly to your hostel. You are supposed to report at the DSW's office tomorrow at eleven. He'll be the one taking care of this. You two are in a heap of trouble."

Mudit thought it wise to bribe Dr Kumar.

"Maybe we could reach a compromise, Sir. Do you want anything?" he asked, making a gesture of smoking a joint. "Maybe I could get some for you."

"What?" asked Prof. Kumar, bewildered.

"Nothing, Sir. We must head back to our hostel," I replied.

Prof. Kumar began to say something, and before he could, Mudit and I rushed out of the mess hall.

"Screw him," Mudit said, as we walked to his bike, this time through the hostel's gate.

CHAPTER II

June mornings are noisy and bright in Chandigarh. The sun has a habit of rising early and birds mistake themselves for professional singers. Dogs enjoy talking to others of their kind. If that were not enough, you can hear constant honking of cars without restrain.

My hostel shared the same characteristics; it was loud - even at the crack of dawn, you could hear people waddling about.

When I woke up the morning after my encounter with Dr Kumar, I had faint memories of my antics from the previous night.

"I am never drinking again!" I said to myself, as I woke up.

Lying on my stomach with my face in a small puddle of my own drool, I was sweating, even though the ceiling fan was doing its best to keep the room cool. I rolled over, took out a cigarette from the box in my pocket, and lit it up. It was 7:45 a.m. and my Economics 442 Class was going to begin at 8.

On finishing the cigarette, I walked out of the room and looked around before I shut the door.

It had to be criminal to make an engineering student live in that scantily furnished room. I could count the number of things in the room on my fingers, and still have a few to spare. There was a foldable metal bed; a brown wooden table; an old ceiling fan that barely worked; and a metal chair, whose paint was withering away. The pallid walls were meant to induce depression, and on the wall opposite to the door, there was a large closet with a blue door and no hangers inside. The management of the college clung to a firm belief that these 'luxuries' were all that a student needed to survive.

I locked the door, pushed it to double check if it stayed locked, and by and by, found myself rushing to Mudit's room.

"Get up! It's almost eight," I shouted, banging on his door.

I heard him slump out of bed and walk to open the door. His eyes were nearly shut and his hair dishevelled.

"What time is it?" he drawled, in a voice heavy with sleep.

"7:50. Go, go, go!"

He picked up the keys to his bike, a battered notebook, and his phone and we ran to the parking lot.

Within five minutes, we were scuttling inside the main college building. Being a government institution, the building was barely maintained; the dilapidated yellow walls matched the old cemented floor perfectly, and the ceiling looked as if it had overseen too many batches of students, and was ready to collapse.

Reaching the doors of our classroom, I peeped inside. The benches were arranged in rows of rising steps and could seat around a hundred. The room had a podium for the teacher on one side, and a certain moist smell, which, I was sure, was due to the water stains on the walls. My contention had been that the air we breathed in there was more mould spore than oxygen.

Luckily for us, we had reached before the professor, so we walked up to the last row and sidled onto a bench.

The academic year was coming to an end, so barely half the benches were occupied. The empty benches reminded us that the rest of the class had skipped the lesson to study for the final examinations. I looked around for Neera but could not spot her curly locks. So I took out my phone and sent her a text message, asking her where she was. After waiting a while for her reply, I put my phone back into my pocket.

Meanwhile, we were joined by our friend Riayat a short, plump guy with droopy shoulders and neatly trimmed beard. His eyes had a certain glimmer, which could deceive anyone into thinking that he was there to gather every shred of information that the world had to offer, although he attended classes only when he had nothing better to do. He studied Aeronautical Engineering with me and we attended most of the courses together. After exchanging pleasantries, I opened my notebook and turned to a new page. The page opposite to it said:

"Breaking the dead silence his footsteps roared,
I caught a glimpse of his old form, as he soared,
Past me, across the floor of the House of Lord,"

It was the first paragraph of a poem I was scribbling a few days ago in another class. I would not call myself a poet, not even an amateur one. I was just a guy who wrote lines that rhymed, and that too only occasionally. I did enjoy writing, no doubt; but I was sceptical to show it to others. Taking criticism was not something that I did very well.

What rhymes with "Lord", I mused. "Ward, marred, fard; 'fard' isn't a word..."

If people could look into my creative writing process, I would be sentenced to never touch a pen again.

Finally, after a while I wrote down:

"Walking in beat to a song with divine chords."

The poem was far from over, but since I had three more classes to struggle through, I knew that I would finish it by the end of the day.

"Still not done?" Mudit asked.

"No, I have a long way to go."

"I don't understand why you don't submit some other poem? You have so many, a lot of good ones."

"Na, man. I want to write something fresh. It's for the magazine, *Panorama,* after all. Getting published in it will be an achievement. The best thing is that they have a section for amateur poets."

"When's the deadline?"

"After our Economics exam."

He nodded, and I went back to my poem.

Not long after, Prof. Verma entered the classroom. Just a few inches above five feet, she was a stout woman with an especially shrill voice. She always had a train of students following her, asking her questions related to the course. Sometimes, I could hardly recognise them, so I had theorised that she paid people to pursue her.

As the class began, Riayat nudged me and mouthed the word 'Bingo' a game we played during classes. The rules were simple; it was similar to the commonly played Bingo, the only difference being that we would call out the numbers to strike out one by one there were no pre-printed cards. I started filling in the squares of my Bingo tile and I felt my phone vibrating in my pocket. When I took it out I saw that it had deceived me; I had received no messages or calls. The wait for Neera's reply was killing me; therefore I sent a text message to Yukti.

"Where's Neera?" it said.

Yukti was sitting a few rows ahead of me. I saw her move to take her phone out of her pocket and type a reply. It said:

"Sleeping..."

That is not so bad, I thought. She is probably tired from studying last night. After all, exams are approaching.

With this conviction, I returned to the game.

Thirty minutes into the class and games were flying; Mudit and I won a few, but Riayat's luck was not with him. There was no monetary reward for winning this game, no laurels, and certainly no fame; but if you did not win, it certainly made you angry.

"Twenty three," I said.

"Bingo! Bingo!" Riayat exclaimed, in a voice loud enough to make everyone in the class turn around.

Prof. Verma looked at us - our gazes buried in our notebooks, like dedicated students wondering, "How very interesting!"

But, she was not the one who could be fooled. We knew what was coming. She could not identify the voice, so she was going to ask a random person in our row a question; the answer to this question would determine whether or not the said person would grace the class with her/his presence for the remainder of the time.

"Mudit, tell me what topic are we discussing," she asked, nonchalantly.

"Economics," he replied, confidently.

"I would need a little more detail, Mr Adam Smith," she said.

"Indian economics," he said, with a smile.

She was not amused. "Get out," was her retort.

Mudit got up and walked out of the class, with a gait full of pride.

I took out my phone and sent him a message that said, "Don't forget, we have an appointment with DSW at 11."

The class went on and after a few games, Riayat and I got bored. So I sat still, yawning and staring at the board. The summer heat, Prof. Verma's endless drone, and the mouldy smell of the room made me fantasise about being back at home in Shimla. The chill, the beautiful hills - I loved everything about that place. I was aware that I would not have a career to pursue after I finished my degree, yet I believed that when I went back home, my life would be better than it was as a student. How wrong was I!

By and by, I received a reply from Neera.

"I am in my room," she had written.

"I was worried, you normally don't miss classes."

After a few minutes she replied, "Did you talk to your parents?"

And the conversation came back a full circle. I racked my brain and finding no suitable reply, put my phone back into my pocket. I could only talk to her after I spoke with my parents.

On conclusion of the lecture, I took leave of Riayat, and met Mudit outside the DSW's office. He stood leaning against a granite wall.

I waved and asked, "Is he in his office?"

Mudit nodded.

The cream coloured door was shut and had a name plate saying "Dr Ananth Naidu, Dean Student Welfare". At 11 a.m. sharp, Dr Kumar arrived, knocked and opened the door. He gestured that we follow him, and we did.

The office was cold, thanks to the air conditioner running on money paid by the citizens of the country in the name of taxes. Dr Naidu was sitting on a comfortable chair, with his eyes staring at a computer screen. On seeing that he had visitors, he turned to us, and looked enquiringly at Dr Kumar.

"Sir," began Prof. Kumar, "as you might recall, I told you this morning that last night I caught two final year students from the first year hostel. Here, I present them to you, for your judgement."

Prof. Naidu nodded and asked us, with an expressionless face, "Why were you two there?"

"We were meeting a friend. My brother, actually, Sir," Mudit answered.

"You are forbidden to visit the first year hostel, do you not know that?"

"We know, Sir," Mudit replied for us. "But, we were not there for anything illegal."

"Do you know that recently a lot of complaints of ragging have been received from the first year students?"

"No, Sir, we weren't aware of that," I stated.

"That is exactly why I conducted the surprise inspection," Prof. Kumar said. "And I caught you two."

"But we were not ragging anyone, Sir," I said. "Like he said, we were there to meet his brother."

"Can you tell me the name of this 'brother' and his room number?" Prof. Naidu questioned.

"We don't want him to get involved in this mess, Sir," I answered. "He won't get into any problem."

Mudit glinted at me and said, "He lives in 2-31, Sir."

"Good," replied Prof. Naidu, writing the information on a piece of paper. "I hope for your sake that he testifies that you two were with him and not ragging anyone. Also, I was made aware that you were drunk?"

We did not answer.

"This is not the first time I am seeing you for being drunk on the college premises, is it? If I remember correctly, last year, you two were caught on the roof of the Department of Architecture." He continued after a pause, "Since you two are repeat offenders, I have no option but to refer your case to a committee of professors. The hearing will take place two weeks from today. Mind you, you will receive punishment for your actions; you can even be expelled from this college. If I were you, I would gather a few witnesses to prove your innocence in the ragging matter."

We nodded and he dismissed us.

As we were walking out of the door, I heard Dr Kumar exclaim, "Very fair, Sir. Very fair!"

"Shit," Mudit sighed, as we walked to his bike.

I shook my head. I knew I should have been concerned, but my mind was occupied with the impending conversation that I had to have with my parents.

"You don't look worried," he said.

"*Meh!* It'll be terrible, probably, but I'll deal with it when we have to cross that bridge, you know?"

+++

Rest of the day was not particularly interesting; I attended a few classes, none of which I shared with Neera or Mudit. Feeling exhausted when I got back to my hostel room, I decided that I would rather sleep than have lunch.

I woke up two hours later, and, on checking my phone, saw that I had no messages from Neera. She had already asked what she wanted to know, the ball was in my court. I could not avoid the conversation of our engagement with my parents.

I lay back on the bed imagining a dialogue with my parents, and a variety of scenarios. "He can marry her and live in a cardboard box outside the house," my father said, in one of my dreams that ran wild.

After smoking a few cigarettes, I finally gathered courage to pick up the phone and call them; my mother answered. She had a standard questionnaire that I had to face every time.

"How're you?" she asked.

"Fine, Ma."

"How was your day?"

"Fine, Ma." It could be the day of the rapture and I would still tell her that my day was fine.

"Did you have your lunch?"

"Yes, Ma," I lied.

"What did you eat?"

"Food, Ma" I said, exasperated. "I have to talk to you about something important."

"OK, tell me."

I paused. None of the conversation scenarios that I had imagined had her say, "OK, tell me." All my planning fell apart; I had to ad-lib the rest of the dialogue.

"Neera and I were talking yesterday and she told me that I should talk to you about our future. Neera and my future, I mean."

"What do you want to talk about?"

"About our engagement."

She said nothing, so I continued, "She wants us to talk about it. I know that this idea's crazy because I don't know about my future, but it's important for her. She wants us to get engaged right out of college. What do you think?"

"I understand," she said. "I think I should talk to your father about this. He's sitting right beside me. Hold on a minute."

I heard her cover the mouth of the phone and murmur something to my father. My father took the phone from her, and after assuring himself of my well-being by asking a series of questions, he said, "You're barely twenty one, Prachur. Don't you think you should wait a little? Maybe you can wait one year, see if you can make something of your life. An engagement at this point is a big commitment."

"It's just an engagement, Papa. We can think about the rest in the future."

"I know, Son," he said, concerned. "But you are much too young for this. In my opinion, you should wait. If you want, I can talk to her family about this."

"No, please don't talk to her family," was my reply. "It's better if Neera does it herself."

My mother took the phone from my father and asked, "Prachur, should I talk to Neera? We're very close, you know."

"No, Ma." I said. "Thank you, though."

"Also, her parents are not your biggest fans", she said.

"Yeah, I am aware of that, Ma."

"Honey, your father thinks you should wait, so do I; but, we'll be with you in whatever you choose to do. If you tell me right now that your wish is to get engaged to her after finishing college, we won't object. She's very sweet and I am really fond of her; your father approves of her too. I am happy with whatever makes you happy. If you and Neera have decided something, I am going to support you."

"Thanks, Ma. So I should tell Neera that you guys are on board, right?"

"Yes, Son. Here, talk to your father."

"Anything that makes you happy, Son," said he, before we bid our goodbyes.

Finally, I had my parents' approval. I sent a text message to Neera saying I wanted to meet her and in the conversation that followed we planned to have dinner together.

My brain was torn asunder by conflicting thoughts. I knew that I should be happy, but I was neither delighted, nor sad; I felt empty.

We live in a world with so much stimulation that I have been desensitised to happiness, I convinced myself.

+++

As I walked to meet Neera, my mind was occupied with the conversation that I had had with Prof. Naidu. I could not stop imagining Neera's face, riddled with shock, sorrow, and disappointment, if I were to be expelled or reprimanded in any way for my actions. There are some people you never want to disappoint; Neera and my sister were those people for me. I decided that I would keep my predicament from Neera, unless it became absolutely necessary to enlighten her.

I was headed to the local market inside our campus; it usually took me about fifteen minutes to walk to it from my hostel. The evening air was pleasant and the sidewalk was beautifully lit. Even someone who loathed walking as much as I did would have enjoyed that beautiful man-made scenery.

The worry about the disciplinary hearing made me fancy a smoke, but since there was a chance that I could run into a professor of mine, I held back. Smokers were regarded as heretics in the academic circles of our college; legality did not justify consumption.

People were swarming the campus, a consequence of a cool evening that follows a scorching day, walking and discussing matters of great subjective importance. There was a particular serenity on their faces, the kind achieved through figuring out the complicacies of life. At least that was the impression I had; maybe they were excellent pretenders, drifting through life as thespians in a play, directed apparently by God. Was I the only one who saw murkiness in his future?

It did not take me long to find Neera after I reached the market. She was sitting inside one of the restaurants that we preferred. I went and sat beside her; she said nothing and just kept looking at me.

"I talked to my parents," I said.

"Oh! That's great! What did they say?"

"That I should do what makes me happy."

"Would our engagement make you happy?" She sounded doubtful; it was precedented, my tone made it so.

"Certainly," I said. Her look told me that I needed to continue, and that I did. "Neera, we have been friends since we were kids. I know that you make me happy, as happy as a human being can make another. And you know me better than anyone, so you understand my problems. I have nothing about my future our future figured out. Ever since we were kids, I was accused of being a bad influence on you; this is one of the reasons your parents hate me." She started to speak but I interrupted her, "Please, let me finish. I know what you want to say that your parents don't hate me. Maybe they don't, but they surely don't like me much. They expect great things from you and they see me as a considerably long detour on your path to achieving what you deserve. I mean, they were so hysterical when you gave up your seat at IIT, Delhi and joined this college. That's why I think that if you were to wait for me to find something to do after I get my degree, I think you and I could have a better future. At least, I would know for certain that I am not holding you back."

I thoroughly believed what I said. It was strange to me how my deepest thoughts came out only when I ruminated aloud in Neera's presence. Honesty is a very important pillar of a relationship; thankfully, we did not suffer from a want of it.

"Prachur," she said, smiling and holding my hands, "I understand completely what you feel. But you are not holding me back; you can never hold me back. I make my own choices. And besides, like you say — it is our life; not my life, not your life, but our life. My life's goals have always included you. You are not someone who would make me choose between my career and yourself, I know that. So, stop being silly."

"You always know what to say," I said.

"This engagement was always our plan," she continued. "It's an emotional thing for me, and I like to believe, especially because you have accepted it a hundred times in conversations before, for you as well. A year ago, I would have never been uncertain of your intentions or your feelings; it is only because of you acting aloof in the past few months that I ask you, repeatedly, about your happiness. I feel awful to doubt you, but I have never been uncertain about our future. Being engaged after getting out of college, getting married in a year or two, having three kids, and living happily ever after — that was always our plan, wasn't it? But these days, whenever I see you, I feel that you have changed your mind."

"Yes, Love, that always was our plan and always will be," I said.

"Two kids, though, not three."

"Three," she said, sternly.

"Yeah, because that's what this great nation of ours needs more people."

I truly felt in my heart that this joke was hilarious, but her straight face told me she was not happy that we were drifting away from our conversation.

"My exasperation has nothing to do with our engagement, Love," I said. "I promise that I will try my best to make sure that you feel that I am inclined to get engaged to you. But, whom should I reveal my feelings to, if not you? Mudit? He's an idiot. Yukti? She only has 'just stay positive' advice in her quiver. You are the only person that I can pour my heart out to; and if I have to pretend that everything is hunky-dory in front of you, my feelings would just drive me insane. So, from now onwards, if you see me act as if I am a little distant, please know that I am worried, or rather, a little concerned about my professional future, and that it has nothing whatsoever to do with our engagement."

She considered what I had said for a moment and replied, looking into my eyes, "My Love, don't hold back your emotions from me. I will not question you anymore about this. And, I am sure you will be amazing at whatever you choose to do. I have always believed that and I will always believe so. Let's change the topic."

"Yes, let's talk about food," I said, jubilantly. "Now, since I am happy, I shall eat something vegetarian and spare a chicken's life."

She laughed and made the day precious. We ordered food and while we waited, she turned to me and said, "I know this might not be the best time to talk about this, but I haven't had my period yet; it should have come two or three days ago." She continued, on seeing the confusion on my face, "I can't help worrying about *that* incident, you know?"

"Ah, that! No, don't worry about that," I reassured her. "I am a pessimist, and, still, I am not worried. It should tell you something."

"My father would kill you," she said, seriously.

He would kill me, I knew that. I nodded.

"Don't worry, there is like a million to one chance of that happening," I said, as food arrived at our table.

"But what if it does happen?"

"Then we have options, you know?" I said.

"I am not going to kill an unborn baby!" she exclaimed.

"I hope your father would share the same sentiments about a young boy of twenty one."

"If it happens, it'd sure be very bad for my IAS preps," she said.

"Yep. It would be. How happy would your family be when they find out that I ruined your future!" She smiled and I added, "But this won't happen. Don't worry about it."

We started eating and our conversation took us in a different direction.

"How's your poem for Panorama coming along?" she asked.

"I will finish it soon."

"You said that two weeks ago. When's 'soon'?"

"I don't know. Look, I am working on it, OK? Can we please talk about something else?"

She sighed and asked, as she was stuffing a dumpling in her mouth, "Do you remember that you used to say that we would never grow older than sixteen?"

"Yeah, I do."

"You were crazy," she said, her speech muffled with the aforementioned dumpling.

"It was a theory, OK? And it nearly worked till my seventeenth birthday. I wish I had been right; we would have spent days loitering around our school, not doing anything."

The feeling of nostalgia for childhood is one of the primary distractions for a lethargic and unmotivated mind. I was one of the common lot of human beings, the one with the habit of summoning alternate past lines to avoid doing chores in the present. Not that I was biased towards the past; a future full of everything I have ever longed for would have sufficed for my procrastination as well. Leastways, when I was with Neera, my mind was reined in by her mellifluous voice.

Returning to the tale, Neera and I had our dinner and walked about the campus, talking about the future we were planning to share together. Finally, at the end of our date, I escorted her to her hostel. After bidding goodbye by stealing a quick peck on her lips, I began my journey to my room, with a happy heart.

Both happiness and gloom are infectious. Thankfully, this particular battle was won by the former.

CHAPTER III

"He was sitting, alone, on a..."

Nope not good enough, I thought, and went on to delete the words I had written.

I was sitting at my study-desk in my room, staring at my laptop. For two years, I had been trying to work on an idea for a book. I had managed to write two chapters during this time, but could not, for the life of me, write any more.

The window of my room was covered with drapes, to keep the sunlight out. I preferred the dark; it is so tranquil, so consistent. The fan was creaking, maybe to distract me from completing my masterpiece. The ash tray on my table was nearly full of cigarette butts. With the intention of emptying it, I walked out of the room.

After washing the ash tray in the common bathrooms, I went back to my room, and slumped on the chair.

"Focus," I started talking to myself. "You know why he's there. You know where he wants to go. Just write it down. Simple, right? Apparently not."

Nothing.

I tried to read what I already had, which was always a risky endeavour. Whenever I would do so, either I would be filled with immense respect for myself or disgust.

The third chapter had been my nemesis for quite a while now. Often I would try to analyse why I could not get past its first line. Maybe I was afraid to proceed: What if I complete the book and end up hating it? What if Neera hates it? What if I am branded as the shallowest writer of all times?

I knew that I had to finish a few chapters before I completed my degree. I had no job, no discernible future, so I needed some other vocation. Not that I ever considered writing as my primary work. I was an unpublished amateur, but I was running out of options.

My father owned a publishing business, so if I wanted, the book could be in print the day it was finished. But, his small enterprise focussed on non-fiction and academic books. If I were to be a successful writer, I would have to write something good enough to be distributed by some reputed publisher.

I lit up a cigarette and started thinking of the day I first told Neera about my decision to start working on a book.

"That's so very nice," she had cheered. "I'm so proud of you. This is what you're meant to do."

"You're the only person who likes my writing," I had replied. "What if no one else does?"

"They will. I know for sure."

As I reminisced, my phone buzzed. It was a text from Neera "Going to my class. Be back by seven. LU."

I could never understand how she could be motivated enough to get consistently good grades, attend coaching classes for IAS examinations, and be as amiable as she was.

Some people are born great, some achieve greatness, and some, like me, are sentenced to seek it all their lives, and that too, in vain.

After spending three hours attempting to write, most of which were spent on YouTube, I gave up.

+++

A major part of the following week went by attending classes, to fulfil the seventy per cent attendance requirement of my courses.

During the final week of class, it was decided by us myself, Neera, Yukti, Mudit, and Yashika that we would watch a movie, before sequestering ourselves to start preparing for the examinations; and after spending a whole evening debating what movie to watch, we settled for an evening show of a middling film, playing in a local theatre. Mudit and I reached there on his bike.

It is customary for a platoon of friends to analyse a film as soon as end credits start rolling; but, on this particular occasion, I refrained from any discussion, to prevent the innocent bystanders from drowning in a flood of profanities. As a matter of principle, I would never use the word 'terrible' to describe a movie, because it is, after all, a collective effort and is created by people after months of toiling. Therefore, when I was asked what I thought of the movie, I described it as 'insufferable'. I continued to pontificate that if I were to meet the creators of this film, I would politely suggest that they find some other vocation. Nevertheless, I had enjoyed the three long hours inside that theatre because I got to cuddle Neera, and laugh at few of Mudit's jibes at the film.

We decided to get dinner before we headed back to our rooms, and while we were enjoying the meal, in the midst of Mudit and Yukti's discussion on the evolution - or, rather, degradation - of Indian cinema over the years, Yashika turned to me and asked, "Prachur, why didn't you tell us that you and Mudit are scheduled for a disciplinary hearing next Thursday?"

"Are we, now? I had no such information. For what, do you know?" said I, not wanting to divulge any more information than she already had.

"I don't really know the reason," she replied.

Neera looked at her and then me. She had a mouthful of rice but she decided that she will swallow it only after observing the course of our conversation.

"Well maybe you got your facts wrong," I droned.

"I am Prof. Verma's TA," Yashika retorted. "I saw her appointments. She is scheduled to be a part of a committee that will meet next Thursday to discuss you two."

"Is this true?" asked Neera, after gulping down the rice in her mouth, her face riddled with worry.

"Yashika *is* the Teaching Assistant to Verma, there is nothing but truth in that," said Mudit, in a vain attempt to save his friend.

"Shut up, Mudit," retorted Yashika.

"Tell me, is this true?" Neera asked me.

"Yes, it's true," I sighed. "It's nothing though."

"What is it about?" she enquired, looking hurt. "Why didn't you tell me?"

"Mudit and I may have been caught drunk at the first year hostel," I answered.

"What can this committee do? Can they expel you?" she asked.

"Yes, they can," Yashika replied.

"No, they can't do that," I said.

Yashika snorted; Mudit and Yukti thought it best not to contribute.

"No, they can't do that," I repeated, glancing sharply at Yashika. "They are just going to drink their tea, and talk about politics. It's a small matter."

Mudit nodded to reassure Neera, although both he and I knew that I was lying.

Neera shook her head and went back to her dinner. I could see that she was feeling miserable. I felt angry, at myself and Yashika.

As everyone moved out of the restaurant, I walked beside Yashika and enquired, "Why the hell would you tell everyone?"

"I thought if you knew about it, you would have told us, especially Neera," she replied, without a shred of honesty on her pale face. "Also, are you angry at me for telling her the truth?"

"Your timing for the revelation was spectacular," I snapped.

"Was I not supposed to talk about this?" she asked me, with a straight face. “I am sorry that you are not straightforward with my friend. You should be.”

I was ready to give a befitting reply, but I noticed that Neera was within earshot.

“There is not enough space inside my heart to contain the hate I feel for you right now,” I said to Yashika, lowering my voice.

At this moment, Neera grabbed my arm and pulled me gently to indicate that she wanted to speak to me privately; for this purpose, she and I fell back from the group.

“You know how much stress I am under, because of that thing,” she said, referring to the conversation regarding the possibility of her carrying a baby. “Yet, you think it perfectly fine to give me more things to worry about? And, worst of all, I got to know about it accidentally; I don’t believe you had any intention of telling me, if you could have helped it.”

“Darling, nothing’s going to happen,” I reassured her. Her expression told me that she did not believe me, so I continued, “I am sorry, OK? I know I should have told you, but since it’s not such a big deal, I thought it was best for me to not bother you with this.”

She looked sternly at me.

After a pause, I added, “And, at least, stop worrying about that baby thing.”

“I can’t. I have tried thinking it over, and even though I understand that the odds of it happening are astronomical, I just can’t stop thinking of the consequences.”

“Look, what if we were to buy a test? I can go to that chemist over there,” I suggested, pointing to a pharmacy, “you can perform it later tonight, and relieve yourself of your worries one of the worries, at least.”

She nodded, rather timidly, in approval, and I hurried into the pharmacy.

The judgemental gaze that I received from the cashier, when he saw the pregnancy test I intended to buy, made me feel as if I were in a shop selling narcotics.

The societal outlook on sex in our country is deplorable, for the most part. It is both ironic and grim to imagine that we are the same culture that, not too long ago, literally wrote a book on love making. I could not help but feel that our rigorous family structure was the biggest hindrance in liberalising our compatriots' views on sex. Our elders expect young people to practise celibacy till the day they get married, and on their wedding night, expect the couple to be masters of the trade. I thoroughly believed that it is this kind of upbringing that stems problems like marital rape.

Young age is often characterised by the habitual simplification of a complex problem and being obstinate to criticism of your own conclusions, and I was a maestro of this art.

I handed Neera the test and she told me that she will perform it that very night. We shared a hug, before she got into Yashika's car to leave for their hostel.

✦✦✦

Later that night, as I lay on my bed preparing to go to sleep, I received a call from Yukti. She wanted to know if I was willing to have a drink with her.

"There's never a bad time for a beer," I said.

She and I met outside her hostel. She had two cans of Budweiser in her hands, and we quietly walked to the football ground of our college. It was poorly lit by a flood light, and we sat on the grass at one of the shadowed corners. Beer cans were scattered all around us. The place was perfect for people looking for the thrill of public drinking without any risk of getting caught.

After returning from the movie she had changed into a purple traditional Indian suit. Rarely did she prefer Indian over Western clothing, and at that instant she looked astounding. Of course, I sat without uttering a word about my thoughts on her beauty.

"So, what's up?" I asked. "If you don't remember, we were just together."

She smiled, "I know. I just wanted to have a drink with you. Is that too much to ask?"

"Of course not. I am known to be great company, generally."

Stray dogs were having the time of their lives, and probably felt like the kings of the streets. The grass was very soft and Yukti and I spent a few minutes, sipping silently, before she turned to me and said:

"Neera's pissed off about the hearing." I nodded and she continued, "Yashika bad mouthed you so much during the car ride, I can't even tell. She thinks you are the cause of everything wrong with Neera."

"I don't care what Yashika thinks," I retorted.

"I didn't agree with her either," she said, looking at the beer can. "I know that you are an idiot sometimes, but overall I think you are a nice boyfriend. Neera is just very emotional and she takes so much tension, you know? I don't mean to say anything bad I love her, you know but a lot of times she is so sullen and often when the exams approach, she starts keeping to herself. These days, she's getting angry over very small things. This whole morning she was lying on her bed before we went out to the movie, and when I tried to talk to her, she just lost her temper and told me to leave her alone. So weird, I tell you."

"She has a lot on her mind these days," I said, slowly. "More than exams, I am sure. It's not important what that is, but I think her anger is justified to a certain extent."

"A lot on her mind? Like, what? Your engagement?"

"Did she tell you about that?" I asked, taking a sip of beer.

"Yes," she droned.

I said, "She is worried about that and our future; her future. She has to work hard for the next one or two years, preparing for one of the most competitive exams in the country. No wonder she is all messed up in her head."

"True," she said, nodding contemplatively.

We drank in silence before she said, "By the way, are you really serious about getting engaged to her? I mean, she says you are, but are you actually going to do it? I had been dying to ask you ever since I learnt about it, but I thought that I would rather do it when we are alone."

"Yeah, I am serious about getting engaged to her," I hesitated. "We've been together for so many years. Marrying her is logical, isn't it?"

"I don't know," she replied. "Aren't you guys too young for that? Are you sure that you two are ready for a mature relationship?"

"I don't think we are too young for an engagement," I said. "I am sure we'll manage."

"Maybe," she said. "But, maybe you can find someone who can make you happier. Neera and you are not compatible. I think if you move forward in this relationship, it'll only end badly."

"I don't agree," I said plainly. "I mean, she is a bit controlling sometimes, but otherwise she's perfect. She loves me; I love her, and that's enough."

"Yeah," she said, "I guess...."

By and by, the clock struck eleven and we knew it was time for us to leave.

During our walk towards her hostel, she was silent and glanced, inquiringly, at me a few times. I could not help but feel that there was something she wanted to share with me, but my repeated enquiries yielded no satisfying answer. On reaching the hostel gate, she turned towards me. The light from the street lamp fell on her face, highlighting her features. Her lips quivered and I could doubtlessly say that there was a turmoil within her, which was aching to come out.

"What?" I asked. "I feel like you want to say something." When she did not reply, I said, "Say it, say it for the sake of our lord Satan," while shaking her.

She smiled and started to utter something, but checked herself. The only discernible words she muttered were, "Good bye." She gently kissed me on my cheek before hurrying and disappearing behind the doors of the building.

Needless to say, I found this behaviour confounding, and as I plodded towards my room, I pondered over the possible implications of it. On finding no prudent explanation, I abandoned my quest, telling myself, "Yukti has always been strange."

+++

When I woke up the following day, I saw that I had a text message from Neera.

"We need to talk!" it said.

I was alarmed by her choice of words and called her. I could sense gloom in her voice; she would not give me any details on the phone and kept insisting that we meet, so I swiftly jumped out of my bed and walked to her hostel. She was standing outside the gates, looking dreary; I took her hand and we walked slowly around the campus, while she kept silent.

"What is it, Darling? Please tell me," I implored, as we approached a quiet and deserted part of the campus.

She said nothing and just handed me the box of the pregnancy test. When I rattled it, I heard that the test was inside; I asked her whether I should open it, and on receiving a confirmatory nod, proceeded to do so. There were two small windows on the test stick: one had a single line on it and the other had a plus symbol.

"What does this mean?" I asked.

I knew what it meant because it was clearly imprinted - next to one of the windows on the test stick - that a plus sign indicated pregnancy; I only wanted her to confirm whether my observation was correct. When she did not answer me, I pulled her in an embrace and she broke into tears; I stood still, with her head buried in my chest, as I had no words to console her. After standing wrapped around each other for what seemed like eternity, we broke away and walked lazily, her head resting on my shoulder, to the park outside our campus, and occupied a bench. I smoked while she sat staring into the distance. The Sun was shining brightly but the light breeze and the shadow of a nearby tree made the heat bearable.

"These tests do give false positives," I said, finally breaking the silence. She looked at me in disbelief. "We need to go to a hospital to confirm these results," I added.

"Prachur, what are we going to do?" she cried.

"I don't know about you, but I am going to die," said I.

"I am serious," she said.

"First, like I said, we need to visit a clinic to make sure that these results are correct. If they are, I think we only have one option."

"I don't want to do that!" she replied.

"Darling, what would you prefer?"

"I don't know. I don't," she said, holding her head in her hands. "My future is over..."

"Don't say that."

We spent the whole afternoon together without speaking much, mostly walking around the city, loitering in coffee houses and restaurants. I did nothing but fixate on her pretty face, imprinting its details in my memory. Occasionally, I would utter a few banalities because this predicament had rendered me incapable of making cogent arguments; after all, barely one day ago, I was sure that we will never face this dilemma. How was I to think rationally?

"God dammit!" she said, suddenly, as we sat drinking coffee in

Sector 11. "We're so stupid!"

I nodded.

"My parents will be furious. I can't tell them. I can't. What now, Prachur?"

I shrugged, and she looked away. Her eyes were swollen, and her nose was red.

As darkness set over the city, she told me that she wanted to go to what we called 'our' spot. It was the parking lot of the Physics Department in the College, located in one of the corners of the campus. It was surrounded by walls on three sides, separating it from the world outside. The building of the department was desolate and locked in the evenings, and often we would sit on a grass patch adjacent to the parking lot for hours, talking and enjoying each other's company. It was not surprising that Neera always preferred this place in tumultuous times, as this was one of the places where we made several joyous plans about our future.

After cuddling for a few minutes, when she looked relaxed, I said, "Dear, clearly, we have two options: either to keep the baby or to, if I put it delicately, not keep the baby. Keeping the baby will entail you to be a mother, which not only is a big responsibility, but a choice that will definitely affect your professional future. It is just more prudent that you abort the baby."

"What do *you* want?" she asked.

"I don't know. I guess I would prefer if we don't have this baby."

"Really?"

"Yeah."

"Is that really what you want? To kill a being?"

"No. Don't think like that. Anyway, what does it matter?" I answered. "It's your life, Neera, that would be most affected by this, both physically and emotionally. I mean, isn't it supposed to be your decision, as a woman? If I were to make this decision for you, maybe I will inadvertently sentence you to ruin your life - I don't know —

what I think is that it's not my call; so stop asking me."

She nodded, sat mulling over the subject, and finally asked, looking at me, "What if I don't want an abortion?"

"Wow! That's a difficult question," I answered, scratching my head. "I don't know. Why would you not want it?"

"It's wrong."

"It's not, Neera."

"Tell me, what will you do if I decide to have this baby?"

"I don't know. I mean, obviously, we are too young to have a child. Honestly, I don't think I am a person responsible enough to be a father."

"But, Prachur, we are in love and we're supposed to get married. Does it make sense to abort our baby?"

I shrugged.

"Say something useful," she said.

"I know I am not being too helpful. I believe we need more time to think this through."

She nodded and we sat quietly, meditating.

"I can't imagine taking a life, Prachur. That would be a sin," she murmured.

"Don't think like that. You have a future to look forward to. Don't think about this ethical nonsense."

She buried her face in her arms.

"We need to think," she finally said, with a sigh.

"Yes, we do. Think about what's important, Neera. We'd have plenty of chances to have a baby, but right now, you need to focus. You need to become an IAS officer. If you don't, your father will blame me."

"He won't."

"Trust me, he will."

As we walked back to her hostel room, she smiled and said, gently, "Although, having a kid won't be the end of the world. The baby might have your nose."

"I hope that is not the case," I said. I had inherited my mother's sharp nose.

"We should confirm these results first," she said. "God!"

Soon after reaching my room, I fell asleep.

+++

The next day, we took a trip to a clinic, located far outside the city. After the test, we were told that the result would be available after one day; there was nothing to do but wait.

When I finally arrived back at my hostel room after walking Neera to hers, I had enough time alone to let the gravity of the situation sink in. It was the end of the afternoon and the sun headed towards the horizon. I lay on the bed thinking and pondering over the implication of a positive result from two perspectives my own and my family's.

"This news will be a blow to Mama and Papa," I said to myself. "They'll flip out. I know they will. Maybe they'll kick me out of the house. No, they won't do that. They love me. I am their son; I am irreplaceable. But, they do have orthodox views. I don't think having a kid before marriage is a part of their standard family design. Anyway, let's say that Neera decides to keep the baby, how would I break this news to them? What would their reaction be? Would they stand by me? Would they ever look at me the same way they normally do? I hope Neera does the right thing and aborts the baby. I don't want things to change."

It is immensely difficult to think coherently, especially when we have no prior experience of a certain situation. I tried to compose myself by walking around the room, but in vain. My anxiety only seemed to increase with time; even tobacco failed to relieve it.

"Anyway, I must be clear about my own intentions in the eventuality of Neera being pregnant; how could I be concerned about my family's opinion before I was clear about what I want? Let me think clearly. OK, calm down. There's one thing I know for sure, I don't possess the financial independence required to start a family. I'm not sure about what I want to do in life. I mean, I'm not even sure about getting engaged to Neera. No, that's not true. I am kind of sure about getting engaged to her that's...better. How the hell could I think of bringing a child into this world? I can't believe how lightly we're taking this. This is a life-altering situation. How could I be a father now? No, I can't."

I got out of the room, and walked around in the corridor.

"I do love Neera, there's no doubt about that. I mean, we have always seen children in our future, may be not at this age. No, don't think on these lines. Obviously, abortion is not wrong, per se, right? I mean, it's not taking a life. Screw morality. It's not even human yet. If Neera's OK with abortion, I am too. Yes. But what would I do if Neera decides to have this baby? Oh God! If she wants this child, I won't ever have the courage to tell her to, as some would say, take an innocent life. But, won't that change my life forever? It will. Neera's crazy sometimes. What if she decides in favour of what I am dreading? Oh God! No!"

Even after spending hours pondering over this issue, I felt no better than when I had begun. My thoughts were interrupted by the ring of my phone; it was Mudit and he wanted to know if I would like to have dinner over drinks with him. He informed me that he was buying a bottle of whiskey and had plans to order food to his room. I readily agreed to this proposal. Maybe I will think clearly after I am intoxicated and in the company of a friend, I thought.

On reaching his room, I found him sitting on the bed, working on his laptop. His shoes were lying on their sides at the entrance and his shirt had found an abode on his table. Empty cigarette boxes were scattered across the floor and the door of his closet had a huge dent, as if someone had kicked it in. He waved to me, carelessly, as I entered the room. I saw that he had bought a bottle of cheap whiskey that we usually preferred. Saving money was a priority for us - why drink expensive alcohol three times a month when you could have a cheaper option to drink every day, for the same cost?

After placing the order for food, I poured alcohol in plastic cups, adding soda to his drink and cola to mine. He kept his laptop on the table and patted on the bed to generously offer me a seat, which I graciously accepted.

"You look like you have been through hell," he said, looking at me. "Is it because of that conversation between Neera and you, that day after the movie?"

I denied that I was gloomy, but a few drinks later, since we were inebriated, I felt less inhibited to tell him my problem. But, as people who are drunk do not pursue conversation with a fixed aim, we talked about every topic that is humanly possible to be discussed.

"We will never have this freedom," he said, during the course of our dialogue.

"Yeah, I mean, we will get old," I replied, stressing on the last word. "We will turn twenty-five soon — that's the age that children start calling you 'uncle'. God!"

"My parents want me to get married by the time I am twenty five," he said, looking into his cup. "Children would surely call me 'uncle ji.'"

"I can't imagine you married, brother," I said, laughing.

"Why?" he asked, feigning pain. "Am I not lovable?"

"No, you are not," I said, plainly, as he got up to pour us another round of drinks and cheered, "Screw Naidu and his committee of bastards!"

You must pardon me, for I cannot recall how the conversation went from Mudit's lovability to the plan of taking a tedious trip across the country.

"We should rent a bike for you and then we can ride to Chennai," he said, getting up excitedly.

"I don't know how to drive a bike, you know that," I said.

"You have to learn," he stuttered. "I can drive alone, with you as a pillion rider, bro. I can, you trust me, right?" Upon seeing me nod, he continued, "But, I want you to learn so that you can take Neera with you, and I can take a girl with big...", at this point he made a vulgar gesture that I would refrain from describing, with his hands, spilling his drink.

We had a plethora of random dialogues that night, but as I staggered back to my room, I realised that I had forgotten to discuss my troubles with him. The only thing I managed to do was to plan a trip and make a promise to always keep our friendship in my memory. It was for the best, maybe. After all, during the years I had known Mudit, he had had three relationships, none of them lasting for more than six months. How could he have possibly helped me? I comforted myself.

CHAPTER IV

My denial of a positive result of the home pregnancy test did not help alleviate the shock I received when I obtained the confirmation from a doctor. Neera was, in fact, pregnant. Our meetings thereof were riddled with discussions pertaining to this subject and of the change that would be brought to our future because of this revelation. Even after many bouts of deliberations, we had no clarity about the course of action that we wanted to take, and since the exams were approaching we decided to postpone our worries. Neera found some distraction in books, and we sparsely met. I found peace by spending most of my time with Yukti, and she was kind enough to bring my spirits up.

Finally, the morning before my infamous hearing, I met Neera and Mudit for lunch. I say 'infamous' because someone had been spreading a rumour that Mudit and I were caught ragging first year students, who allegedly stood without their pants at the moment Prof. Kumar apprehended us. I was enjoying the notoriety this whole predicament was garnering for me, but Neera had conflicting views.

"This whole situation will come back to haunt you in the future. Like during an interview, I am telling you," she kept insisting.

Returning to the lunch, I had an ample serving of Maggi and tea. Neera's appetite was affected by her worries and she barely ate. She kept looking at me and embracing me every few minutes.

"I could use a hug too," Mudit pleaded.

Neera shook her head.

"Wow! That's so mean," Mudit lamented. "I am going to be expelled in a few hours and no one would hug me."

"Can you guys be expelled?" Neera enquired.

"No, we can't be," I said. "Mudit, you ass, can't you keep shut for a few minutes?"

"What if you are?" she murmured.

"We'll see what to do, when and if that happens."

This reply, of course, did not soothe her nerves.

"You know how bad a situation we are in," she whispered. "You'd better start taking this seriously. If you get expelled or something, we're in for even more trouble."

"OK," I replied, lazily.

We reached the Academic Block on time, climbed a flight of stairs, and entered a dark hall, to find Prof. Kumar nervously walking across the breadth of the room.

"Ah! Thakur and Garg, there you are," he squealed. "On time, I like it. Ready for the consequences?"

Neera's grip on my arm tightened.

"Yes, Sir, we are," Mudit jested.

"Good, good. Did you tell your parents?" he asked, clearly enjoying himself.

Mudit looked at me with the look that said, "Why would we?", and answered, "No...Sir."

Prof. Kumar nodded and went inside the Seminar Room, which was at the end of the hall.

Soon thereafter, I saw his head peek out of the door and he beckoned us to join him in the room.

"I'll pray for you," Neera said.

"No, there's no need. This will be over in a jiffy," I replied.

Mudit and I walked inside.

The room was carpeted and chairs were arranged around an oval teak table. Prof. Verma, Naidu, and Kumar were sitting at the table, and gestured us to take seats. They had been enjoying tea with warm samosas, and Prof. Kumar was happily dipping a half-eaten samosa in chutney.

Mudit and I sat still, looking around the room, as Prof. Naidu licked his fingers clean. Finally, when there was no flavour left to savour, he looked at us and asked, "Shall we start?"

I shrugged.

For this memoir, I will skip the initial part of the hearing, which included the three reading out accusations, after which, Mudit and I laid out our defence, that is, we told them we were meeting Sanchit that fateful night.

"Do you have any witnesses to prove that you were not ragging anyone?" asked Prof. Verma.

"We do have witnesses, your honour," Mudit quipped. "But they are running late. They should be here any minute."

"They'd better be here," snapped Prof. Naidu.

We nodded and Prof. Kumar smirked.

"While we wait for your witnesses, when you two were apprehended from the DOA's roof, you were let off with a warning and were told that the consequences would be severe if you were caught another time. And, here you are. Why should we not reprimand you severely?"

We chorused that we were aware that our actions were uncalled for, but we never engaged in any behaviour that caused any monetary destruction of the college property.

Meanwhile, Mudit received a text from Sanchit saying that he was waiting outside the Seminar Room. We took leave of the committee to produce our witness.

In a few minutes, the room was swarming with first year students, all of whom testified that Mudit and I were people of unblemished character, and that we were only in their hostel to meet Sanchit and share a bedtime snack with him. I did not recognise most of the 'witnesses'. Some of the unfamiliar faces belonged to those who were not even in town the night of the incident. Needless to say, I had my doubts about the effectiveness of the 'battle plan' prepared by Mudit.

By and by, they left, and the professors looked at us with doubt. Finally, Prof. Naidu blurted, "Anything else you want to say?"

I shook my head and he said, "We will now deliberate the result, you will be called in when we're done. Go wait outside."

And that was what we did. Neera hugged me as soon as I walked out of the door. Yukti was sitting on a wooden bench, on the far side of the hall. She walked to us.

"How did it go?" she asked.

"Fine."

"Who were all those people who went in after you?"

"Juniors," Mudit replied. "Our witnesses. We proved, conclusively, that we were not ragging anyone. I think I could make a terrific lawyer."

We were eventually called in and let off with a warning and a hefty fine of ten thousand each. Obviously, arranging the money without telling my parents why I needed it was difficult, but I was happy with how the whole situation concluded. Neera was ecstatic about the result, and assured me that she would arrange the money, somehow.

I have nothing to worry about, now, I thought, as I descended the stairs with her, Mudit, and Yukti. Oh wait, the pregnancy...

+++

I drudged through most of the examinations, and believed that I had performed well. Anyway, given my shallow preparations, I had no datum to measure the quality of my performance.

It was the evening before my Economics 442 examination that Riayat visited my room.

"How is your preparation coming along?" he asked, as he sat on the chair.

"Not great, man," I said, rubbing my eyes. "I haven't really started reading 'The Elephant Paradigm'. I can't get myself to do it. I tried to read a few pages but then I just stopped; it's just so dry. What about you?"

"About the same. I took a nap this afternoon, then I thought that it's better that I come here to study with you. Do you have the photostats or do we need to go to the market?"

"I have them. Here, take some," I said, passing him half of my notes.

Cramming information that I had never seen before was tedious. Every few minutes I looked around to find something more interesting to see than reading plain words in black on a white page, but I found nothing — an occasional cough or sound of Riayat moving in his chair was the only symptom of the presence of life in the otherwise quiet room.

I knew that I had an academic duty - to carry forward the legacy of the Wright Brothers. And here I was, trying to plod through my exams, without any intention of actually learning the material: shameful, yet necessary. Ever since I had finished my tenth grade, I had accepted that I was to be an engineer, and had actually grown to like the field. So during the last year of my college, I often tried to figure out how I had reached a place where I was so unfathomably bored of the very thing I loved. It was easy to blame the education system, but the reality was that I had lost interest in learning. It had happened systematically. I had whiled away four years of my degree.

There were only a few things in my life that I actually enjoyed. Writing was one of them. I sat back and reminisced about the first time I wrote a poem:

It was in the third grade. I and a few other classmates of mine were supposed to each draw something on a chart paper to be decoratively displayed in class. I was very enthusiastic about the opportunity, and wrote my first poem, about how trees protect against pollution. Happily, I took it to class the next day, but when I saw what other people had created, I was embarrassed. Maybe I was afraid of getting criticised. I hid my poem in my bag, and told my teacher that I had forgotten to bring mine. The next day, I submitted an illustrated biography of the then prime minister. I had no courage to show my poem to anyone, and kept it in the bag for days. It was Neera who accidentally saw it one day after we returned from our Games period.

"It's so sweet," she said.

"It's not polite to take things out of someone's bag without asking, you know," I squealed, snatching my work from her hands.

"It was already out. I could see its corner." I shoved the poem back in my bag, and she added, "You're so talented. I could never write something."

Having a girl with big kind eyes give me a compliment made me blush. From that day, I started writing poems to impress her. I would show my work to no one but her. Two months later, I fell in love with her. I was a child so most would classify my attraction as infatuation, but I knew it was love.

Thinking about Neera made me smile, and Riayat asked me, "What?"

"Nothing."

"You're smiling. What is it?"

I shook my head and went back to my notes.

After a few minutes of studying, he turned to me and said, "So, my father told me that I could work for him, after I finish my degree. It's not much - I mean, he dignifies the job by calling it inventory management, but it's just overlooking his warehouse. But something's better than nothing, right? And, you can join me if you want. There will not be a lot of work involved and most of the time we will just sit around doing nothing."

I nodded and told him that I would consider it, even though I did not mean it. This small exchange of words opened a gate, and by and by, temptation of procrastination managed to seduce us. During the hours that followed, we chatted more than we studied. As the clock struck one, he finally got ready to leave.

"How the hell would we pass tomorrow?" he chuckled.

We bid each other good bye, and I went to sleep after he left.

The following morning, I met Neera and she wished me luck for my examination. Sitting on my assigned seat, I looked around but could not find any trace of Riayat; he had decided to skip the exam.

When the examination finished, Neera asked me how it went.

"Meh," I replied. "I think I will only get a 'D' grade, but I will pass, no doubt."

"Good," she said, and looked at me. She looked tired.

"Have you made up your mind about *that,* Neera?" I asked.

"Nope."

I nodded and hugged her. "I am so lucky to have you in my life. We'll figure it out. Don't worry."

+++

In the evening, I managed to finish my poem for submission to *Panorama* magazine, and I wrote an email to Neera to show her my final draft.

Love,

I finished the poem, finally.

Here it is:

House of lord

Breaking the dead silence his footsteps roared,
I caught a glimpse of his old form, as he soared,
past me, across the floor of the house of Lord,

walking in beat to a song with divine chords.

He stopped as he reached the fence, golden and cold,
the only thing material keeping God beyond his hold,
He closed his eyes and on his feet he gently swayed,
and as the time passed by, I heard his words fade.

Maybe, he was wishing for healthier coming days,
or looking for the answers to his deep mental haze,
He could be asking for an easy painless death,
murmuring, in a foreign tongue, under his breath.

After a while, he turned around and walked away,
I followed suit but soon he took a different way,
Even as he staggered, with hope his eyes were glistening,
All I could hope was that as he prayed, God was listening.

What do you think?
Yours,
Shyny

On receiving her approval and basking in her praises, I submitted the poem.

+++

I was lying on my bed, thinking about the predicament Neera and I were in. I became conscious of my breathing. It became hectic. I felt as if someone had parked their car on my chest. I gasped. A sudden dread overtook me.

A thought darted through my mind: I'm going to die.

I scuttled out of the room. My legs could barely support me, and I felt them shaking. A few moments later my whole body was shivering.

I could hear my breath clearly, and my heart pounding. Although my eyes were wide open, I could barely understand what I was seeing. I wandered around the dimly lit corridor. Everyone was sound asleep.

"Must I get help?" I asked myself. "No. Forget it. This will be over in no time. Soon, I will get to see whether God exists or not."

A few minutes later, I was calm. When I went back to bed, the clock had struck four.

CHAPTER V

The relief I felt after I finished my exams is quite difficult to express in written words. Simply put, my degree was finally over and I had not perished.

As the semester was ending, goodbyes and hugs were rampant around the campus. Our hostel shared the same ambiance everyone was busy packing their belongings and nostalgia prevailed. Mudit and I were helping each other pack; this gave us precious time to spend together. "I am going to miss you," he kept saying repeatedly. "Stop being a sissy," I would reply, every time.

I had always lacked the ability to feel the absence of familiar human forms around me. "Out of sight, out of mind," was my motto. I tried to play along with Mudit's concern of losing touch with other classmates of ours, but honestly I did not care. You lose friends and you make new ones; that was what life meant for me. At that moment, I was more concerned about the situation Neera and I were in.

Since we were going to be separated, our crew had planned a party and as per the plan, Mudit and I rode to a tavern — better described as a *Theka* called 'Yaroon da Mela', which when loosely translated into the Queen's tongue, meant 'Fiesta of Friends', located about twenty minutes away by bike from Sukhna Lake.

The tavern had tables under the open sky and was full of people looking to consume poorly brewed drinks. We preferred this place because of the food, which was out of this world; and the fact that this place served drinks very late into the night only made it more attractive an option for us.

Mudit and I walked to a table occupied by Neera, Yukti, Yashika, and two other people who although hitherto have not found a place in this memoir, were close acquaintances Pranay and Taara.

Pranay was a short guy from Andhra Pradesh, with bushy dark brown hair, wheatish skin, and a square face. I would not describe him as buff, but he made every effort in the world to make people describe him so. In short, he was addicted to exercise. He was wearing an obviously new green shirt. Taara was a girl with velvety dark skin and short hair. Her face was bewitching and her good nature made for decent company. She was thin, and on some days looked as if she was suffering from malnutrition. Both of them studied Civil Engineering.

I went on to occupy a seat next to Neera; she looked at me and smiled, and for the rest of the night, we sat holding hands.

Neera refrained from drinking alcohol, because it might have been bad for the little being growing inside her. Being an occasional drinker no one interrogated her on her repeated ordering of plain aerated drinks throughout the night. Had it been me, I would have had to answer a barrage of questions.

Anyway, the conversation of the gathering spanned across a variety of topics and after mocking our professors for a while, Mudit suggested that we all take a trip before proceeding with our lives; and when his idea was not applauded, he felt a little betrayed. Planning a journey with so many people is a hectic task, but I must say that I was amused at his determination. We had to discuss the destination, the mode of journey, and the number of days we were to enjoy ourselves. Mudit kept the group focused and forced us to talk about all these parameters.

"McLeodganj is the best place to visit, I am telling you," he said, losing his patience.

Yashika had erred in suggesting Shimla as an option for the trip.

Mudit was an ardent supporter of McLeodganj.

"Shimla is closer than McLo or Kasol," replied Yashika.

I would have preferred Shimla, because I hated travelling. The closer the better, I thought. But since it was Yashika who was on my side, I wanted her not to get her way. Therefore, I stayed out of the rhetoric.

"Maybe, but I know a few people in Kasol, and we can do LSD," said Pranay to Mudit, winking.

Mudit thought for a while, then nodded indicating that he would not mind going to Kasol, and looked at me with a smile. Neera pinched me and I shook my head to indicate that there was no way I was going to partake in their endeavour to consume drugs.

After Mudit threatened several times to flip the table over, we selected McLeodganj, as the destination for the trip. A hill town, around six hours from Chandigarh by car, it is located in the state of Himachal Pradesh. Pranay felt contented with the choice of destination as McLeodganj was a famous market for certain herbs, which according to some have been wrongly characterised as narcotics. As the discussion progressed, it was decided that Mudit would borrow an SUV from his cousin that could seat eight people and we would drive to our destination.

Finally, after settling all the details regarding the trip, Yukti, who was sitting beside Neera on the other side and was silent during the whole conversation, turned to Neera and said:

"What is in your future?"

"You know that I am going to prepare for civil services," replied Neera.

"I meant, what's up with you and him," Yukti said, referring to me. "When do you plan to get engaged?"

"No idea," Neera replied. "We'll decide soon."

"What will you do to earn money? Don't you need a job?" Yukti asked me.

"Na," I replied, plainly. "Neera will work and I can be a house husband. I don't have a problem with that. Do I need to work just because I am a man? That's sexist!"

Neera and Yukti kept talking to each other late into the night. Occasionally, they giggled making Mudit and the rest enquire about the subject. The night progressed and I sat talking to the rest of the party, before turning to Neera and Yukti and starting to overhear their conversation.

"We will visit a psychologist, probably," Yukti said to Neera.

"Psychologist, what?" I enquired, joining the discussion.

"I don't know what is wrong with my brother," Yukti replied. "He sleeps all day and eats nothing. He has been a recluse ever since my parents made him quit marijuana. They caught him smoking one day, near his school, and have kept him as a prisoner since that day. I have no idea what to do. He says that he wants more freedom and I do understand that, but what can stop him from smoking again?"

"That's a problem," I said, admiring a kebab before putting it in my mouth. "Going to a therapist would help, I suppose."

"Yeah, but he is such a changed person," Yukti said, gloomily. "He was so full of life before this. I want to know who got him to start smoking and kill that person."

Obviously Yukti lacked the courage to accept the fact that her brother was responsible for his own actions. I could not say this out loud it would have been rude but I did understand the situation and my judgement was not hollow; I possessed prior experience of this ordeal.

If I ever think back about the time I drank alcohol or smoked a cigarette for the first time, I cannot help but blame myself. Certainly, if parents are more communicative with their children, it reduces the chances of the kids taking up the wrong path; but, we all make our own choices and mistakes. My parents had always been supportive and loving but I would not exactly classify them as communicative.

We used to have dialogues during meals, but our discussions only spanned politics and topics of religion or general philosophy. Nevertheless, their parenting could not stop me from getting addicted to alcohol or tobacco. It is true that my friend, Subhag, bought me my first cigarette, but he did not hold a gun to my temple to make me smoke, figuratively speaking. I chose it, and if I end up dead on a curb someday, my blood laced with cocaine or heroin, it would be my fault, not the society's or my parents'. But, how could I say this to Yukti?

"I think depression is a common side effect of marijuana withdrawal," I replied.

"I don't think he is depressed," she said.

"A psychologist will help you there, I guess," I said.

"At least he stopped smoking that god awful *maal,*" Yukti sighed. "Whatever the consequences, we can deal with them. I would have a few months to spend with him, before I join my job. I hope he feels better by then."

"When's your joining date?" Neera asked Yukti.

"14th December."

"That's pretty far away," Neera said. "So, would you come to McLo with us?"

"I don't know," replied Yukti. "Maybe not."

"Oh! It would be awfully sad if you don't come. The trip is still a few months away. Maybe your brother would feel better by then, and don't you worry, everything will be OK, sweetheart," Neera said, hugging Yukti.

Neera's warm embraces, unlike jet fuel, could melt steel, and Yukti could do nothing but cheer up.

CHAPTER VI

It was on a Sunday in July that I looked around my room, for the last time. Without my personal things it looked deserted, eagerly waiting for the next occupant. I sensed mournfulness in the morning air; whether it was a feeling of loss that filled my heart or the thought of bearing the inconvenience associated with relocation, I could not tell.

The hostel was deserted as most people had left for their homes. Mudit had set off for Gurgaon the previous day. I had found that Yukti had departed for Meerut, her hometown, without even bidding me goodbye. Pranay's brother arrived in the morning to take him home.

On hearing a car's horn, I dragged my bag out of the room, closed the door, and slowly walked to the parking lot. It was Neera, sitting in the driver's seat, waiting for me to bring out the last of my belongings. With great difficulty I shoved my bag into the trunk, which was already jam-packed with our luggage.

After closing the trunk, I slumped onto the seat beside the driver, and closed the door. Neera looked at me and asked:

"What took you so long? You went to bring just one bag."

"Sorry, I was just looking around the room for anything that I might've left behind."

She slowly pulled the car out of the parking. As the car crossed the college gate, I felt a sudden feeling of dread, knowing that I would not be in a protected environment anymore. When you are in a college similar to the one that I attended, you are somehow encapsulated from the world and its problems - be it politics, religion, or the economy - you just do not feel the negative effects. It dawned on me that the problems that I faced in college, which seemed gigantic, were minuscule in front of what was about to come. I clearly saw the darkness in my future and the tumult that would be added to it by the fact that Neera was pregnant.

My days as a student were over; I was an adult.

By the time we were about half way to Shimla, our destination, Neera did not say anything. Her eyes were fixated on the road, and we only spoke when it was absolutely essential.

"It was nice of your father to send this car," I uttered, trying to defuse the tension.

"Yeah, it was," she said, glancing at me. "He wanted Rajesh Kaka to drive us to Shimla, but I told him that we could do it ourselves. I thought that would give us some time alone to talk."

"Talk about what?"

"You know."

We kept silent for a while and as we entered Solan, a town located between Chandigarh and Shimla, she turned to me and said, "Prachur, I thought a lot about our situation and I have made up my mind. I want to tell you, but first, I want you to promise me that you will support me no matter what."

"How could I say that I will support you no matter what? What if you were trying to plan a robbery? Wouldn't blindly agreeing to your plans criminalise me?" I asked, chuckling.

"I am serious," she said, with a grim face.

"OK, dear. I will support you, no matter what."

"I want to keep the baby," she said, and then looking at me, when I said nothing, continued, "I know it sounds crazy, but I have been thinking so much about it. I know having a child is not something I should be doing at this age, but, for the life of me, I can't entertain the possibility of an abortion."

"Really? Don't you think you'd be screwing yourself? I mean, don't you have to study? This will require you to give up all your dreams. I don't think I am comfortable with that. Also, most importantly, how could we manage to be parents at such a young age?"

"I don't know anything about that. We could do anything, I could stop preparing for IAS and get a job — anything — but, please, don't make me kill our baby. It's a child of love." Although she tried her best to suppress her emotions, her eyes were filled with tears by the end.

Melting on account of her passionate appeal, I said, "I would never make you do anything that you don't want to."

"Then let me have this baby."

"Neera, you're just thinking emotionally. Please, take some more time, and think rationally about this."

"No. I took as long as I needed. I have made up my mind."

"Neera, don't be crazy..."

"Prachur, you can do this with me, or I can do it alone. I am not going to kill my baby."

"Neera, what about your future? Your dreams? Your aspirations?"

"I don't care. I want this. I'll figure a way out to balance the two things."

I sighed. I realised that there was absolutely no chance of changing her mind. Still, I decided to give it a last try.

"What if I don't want a child?"

"I don't know. You don't have to be a part of this. I won't bother you."

"So, you'll leave me?"

"If you can't accept this, then I would have no choice."

"Neera, you've gone completely crazy."

"I want this."

"Neera, I don't want to lose you, but I think this is ridiculous."

She said nothing, and we did not speak for the next half an hour.

"There's no way you'll change your mind?" I enquired, finally.

"No."

"Then what other choice do I have? Let's do it," I said, without enthusiasm.

"Not like this, Prachur. Either you do it with your heart, or you don't do it at all."

"How can I not do this? I love you. I can't lose you. Let's have a baby together. OK?"

"That's not cheerful, at all," she said.

"That's the best you're going to get."

She shook her head, and stared at the road.

After a while, I said, meekly, "Look, we can have the baby, we can do anything you want. I love you and I would support you. Also, forget this silly business of giving up your goals. If you really want to do this, I will take up a job. I'll figure something out soon, OK? Don't you worry."

"Are you sure?" she asked.

"Yes, a hundred per cent."

She stopped the car on the side of the road and, while we held each other, she wept profusely. On breaking the embrace, she said, while I wiped tears off her face, "I was so scared that you'll leave me. Last night, I could not get any sleep."

"Is that why you broke this news to me in a moving car, so I won't jump out? Good call because I actually considered that option." She gently pushed me away, to look up at me and smile.

She said, "I am happy. Are you happy?"

"Yes, Love," I replied promptly, so she could not sense my indecisiveness. "I am fine."

"Kiss me, please," she whispered.

Our lips met and I felt ecstatic. Her fragrance enchanted me into a trance; what would I not give to smell this every waking moment of my life! I could not lose her, whatever the cost.

After a few minutes of adoringly gazing at each other, we restarted our journey.

"So, are we going to tell our parents?" I asked her.

"Yeah, obviously, my Love," she replied.

"Really?"

"Yeah."

"We could hide it. We could tell them you are just getting fatter and act really surprised when the baby is born."

She smiled. "We have to tell them soon. The more we hide, the angrier they're going to be when they find out."

"True, true. But, you know that they're going to be very upset whenever we tell them, right? They care about society and stuff too much. They'd think of what our neighbours would say before they even consider our happiness. This is not a decision that concerns our career; it is about our future family life, the most important part according to them. Apart from that, there is still a billion to one chance that my parents might accept this, but yours, I am sure they will murder me."

"Yeah, I am worried about that too," she said, "but we will figure it out, right?"

I nodded. Fate and Neera had decided my future for me — all I could do was accept it.

+++

The majestic Himalayas laden with ample greenery greet any traveller entering Himachal Pradesh. The air is cool and the environment serene. Apart from the flora in this part of the nation, the kindness in the people residing in these hills was something I never found in other parts of India that I had visited. Clean streets run through the towns, which is a spectacle to most Indians.

"Shimla, 12 KM," said a board in green. The sun was shining

mildly because the afternoon was about to retire and hand over charge to the evening. We had reached Shoghi. This town marked the boundary of Shimla for me, and as we passed through it, I finally felt that I was close to home.

During the rest of the trip, I occasionally glinted at Neera. She was brilliant, funny, and beautiful. Her placid mind had often made me suggest that she should not waste her time joining the mindless drones in our bureaucracy. Research or academia were the fields starving for an intelligent person like her; but her parents had absolutely no respect for any profession practised by human beings except medicine, bureaucracy, and the armed forces.

Although she was occasionally emotional and timid, the clarity with which she tackled her problems was unparalleled, and I had always admired her determination. At the moment, she was bent on telling our parents that she was pregnant and was going to have our child no matter what people would say; her resolve was unrelenting, so I could not talk to her about my apprehensions. Leastways, my parents were expecting Neera and me to move forward in our relationship, but her parents were oblivious even of the fact that Neera had talked to my mother about our engagement last night; how could they endure such a turn of our fate?

I turned to Neera and enquired, "When are you planning to tell your parents?"

"I don't know," she replied, shrugging. "Soon, probably."

"You said 'soon' earlier as well. I meant, how soon? Like, today?"

"No, Prachur," she said. "I have not really planned everything, yet. I will tell them when I feel the time is opportune; maybe in a day or two."

"Please, inform me before you do, so that I have time to prepare myself for a considerable mental ordeal."

"Yeah. Of course, dear," she said, smiling. "And why are you worried about it? Are you not used to my parents thinking that you are the worst person in the world?" she joked.

"Yes, I am, but in things like not attending classes, loitering around the city all the time, or smoking. This...this is huge!"

"I guess, so," she said, nodding in approval. "Everything will be OK, darling. We are together, aren't we? As long as we love each other, we can solve these problems."

"I need to write a letter saying that if I go missing under suspicious circumstances, your father will be responsible," I said, half-jokingly. "Will you continue to love me after he kills me, or will you find someone else?"

"I will find someone else, obviously," she said, with a straight face. "I am too young to live my life by myself." When I shook my head, she laughed.

"Finding my troubles amusing, are you?"

How could she be as calm as she was? If my girlfriend — my future companion — was so tranquil about such an uncertain future, then why was my mind so uneasy? My anxiety increased as our destination drew closer.

The next few months are going to be harsh, I thought.

CHAPTER VII

After a four-hour journey Neera and I reached my parents' home, which was located on the outskirts of the city aptly named 'The Queen of the Hills'. I was not very fond of travelling and I felt a sense of relief when Neera pulled the car over, outside the gates of my house.

The ill-maintained street was lined on both sides by houses. The black metal gates were dusty, not due to neglect, but because of the clouds of dust that followed all the vehicles running on the battered street. A black plaque on one of the pillars, which held the gates, had the inscription, 'Shanti Niwas', which meant 'Shanti's Dwelling'. My parents had christened the house after my grandmother. It was a beautiful four-storeyed building, on a sloping hill, with only one floor above the level of the street. A red slanting roof graced its acme and the white coloured walls proved a sharp contrast to the lush greenery that surrounded them.

Shimla is a city that has sprung up despite the obvious hardships offered by the tough mountainous terrain, and most of its parts are not particularly planned. Houses have been constructed wherever people found land suitable enough to create an abode, even then, the density of population had grown exponentially. At least there was no other house in the immediate vicinity of our home. My parents had bought the land, on which the house stood, several years ago. I had always been glad that they had chosen a site that offered solitude.

Most parts of this city or town hardly have addresses that follow any logical pattern. It was my contention that the only reason residents received mail at home was because the postmen were familiar with everyone living in the area that they served.

Getting back to the tale, we got off the car, and I stood stretching while Neera went and rang the bell. The door was opened by my sister, Innaya - a lanky girl with a broad face, a feature she inherited from my father, and a round chin. Her eyes were full of kindness and she wore her hair short. A self-described feminist, she was pursuing a master's degree in Women's Studies at the local university in Shimla. She and I shared brown eyes and during our lives, numerous observers had pointed out that we looked alike; but I could never accept this fact.

She was jubilant on seeing us and rushed out of the door to hug Neera. They chuckled while exchanging queries about each other's well-being, before Innaya turned towards me and clasped me in her arms.

"Hi, Brother," I said. "Is my sister home?"

"I did not miss you at all," she replied.

"Neither did I," said I, smiling.

Our way of coping with an extended separation was to engage in friendly banter; tears are for the weak willed, we believed.

She was two years older than me but we had always been very close since childhood. During my adolescent years, she and Neera had been my sole company. For keeping the record fair, I must quickly state that she loved me more than I loved her, as she would often point out.

"Where're Mummy and Papa?" I enquired.

"Mom's out shopping, to get stuff for you - your favourite pastries and other things - and Dad's at work."

She and Neera went inside, holding hands, and I followed. We chatted about a variety of topics from the latest happenings in my sister's life to Neera's future plans. Neera and I refrained from speaking about our marriage. We had decided that I would break the information regarding her pregnancy to my sister in private.

The clock struck seven and we heard a car stop outside the gate. It was my mother returning from her shopping spree. I walked outside to help her with her bags; Neera and my sister followed me.

My mother was a typical Indian matriarch: short and plump - or rather stout, with a round face. She wore the traditional Indian *Salwar Kameez* with running shoes, which to an ordinary human being might sound like a bad fashion combination but the shoes were actually very useful to scale the slopes of the Himalayas. She had, as I had already stated, a pointed nose, and her hair was always tied in a bun. Beside the nose, she had also blessed me with a round chin, similar to hers.

She too, like my sister, hugged Neera first; my family preferred Neera to me - it was a fact that I had always known and loved. I bent down to touch her feet, like a morally sound Indian boy. However, since she was aware of my apprehensions about traditional practises, she was taken aback. After she quelled the rising anxiety in her heart about the change in her son's habit by asking a lot of trivial questions, we all went inside.

Neera and my mother chatted for a while before Neera's phone rang; the call was from her mother. I pointed out that we must unload my belongings from the car before Neera heads to her home, which was a few minutes' drive away. Before Neera and I walked out of the house to her car, my mother suggested that Neera drink tea with us. Even though Neera mentioned that she should really be hurrying home, my mother kept insisting until the offer was accepted.

"Please tell me what Innaya Di says after you break the news to her," Neera said to me, as she was helping me unload my belongings from the car.

"Of course, Dear," I said, taking a small black trolley bag out of her car's passenger seat. "She will take your side in any case. 'Women are always right' is the motto of these feminist retards."

Neera punched me in my arm; she hated to hear anything negative about Innaya, even if it were in the form of a hilarious joke.

"I hope she doesn't think badly of me," she said, concernedly.

"She wouldn't, I am telling you."

I was trying to console Neera but I was anxious myself. My sister supported me in everything, but I was afraid that the magnitude of this particular problem might cause her solidarity with me to waver. I would have found great comfort in my sister's support. She was one of those people who fight with all their strength for something they support or believe in.

By the time I was done unloading most of my luggage from the car, Innaya came out of the house and informed that hot tea was waiting for us. Neera and I hurried back inside.

"I talked to your mother," my mother said to Neera, while handing her a ceramic cup full of tea. "We will be joining you people for dinner tonight. It has been so long since we did that together. When was it, let me remember, last December, maybe? Yes, it was after you guys came back from your industrial tours. I sure miss your company, sweetheart."

"I miss you too, Aunty" Neera replied.

"At least, you call me," my mother said. "This mister never speaks to me, never picks up my calls. She is way better than you," she said to me, "she talks to me, every day. She is more of a daughter to me than you are a son."

Neera got up and hugged my mother.

"What are you talking about?" I exclaimed. "I called you every day! Have you ever heard of a college-going boy talking to his parents every day? I am the only one in the whole batch who did it. All my friends talked to their parents like once every two weeks. They call me a 'mama's boy.'"

"I don't care what the boys who don't love their parents say," she retorted. "I want you to talk to me, every day."

"Yeah, Prachur, my boy, you should talk to the lady who gave birth to you," my sister laughed. Neera smiled and nodded in agreement.

At this point, it dawned on me why a small part of me was dreading coming back home. My mother, sister, and Neera would often band together in making fun of me. What was I to say if all of my adversaries were ready to twist facts and ignore general logic during the course of our debate?

"When will Papa return?" I asked, in an effort to change the course of the conversation. Thankfully, the manoeuvre worked.

"He'll join us after he finishes his work," my mother replied.

"Are we going to Neera's house?"

"No, we will go to *The Great Indian Palace,*" she replied.

By and by, we finished our tea and after some warm adios, Neera and I walked to her car. I wanted to kiss her to show her that I will miss her, but since we lived in a country where a consensual meeting of lips in public was generally regarded as a bigger crime than rape, I only hugged her. She whispered, "I love you," in my ear, as I embraced her strongly. "And I you," I replied, before she got in her car and drove away.

✦✦✦

Two hours after Neera left, my mother drove us to *The Great Indian Palace,* which was located on Shimla's famous Mall Road. The place was bustling with people and we had to wait for a while before a waiter led us to a table that could seat eight people. The plastered walls of the restaurant were lined with polished wood, and hanging lamps set the ambiance. Tables were closely arranged together and there was barely space to walk around. It was nothing short of fantastic to watch the waiters fight their way to deliver orders to the starving customers.

As my mother, Innaya, and I sat discussing options for appetisers, Neera walked in through the door, followed by her parents.

Her father, Mr Rana, was a pot-bellied man in his fifties, who walked with an air of authority. His head initially seemed bent on balding but had decided against it after reaching half way. He was wearing a chequered shirt, which was tucked into his navy blue pants. He kept a 'handlebar' moustache, as a sign of his Kshatriya class of the archaic and discriminatory caste system of the Indian society.

Neera's mother was a petite woman who dressed in Indian suits. She shared a lot of her facial features with Neera. Although highly educated, she was a staunchly religious woman. She wore the traditional Indian *bindi* and a *mangalsutra*, marks of a married woman. She wore glasses, which made her face look smaller than it really was.

Both of them were officers in the Himachal Allied Services. After the ceremonial exchange of *namastes,* they took seats around the table; Neera sat opposite to me.

Neera's mother, who was sitting next to her daughter, turned to me and asked, "How're you feeling, Prachur, now that your degree is over? Excited? Scared?"

I was certain she was not expecting a reply; all she wanted was to vent her thoughts to a receptive audience. Nevertheless, I started to answer, as a mark of common courtesy, but she continued:"Neera is so tensed about her future, and I always tell her not to be worried all the time. But, kids these days are so competitive. In our days, we would study for eight hours a day and not give any thought to the outcome. Do your duty and don't worry about the results, I always say."

I could do nothing but nod.

"Prachur," Neera's father said, "what was your final grade point, eh young man?"

"6.3, Uncle."

"Were you eligible for the campus placement process?" he enquired, condescendingly. Neera's GPA was '9.6'; no wonder he was flaunting it.

"I was, yes."

"But, you did not take a job?"

"No, Uncle."

"Why? What is that you plan to do?"

"I don't really know what I want to do, but I am sure that the absolutely last thing I want is to take a job and drudge day and night to make a heap of cash for someone else."

"Maybe that is the way you justify it; maybe, you are just lazy and you are inventing these explanations to hide that very fact."

"Yes, Uncle," I replied, sitting up in my chair. I expected this conversation and I was adequately prepared for it. "It could be true that I might just be lazy and that I loathe a job just because I am not a hard working person. But, if this were true, the last thing I should do is get a job. I mean, if I have no intention to work and I only take up a job because of the sole reason most people do it - to earn money - would that not be unfair to my employer? They'll ask me, 'Why do you want this position?' and I cannot just say, 'I need money to eat, Sir, like the rest of the world, as you might have noted, needs.' I would have to concoct a reason to explain why I deserve that particular position and of course my reason would be untrue. So, a lazy person can bag a job that he does not want by inventing a web of lies, solely to deceive an interviewer; in what way is that beneficial to anyone?"

"Kids these days," my mother interrupted me, "have their own mindset."

"Yes, that may be Mrs Thakur," Neera's father replied, turning towards my mother, "but, what does this kind of mentality achieve? I mean, you have to earn money, and you need to work to contribute to this country. If every young person starts thinking like this, the country would go to hell."

As far as I had observed, the country had already gone to hell, and it was his generation that had contributed more than mine to bringing this nation to its current predicament.

"Yes, that is true," my mother replied, looking at me.

"If every young person works half-heartedly, Uncle," I replied, "then, this great nation of yours would head towards downfall."

"So, doing nothing is better than doing something?" he asked.

Neera's expression told me that I should stop the train of this particular conversation, but in the heat of the moment, I found myself too deeply engrossed in it to care about consequences.

"Yeah, of course it is, Uncle." I replied, with a straight face. "I'd prefer failure to mediocrity, any day."

"You're just a kid," he snapped. "You have not seen anything. When you'll see the world, you'll understand that you have to think practically. Life is all about sacrifices and compromises, son. Don't think that you can get through it based on just some foolish ideology."

"I do agree that life probably is about compromises, Uncle. The thing I want to add is that if you accept this as a fact, then you have no right to criticise the way things are running — the government, the electricity department, the police, or anything else. I mean, if politicians represent us in the local assemblies half-heartedly, it should be no wonder if the streets are littered with potholes."

Neera kicked my leg, under the table, and was shaking her head. Taking the hint, I added, "But, like you said, life is all about sacrifices, and in the next few days I'd be exploring the options available to me, including finding a job. After all, I must be prepared for the future, and everything it will throw at me."

In the meantime, my father had joined us at our table. A tall man with short hair, he did not keep a moustache, which made his proportionally big nose stand out. His forehead was riddled with wrinkles. Innaya inherited his wheatish colour. He was well built, a consequence of his daily exercise, and would often suggest, to my discomfort, that I get up in the morning to jog as well.

"Namaste, Mrs Rana," he said, before shaking hands with Mr Rana.

"That's what I want to hear," Neera's father said, turning to me.

Finally, now that the atmosphere had become placid on account of my father's arrival, I realised that I did want Neera's father to be pleased with me at the time the news of the development between Neera and me was revealed to him. Gentle flattery is the right path to take from now onwards, I thought.

"What are you guys talking about?" my father asked.

"Nothing much," replied Mrs Rana. "Prachur was enlightening us regarding his views about the world."

"Really?" He looked at me, enquiringly. "He does have strange views."

"That's an understatement," replied Mr Rana.

"But, no matter what, he *is* my son," replied my father, smiling. "What can I do?"

The conversation then shifted to the typical topic prevalent among people in Shimla - local politics, which I will refrain from detailing as I found it pointless and, quite frankly, plebeian.

Following dinner, the rest of the evening progressed smoothly, as we all took a walk in the calm and cool summer air of Shimla. It was late into the night, but since the city was swarming with tourists from the plains of Northern India in the hot months of the year, shops were still open.

Neera and I walked behind the rest of the party.

She clenched my arm and said, slowly, "We should tell them, like, tonight."

"No! What? No!" I exclaimed.

"Yeah, everything's calm, my father is in a jolly mood, and they're all here. What more do we need?"

"You want to tell our parents on Mall Road? That would be some scene! I don't know about you, my crazy Love, but I do not intend to die today, and that too in full public view."

"Not here, darling. What I mean is that we can tell them after we reach home. You could tell your parents to visit my home, for five minutes."

"No, no! Not today, please."

"Why not? The more we wait, the worse this situation is going to get. What exactly are you waiting for?"

"I want to talk to Innaya first. I will tell her and then we can talk to them."

I would have preferred to conceal this secret forever, but that would have been impossible. I assured Neera that I would speak to Innaya that very night.

+++

When we reached our home, I told Innaya that I had to tell her something important, and suggested that she join me in my room.

My poshly-furnished room had a computer table placed along the wall opposite to the door. To its left was my bed, laden with quilts and blankets. The marble floor was sparkling clean, except for the parts that were dotted with my possessions, which I had brought from my hostel room. There was a picture frame above my table on the wall, with photos of my family and Neera. Apart from that the creamy walls were mostly bare, as I did not enjoy having posters in my room. The closet doors were shut and my clothes inside were neatly organised - something that would soon change with the course of time due to my recent occupation of the room.

Innaya sat on the bed, while I took my place on the chair next to the table.

My mind was riddled with questions: How must I divulge this shocking piece of information? Should I lead her to it or should I blurt it out suddenly? My experience had taught me that the most sensitive information is better revealed quickly and painlessly, exactly how I would prefer my death. I must pour out my heart and expect that it would not be trampled upon.

"What?" she asked me, as I sat pondering and staring at the door, which was slightly open. "Say something. Is everything OK?"

"Don't go crazy when you hear what I have to say," I replied, "and keep your voice down. I don't want Mama and Papa to know right now."

"Oh my God!" she exclaimed, but checked her voice suddenly. "What the hell did you do? Is your degree not finished? Would you have to retake some of your subjects? Tell me!"

"No, it's not about my degree," I answered, impatiently.

"Then, what?"

I got up, shut the door, and sat down on my chair. After taking a deep breath I said, "Don't freak out, OK?" Upon seeing that she mouthed the word 'OK', I said, "Neera's pregnant."

"What!" she exclaimed, and put her hands on her mouth.

"She's pregnant, we found out like a few days ago."

"Is this for real? You're making a fool out of me, aren't you?"

"Na, it's true."

"Oh my God!" she said. "How could you do it, you fool? You idiot! Mom and Dad are going to freak out! Oh my God!" All this while, she was punching my arm.

"Ouch, that hurts!"

"Yeah, it should," she replied, punching my arm again. "Prachur, how could you be so stupid?"

"It happened, OK. I am sorry. Now I want you to support..."

"Support?" she snapped, getting up from the bed. "Support you in what? Oh my god! My little brother, what have you done?"

I said nothing while she walked around the room, recovering from the shock.

"This is going to bruise," I contemplated aloud, examining the place where my sister had let out her shock-driven fury. She ignored my concerns.

Finally, when she sat down, she whispered, "How's Neera? What does she want to do?"

"She's fine."

Before I could answer the other question, she punched me, thankfully, in my other arm, and enquired, "How dare you put that sweet little girl in this situation?"

"Put her in this situation? I did not force her. It happened."

"It happened? How can this just 'happen'?"

"You want me to explain how a girl gets pregnant? I think you should rather consult a sex education class."

"Stop kidding around, you ass."

"Sorry. Look, she took a pill afterwards, alright?"

"Couldn't you have controlled yourself, and waited to buy a condom, you sex-crazed monkey?"

"We didn't risk it due to non-availability of a prophylactic, my dear madam. The choice was based on other reasons, but that is not important. What matters is the course of action we need to pursue now."

"What reason could you possibly have?"

"We wanted to do it, without anything between us. That sounds stupid, I know. It was an emotional thing. And it was not the first time that we did this. I mean, nothing had happened before; how were we supposed to know that it'll happen this time?"

"Wow!" she cried out, shaking her head, and sat quietly for a while, holding her head in her hands. Minutes fleeted by before she asked, "What the hell do you expect me to do?"

"I don't know. Resolve this situation. That's all I need."

"What do you guys want? What does Neera want?"

"She wants to keep the baby."

"And what do you want?"

"I want what she wants."

"Really?"

"Yeah," I mumbled.

"You don't sound decisive."

"I am, though."

"You want to have this baby out of wedlock?"

"We haven't talked about that yet, but she wants to have this baby."

"God, please give this boy some sense!" she said, before she got up and left the room.

I felt as if I had been relieved of a huge burden. There was no way that Innaya would do something that would compromise my happiness. At least, now I had someone sharp and sober to help me survive this predicament; I had outsourced my worries.

I lay on the bed, and wrote a text to Neera, which said:

"Told Innaya..."

"Was she angry?" she replied.

"Yeah, kinda. She'll be fine, though. Don't worry."

"Can we tell our parents now?"

"Can't that wait?"

"No."

"I don't know what to say, Neera."

"I'll tell them over the next few days. Don't worry. GN. ILU."

I was amidst typing a reply when Innaya entered my room.

"A knock would be appreciated, very much."

"Shut up, you ungrateful piglet, and listen," she replied, sitting on the chair. "I thought about this and I think you guys should abort the baby. I think that is the best resort for you. There's no way you guys are mature enough to have a baby."

"Neera doesn't want that."

"Prachur, don't be silly."

"She does not want that, I am telling you," I replied.

"It's crazy!"

"I know."

"Should I talk to her?"

"You can do whatever you want, but she's not going to change her mind. I am scared about the consequences as well, but this is what she wants."

"Let me talk to her, wait," said Innaya, before she left my room.

+++

The clock struck eleven. I was looking around the room, carelessly. Innaya sat staring at the wall opposite to the bed, and finally, rubbed her face and said, "Neera is so determined to do this. I can't believe it."

"Told ya."

"Prachur, do *you* want to do this? This sounds nothing like you. You live so irresponsibly."

"Innu, I can't lose Neera. I'll do whatever it takes to keep her in my life."

"But, this... Prachur, what can I say? If you're bent upon pursuing the course you want, even after knowing what's best for both of you, what can I do? I will help you, my stupid brother."

I nodded.

She added, "I just suggest that you should tell Mom and Dad as soon as possible, and I will be there when you break this shocking piece of info. It'll be tough at first, but they'll have to accept eventually. I mean, what else could they do? They could throw you out of the house - yes, they could," she continued after a pause, "but I don't think they will try anything that might hurt Neera, so that is not an issue you should be worried about."

"Thanks, babe," I said, hugging her. "I knew you would support me. You are the greatest sis in the world. Make sure that my will be done."

She shoved me away, and walked out of the room. "Good night!" I said as she closed the door behind her.

CHAPTER VIII

I had always despised uncertainty. It makes one vulnerable. How can people expect to move on when they cannot see where they are headed? It is like driving with a blindfold. If everyone did that, save maybe a tiny minority that might never have an accident, most of us would be dead very soon.

Why could we not get a script of the part we were supposed to play in this life? I would much rather memorise the lines I was supposed to say, than try to figure out my place in this universe.

I always liked being in the know — it was one of things that made me like science. After revealing Neera's pregnancy to Innaya, I was feeling uncertain, and therefore uncomfortable. Innaya's support, howsoever reluctant it might have been, did lower my anxiety, but still I had no idea about the events that might follow Neera's conversation with her parents.

Mr Rana had always had a bad temper, something I had always been afraid of. He saw me as a leech on the economy and a worthless excuse for a human being. I am not even paraphrasing; I had heard these words from him over the years. Mrs Rana's behaviour towards me was no better.

I knew perfectly well that howsoever gently Neera managed to break the news to her parents, they would be angry. But, I had to deal with it. Neera had left me no choice.

+++

"Where is that little piece of crap?"

I rolled over. The cool morning air and my laziness insisted that I stay in bed rather than welcome the sunny morning with open arms. My dream woke me, but strangely I remembered nothing of it. I sat up and ascertained, by looking at the clock on my table, that it was 8:22 AM. Birds had started singing, as is their vocation, and monkeys were frolicking over the roof. Sunlight somehow found its way through the drapes and was pouring in through the windows.

"Bhai Sahab, please calm down," I heard my mother say.

"No, I am not going to calm down! I want to know where he is."

The other voice was of Neera's father. He sounded furious. I checked my phone and noticed that I had missed a few calls from Neera.

"Prachur, Rana Uncle is here, and he is really pissed off," Innaya said, as she burst in through the door.

We both knew why he was there. I got out of bed and Innaya disappeared downstairs. I *had* to go down, what other option did I have? I looked at the window of the room, as a possible escape route, but a metal grill stood between me and my safety. Reluctantly, I walked out of the room towards the bustle.

"Rana Ji, what is the matter?" I heard my father enquire.

Mrs Rana was barely holding back her husband. Neera stood behind them, tears streaming down her face. They were standing in the living room, near the coffee table surrounded by sofas. There was an oak dining table in one corner of the room. A TV was on the wall directly opposite the stairs, and although it was muted, I could see that some anchor was struggling to get through the morning broadcast. My mother was at the dining table, hurriedly pouring water in a glass.

"There he is!" Mr Rana shouted, as he pushed his wife aside, and started moving towards me.

I halted at the last step of the staircase. Luckily, my father stopped him. Mr Rana's eyes were shot red and his face betrayed a blood lust.

So, this is how I die, I thought - no parades, no ceremonial firing of twenty one guns, just an angry father and a dead boy. What would I be remembered for? Being a staunch cynic? Being lazy? I was clear about the fact that I had not contributed to this world enough to justify building of statues after me.

"At least, tell me what the matter is, Rana Ji," my father said, repeatedly.

"Ask, him," Mr Rana thundered, pointing at me.

"Prachur," my father looked at me, "What did you do to make Rana Ji this angry?"

"Nothing that I remember, Papa."

"He knows, this lethargic no-good moron knows!"

"Prachur, what did you do? Tell me!"

I looked at Neera and she mouthed the words, "I am sorry."

"I don't know, Papa. Maybe some context will help."

"Context, this dog needs context," Mr Rana barked. "Neera, tell Thakur Sahab."

Neera wiped tears off her face and stood looking at the floor.

"Tell him," shouted Mr Rana, as my mother offered him a glass of water, which he refused.

"I am pregnant," Neera mumbled.

"What!" gasped my mother as my father let go of Mr Rana.

There would be no beating around the bush, anymore. The truth was out. I was aware of the graveness of this development, but the first thing that my brain told me to do was to joke, "With whose baby?" and expect people to calm down as they laugh their heads off.

No Prachur, no kidding around, not now, I told myself.

"You knew this?" asked my father.

I nodded slowly, in an effort to be ambiguous, but the message was received unabridged.

Silence dawned on the room. My parents stood still, while Neera's father sank into the sofa, and stared at me. He was expecting some form of corporal punishment for me in lieu of my actions, but my parents did not believe in beating the life out of their children for any reason, whatsoever.

"Prachur, oh Prachur!" my mother said, as she kept the glass full of water back on the table.

"He destroyed our daughter's future," Mrs Rana pointed out.

"No, Mummy, he..." Neera said, feebly.

"Shut up!" Mr Rana interrupted, glaring at Neera.

"I don't know what to say," said my father.

"I know what to say, Mr Thakur," replied Mr Rana. "I know. I don't ever want your son to see my daughter. I hope you'll understand."

"But, Papa," Neera began, but Mr Rana told her to keep quiet.

"Uncle, you can't do this," Innaya said. "You can't separate them, not after this."

"Young lady, they are obviously too stupid and naive to see the difference between right and wrong," replied Mr Rana. Turning towards me, he added, "If you ever try to contact Neera, I'll kill you."

"What do you want to do about the baby, Uncle?" Innaya retorted.

"That's none of your business," Mrs Rana replied for her husband.

"It is, actually, Aunty," snapped Innaya. "Neera is pregnant with my brother's kid, so it is my business."

"Your brother does something wrong and you are taking his side?" replied Mrs Rana. "Terrific!"

"Yes, I am. Now, tell me. What exactly do you want to do about the baby? Kill it?"

"You shouldn't concern yourself with what our daughter does," said Mr Rana, getting up agitatedly.

"Dear, please, stop it," said my mother, to pacify Innaya. "We can talk about this later, when we've all cooled down."

"Not now, Ma," said Innaya.

"But..."

"I said, not now, Mom," shot Innaya.

"We're leaving," said Mrs Rana, grasping hold of Neera's hand.

"No, you aren't," said Innaya. "Are you going to force Neera to do something against her will? I swear, I would get you guys put behind bars!"

"Look at her courage!" exclaimed Mr Rana. "Her brother violated our daughter, and she wants to make us feel guilty about making the right choice."

"My brother didn't 'violate' your daughter, Uncle," yelled Innaya. She took a deep breath, and continued slowly, "They've been a couple for years, and you know that. Whatever happened, happened with consent. We can only guide them; we can't force them into something they hate. Please, Uncle, think about their happiness."

"Happiness?" Mrs Rana said, letting go of Neera's hand. "Did they care about us, before they did something so heinous? What are we supposed to do now? Whether or not we kill this *thing*, everyone's going to know about it. This is a small town; gossip travels very fast here. You have no idea about the things that people are going to say about my daughter. Do you have any idea how big an issue being pregnant before being married is? Have you lost your mind, silly girl?"

My father stood silently, observing the conversation. My mother had taken a seat near the dining table, and was crying her eyes out.

"Aunty, I know people will talk," Innaya said, calmly. "But, would you risk your daughter's happiness for the opinion of your neighbours? Do you even know what your daughter wants to do?"

"Yes, she told us," retorted Mr Rana. "She has lost her mind. This little pest here," he said, pointing at me, "has corrupted the mind of our daughter."

Adulthood does not begin at eighteen in India, you only get the right to vote at that age; it begins when you become financially independent. Neera and I were not earning, and thus, we were not allowed to think for ourselves.

"Papa, he did nothing wrong, it was my..." started Neera. She was, yet again, interrupted by a "Shut up!" from Mr Rana.

"Stupid girl, you must keep your mouth shut. Let us talk," said Mrs Rana severely to Neera.

"Ma..." Neera began to speak.

At this moment, Mrs Rana moved towards Neera, in an apparent rage to slap her. Sensing this, Innaya jumped between them. "Aunty, have you gone crazy?" she exclaimed.

"What right do you have to talk to me in this way?" Mrs Rana asked Innaya, sternly.

"Aunty, please," I said, finally finding courage to contribute to the dialogue.

"Prachur, go to your room," my father said.

I hated to see Neera cry and seeing tears in the eyes of the love of my life was making me furious. But what was I supposed to do? We were not married, ergo legally she was not mine. The only thing that could give her some topical relief at this point was the support of my parents. Therefore, I thought I would make an appeal for the same.

"But, Papa, you can't let Neera be treated this way," I replied, with a cracked voice.

"I said, go to your room!"

"No, stay Prachur," said Innaya. "Let him stay, Papa. He's right. The way they are treating Neera is just plain wrong."

"She is their daughter, we have no right to interfere, Innu," replied my father.

"I don't even know why we came here," said Mr Rana meekly. "We should have taken care of it ourselves. Mr Good-for-nothing here had no intention of telling either his parents or us."

"They were going to tell everyone soon," said Innaya.

"Since when have you known?" Mrs Rana, enquired. "Incredible! How deceptive could you kids be?"

"Prachur told me last night, OK?" answered Innaya, apathetically. "What does it matter, anyway?"

There was a few minutes of silence before Mrs Rana said, addressing everyone, "You know, how crazy he has made our daughter? She came to us this morning and said, 'Mama, Papa, I am pregnant with Prachur's child. And, we want to have the baby.' No shame at all in kids these days! On the contrary, she sounded happy; can you believe it? If something like this happened with me, I would have died of guilt before telling my parents; but, she was explaining how they could raise a bastard child."

"It's not a bastard, mind your language, Aunty," snapped Innaya.

"Yeah?" replied Mrs Rana. "Then what is it? A gift from God? I pray two times every day, yet this is what I am 'blessed' with? What could I have done wrong?" wailed she.

"How about you see this as a token of their love?" Innaya asked Mrs Rana.

"This is a blot on our dignity!" Mr Rana said, sitting back on the sofa. "That's what it is, nothing else."

"You have a choice of seeing this either way, Uncle," Innaya pointed out.

Mr Rana rolled his eyes, and turned to my father, "What did we do wrong, Thakur Ji? We gave them everything. Where did we go wrong? What could we possibly have done in this life or the last to have our kids go out and make a mockery of us in front of the whole world?"

My father just shook his head to indicate he was short of words on the subject. Silence prevailed. Neera stared at the ground, and I fixated on her.

"We have to do what's right for us," said Mr Rana, his voice barely being audible.

"I know," replied my father. "Do what you think is right, Rana Ji."

"Papa, you can't possibly let Neera go through this, please!"

Innaya cried out. "Please, Uncle," she said, seating herself on the floor, next to Mr Rana, "do you really think Neera can go through this and be happy?"

"She'll do what I say, if she wants to live under my roof," Mr Rana said, looking away from Innaya. He sat contemplating for a while, then moved towards the door saying, "This conversation is over. I hope you'll make sure that your son doesn't see my daughter anymore, Thakur Ji."

My father simply nodded his assent. Mrs Rana followed her husband, dragging Neera along with her.

"God! How stupid can you be?" shouted Innaya, from the front gates of our home, as the Rana family walked to their house.

"Please, don't make a scene," my mother implored Innaya.

Innaya returned from the door mumbling profanities. I was still standing on the staircase.

"Ma, Pa," I said, before I was interrupted by Innaya.

"Go to your room, Prachur," she said.

"But.."

"Go to your room!"

My parents did not even glance at me. With my head hung low, I walked back to my room without closing the door behind me. I was sure that they were going to discuss the latest development and I wanted to know what my parents thought of the issue, so that I was well prepared for my next step.

"Kuldeep," said my mother, feebly. "What has Prachur done! What now?"

"I don't know, Tara," my father replied.

"The whole world is going to find out soon," cried out my mother.

"No one's going to find out, Ma," said Innaya. "Who is going to tell people? You are never going to talk about this and there is zero chance that Rana Uncle will mention it to any soul, living or dead."

"Yeah, she's right," said my father. "But, we still need to think what to do? How could this boy be so stupid? We've always given him all the freedom he has ever wanted, maybe that was the problem. I understand all about not wanting a job, but taking a huge step like this!"

"Rana Ji is going to do that thing to the baby, I am sure," said my mother.

"Yeah, probably," my father replied. "Innu, I want you to stay out of this, OK? This is their family matter, not ours. Besides, doing what Rana Ji wants to do is probably good for us too. I mean, what if Neera has this baby? She will be humiliated in the society and so will our son. No, No! We must keep mum about this business."

"You're right," said my mother.

Innaya did not object, it would have been futile. Instead, she calmly said, "That's your grandchild."

My parents fell silent.

Finally, my mother said, "Let Rana Sahab do what he pleases. You'd better not interfere, Innu."

Innaya climbed up the stairs and entered my room. I was sitting on the edge of the bed.

"Let'em calm down, then we'll see what to do," she said.

"What if Rana Uncle forces Neera to do it within the time we are waiting?" I enquired, concernedly. "I tried calling her, but her phone's switched off. I am sure her parents have forced her to do that."

Innaya nodded and said, "I can try to meet Neera, in a few hours. You should stay here. It's better for everyone if there is no drama outside on the streets."

"So I am supposed to sit here, while she is being tortured there? They obviously hit her - I swear I saw bruises on her face."

"I know, Prachur. I did too, but if you try to meet her, you'll only make things worse. Let me go there after lunch, and I will talk to them peacefully."

With these words, she retired to her room.

I noticed my hands were shaking. Numerous emotions had taken possession of my mind. I was angry with the Ranas and with myself for not speaking when the time was right. My sadness was tormenting me physically and I felt nauseated. I walked around the room agitated and desperate for a smoke, but I never smoked at home. My eyes were wet, and I felt helpless. I contemplated various ways in which I could make Neera's life better; most of them were filled with imaginary scenarios involving heroic antics, but none of them involved a logical course of action. I was not financially secure myself, and my parents were clearly not going to support me.

"What should I do?" I whimpered, as I sat back on the bed, and pulled my hair.

CHAPTER IX

Hours had passed since Neera and her parents left after that horrendous scene. Innaya went to their home after lunch and returned without any substantial information. Mrs and Mr Rana had been adamant and had not allowed her to meet Neera, so she calmed herself down by shouting profanities at them before walking back home. She assured me that she would try again in the evening.

I had breakfast and lunch in my room, alone, as my parents appeared to have forsaken me. They avoided looking at me when they passed by the door. I knew I had disappointed them, but I would have loved some consolation; I might not have deserved their embrace, but the boy inside me longed for it.

I called Neera every five minutes, but her phone was switched off. I was lying on the bed, staring at the beige ceiling, with my arms crossed under my head. The house was quiet; I could clearly hear the vehicles outside and the noise of people talking on the street, but I did not hear much from my parents. Even though the Sun had set, I could still see the sky and the buildings on the hills opposite our house through my window. During my childhood, I would spend hours looking outside, avoiding my school work, and that time, I preferred reclusion; but now since that was all I had, I felt lonely. I am not a creature who desires abundant attention, but on occasion, I certainly love to be pampered.

I could not help but feel that if Neera had agreed to abort the baby, none of this would have happened, and I lost a bit of respect for myself. How could I not stand by her? She had done the same for me, so many times.

With an urge to write, I sat at my laptop. A blinking cursor greeted me. I took a deep breath and jotted down a poem.

Dark Days

Glaring at the dark abyss ahead, I learn,
Our fate is never what we yearn.
It happened when I thought I held the wheel,
The harsh blow of destiny made me kneel.

Thinking back I ask myself again,
How could I deserve such pain?
To accept this is my only choice,
There is no way fate can be enticed.

And here I stand, before the gates of my dream,
My hopes locked away, I hear them scream,
I hold the lock but I don't have the key,
Indeed, there are very dark days ahead of me.

After reading the poem several times, and on conceiving no way to improve it, I fell back on the bed, and quickly fell asleep.

As the clock struck seven, I heard Innaya climb the stairs to our floor; she had returned from Neera's home. I hurried to the door, and asked, "How did it go?"

She said nothing, entered my room, and closed the door behind her.

"How did it go?" I repeated.

"Not great," she replied. "I did meet her but her parents were in the room with us all the while. She has obviously been crying a lot and looks awful. She barely had the courage to speak, and her parents were interrupting her at every sentence. Maybe she wants to abort, I don't know, Prachur; I *think* she does. She did not say it clearly but she did agree to her father saying that an abortion is the best option for her. I couldn't change her mind; I kept telling her that everything will be OK if she has this baby, but she said she'll do what her parents want. I am so sorry. I really am."

"I can't believe that she agreed to it," I said, shocked by what I heard. "She wanted to have this baby so badly. I can't understand how she can change her mind so quickly."

"This is the truth, Prachur," she mumbled.

"They obviously broke her spirit, somehow," I said, standing up, hurriedly. "I swear to God if they hurt her, I would elope with her. I couldn't care less about what people would say. I would work as a coolie or a janitor, but I am not going to let some pretentious idiots destroy my future to save their imaginary reputation. But first, I have to hear what Neera thinks, myself." After walking excitedly around the room, for a few seconds, while Innaya silently looked at me, I asked her, "What did she say about us, about our relationship? Does she want to meet me?"

"She didn't say much about you," Innaya said, "but, I don't think she wants to be with you anymore. I asked her if she would want to meet you, to talk to you, but she did not reply. Of course, her parents hate your very name. They cringed every time I brought it up in the conversation."

I stood, looking out of the window. I had nothing to say. I could not believe that Neera wants to end our relationship, even if I heard it from a person I trusted more than myself.

Innaya hugged me and said, "I am sorry, brother."

"I don't know what to do," I said, sulkily. She tightened her embrace.

After she consoled me and told me that she will talk to our parents about this matter, she went to her room, as she and I both felt that peace and seclusion were the best remedy for me.

After ruminating for a while, I made up my mind to meet Neera. I had to find out for myself what her heart wanted.

I decided that I would go to her house after midnight, come what may.

+++

I sat on the chair, with my eyes closed, in my room amidst darkness. Midnight had passed, but I was not sleepy. I checked my watch and decided it was time for me to leave. Slowly, I got up and walked to the door. I opened it, and put my ear out to catch any noise. Deathly silence prevailed, so I crept out of the room, and walked down to the living room. I lit up the screen of my phone and, in its light, found Innaya's car keys. Stealthily, I walked to the outer gate of our house and climbed over it.

The street was deserted and most of it was poorly lit in the Moonlight. I walked to Innaya's car, which she parked some fifty metres away from our home, because that was the only place where parking on the side of the road was possible. Innaya owned an old black Maruti car. It was the first car that my parents had bought decades ago and was still in good condition. As Innaya was fond of it, she took good care of it. I opened the door, carefully, and looked around to make sure there were no witnesses to my act.

I had done this numerous times. When I was in school, I would often sneak out to meet Neera. We would find privacy in the comfort of this car. What better place to engage in acts of love other than inside a vehicle parked in a desolate place?

I pushed the car slowly to a point that I felt was safe enough for me to start it, without waking up anyone in my house. Doing this was easier now that I was grown up and physically stronger than when I was a kid. I drove without headlights for some distance before I turned them on. I knew it was dangerous, but what else was I supposed to do in a society with so many constraints?

Within a few minutes, I found myself in the vicinity of Neera's house. I stopped the car around a blind curve, turned the lights off, and walked towards her house. All of its three storeys stood below ground level. It was barely possible to discern the green colour of its wall in the moonlight. Two cars were parked outside. Therefore, I was sure that the Rana family was home. No light seemed to be on inside the house, a fact which I found comforting.

Neera's room was on the second floor. I swiftly climbed over a small white brick fence that surrounded the house. From there onward, I had to scale down a retaining wall that was built in the form of steps, which I did without making any substantial noise. Soon, I had reached the level of Neera's room. I carefully stepped on the ledge outside the house's wall and walked to the balcony, which had a door that led to her room. With practice comes confidence, and even though I had mild acrophobia, I never felt scared performing this particular feat.

Once on the balcony, I looked in through a small window next to the door, which was not covered with drapes. I saw that Neera was sleeping in her bed. I took out my phone, and with my fingers crossed, dialled her phone number.

"The number you're trying to reach is switched off."

I exasperatedly put my phone in my pocket and gently tapped once on the glass of the window. Thankfully, she sat up in her bed and looked in my direction. I waved at her, and gestured for her to let me in. She jumped out of bed, and opened the door.

Moonlight fell on her face. Her brown eyes, full of surprise, gazed at me. All the anxiety and fear in my heart vanished, as happiness and determination took their place. I could do anything for those eyes.

"Neera, I wanted..." I started, but before I could finish, she had wrapped her arms around me, and we were kissing passionately.

"I missed you so much," I said, barraging her face with gentle pecks.

"Me too," she replied, and we locked our lips again.

We heard a car pass by her house and I gestured that she follow me. She put on her shoes and her jacket, and within a few moments, I was helping her climb down the ledge outside her room to the retaining wall. After she quietly closed the door on her side of the car, I drove us away.

We both knew where we were going. Before we joined college, we would often drive down a secluded road connected to the street my house was on, till we reached a natural pathway heading into the forest surrounding the road. This led us to a clearing, a place that we found peaceful and private.

I stopped the car on reaching our spot and after turning off the engine, looked at her, and brushed her hair from her face.

"Please tell me you're not OK with what your parents want," I said.

"I am not," she said, tearfully.

"Innaya told me that..."

"My mother told me to choose either my family or this baby. She told me that if I have this child, she can do anything before I shame our whole family; even kill herself. I was so scared!"

I hugged her and said, "She'll not do anything, darling. She's just emotional." I wanted to say 'crazy', but 'emotional' seemed more appropriate. "Please calm down. Nothing bad is going to happen."

"No, Prachur," she sulked. "Day after tomorrow, they have arranged to visit a family friend, who's a doctor, in Solan. I am sure they want to kill my baby."

"No one is going to do anything," I said. "You need to tell me, what you want to do. Forget what your mother wants, forget the world, forget any consequences of your choice; just tell me, what do *you* want?"

"I want to keep the baby," she said, firmly.

"Then, there's nothing that'll stop us from doing that, darling," I replied, with a smile. "Your happiness is everything to me."

"But, what about my parents?"

"We'll try to talk to them and convince them to support us. If they don't, what can we do? Look at this," I said, leaning and picking up a dark blue side-bag from the back seat. I opened it and displayed its contents to her. It had the picture frame that was on the wall of my room, above the table; a box with pictures and cards that Neera and I had accumulated over the years; and a pack of cigarettes. "I am ready to elope with you right now. I have everything I need in this bag and I have a plan, as well. We can wake Innaya up and ask her to drive us to the bus stand; then we take a bus to Chandigarh and live on our own. I can take a job with Riayat's father. We can do what we want, Love. I just want to see you happy."

She smiled and kissed me on my cheek.

I continued, "I know you're worried about what your mother might do. I don't want to hurt my parents either. That's why we will keep this plan as a backup. I have decided that tomorrow morning - well, today morning - I will talk to my parents about us. I'll tell them that they can either support us or we can go off on our own. I love them, but I can't harbour the thought of being separated from you."

"What if they don't agree? What if they make you choose between me and themselves?"

"Then, I'll choose you," I said, without a pause. "Look, they're my parents and they have done a lot for me. I am indebted to them for my whole life, without a doubt. But, I am their child; I am allowed to screw up. They're the ones who have to forgive me. They don't have a choice. This bond does not come with a termination clause. And I am not saying this because I am selfish, if someday this little one," I kissed Neera's belly and continued, "does something that makes us sad beyond words, we won't just stop loving our child, now, would we? Children err, parents forgive; it has always been so. If we choose to have this child, of course our parents would be hurt at first, but eventually they'll come around. Who can resist meeting their grandchild?"

"You're right, I guess," she said, visibly relieved.

"We should avoid hurting them intentionally. Rather than elope, it is better that we talk to them calmly, at first. We can tell them that we'll do anything that'll let us be together and save their 'pride' at the same time. It'll be like a negotiation."

She nodded and said, looking out of the window, "I don't know what I would have done had they forced me to kill this baby. How could a girl go back to her life after a forced abortion? What do they expect? Did they think that the day after I see my child killed, I would go back to their home and pretend like nothing happened? Sometimes I think all my parents care about is their pride. They don't care if I'll be happy as an IAS officer. They just want to tell people that their daughter is trying to become one. Their behaviour on this latest matter is so strange, I can't understand it. Everyone knew we were destined to be together, still all this drama. You know what? My parents were so angry and surprised that I let you have sex with me before we were married. They have known you for years, and our families like each other. I don't see any problems, what do they see?"

"I know," I said, after being silent for a few moments. "Maybe, they thought that us being a couple means that we study together or something. Do you remember that we were not even allowed to close the door of your room when I used to visit you? I have struggled a lot, honestly. I mean, I guess I'm one of the few who know what it is like to pee in your pants whilst you're kissing a girl and you hear a creaking door. Brutal times!"

She burst out laughing and said, "Yeah, remember that time when my father saw us walking holding hands? 'Neera, do you have no shame? And Prachur, get away from my daughter!' he had yelled from his car. The way you ran and the way he chased you was hilarious!"

"Yeah, you think that's funny? I don't," I said, grimly. "He chased me right up to the Kasumpati market. Thank God Subhag lived there! He told my parents too. I mean who does that to a school boy? He's an ass," Neera shot a look at me and I quickly added, "asymmetric person. That's what I wanted to say. He's an asymmetric person."

"What does that even mean?" Her cheerful laughter filled the car.

I looked at her and said, "Our memories are so beautiful. You make me so happy."

"You too, dear," she replied. "Will we be together like we dreamt of?"

"Yes we will be," I said. "I promise."

We kissed and she climbed on to my lap.

"Do you remember what we used to do here?" she whispered in my ear.

"Yes, I do."

"Make love to me!"

"Well," I said, smiling, "you already are pregnant. What else could happen?"

+++

By three in the morning, I was already in my bed after dropping Neera back to her house. The anticipation of the coming day kept me from sleeping. Every ten minutes I would get out of bed and stare out of the window for any sign of the advent of sunlight. I constantly reminded myself, lest I should forget, that I would have to call Riayat to make sure that I could work for his father, in case my parents were unmoved.

I looked around my room.

This could be the last night I spend here, I thought. My parents could not possibly hate me for more than a few days. Things would be back to normal in no time.

Neera was my future and to be with her, I was ready to face any obstacle.

CHAPTER X

Sunlight fell on my face as I rubbed my eyes. I was looking out of a window in my room, watching the sunrise. The green hills far away stood unmoved while the mist on the glass of the window knew it was time for it to go. The view was breathtaking. Warmth filled the room, and I felt ecstatic. What a perfect day, I thought, if only I could get to enjoy it with a free mind! We are often looking away from the present when it gifts us the best moments.

I was determined to lay down my cards in front of my parents, and deal with the consequences. A mild anxiety overtook me and I started walking around the room, rehearsing my opening line.

On hearing my mother call my father to have tea, I closed the door behind me and walked downstairs. It was time for the conversation that would change my life, for better or worse, I knew not.

My father was sitting on the dining table, lazily stirring his tea, while my mother stood in front of the television, flipping through the channels. As soon as she sensed that I had descended from the stairs, she switched it off, and turned towards my father.

“Mama, Papa, I have something to say,” I said, softly.

They did not reply.

“Ma, Pa,” I said. They gave no reply and the room was so silent that I could clearly hear my breath. “I know you don’t want to talk to me and I understand your reasons, but I have to tell you something. I met Neera last night.” They looked at me in surprise and I continued, “We talked about our future, and we want to keep the baby. I don’t know whether or not you guys will support us, but we are going to do it either way. I love you, but this is what we want."

My parents looked at each other in disbelief. I waited for a reply, but on receiving none, I started walking towards the door.

"Where do you think you're going?" asked my father.

"Neera's house," I replied.

"Have you gone crazy? This boy has lost his mind!" my mother exclaimed. "For what purpose, mister?"

"To tell her parents the same thing that I just told you," I said, plainly.

"My God! Isn't what you've already done enough?" she asked. "What do you hope to achieve by this?"

"I have to do this."

"You are not going anywhere," said my father, strictly.

"I have to do this," repeated I, opening the door.

"Prachur, at least clear this with us, before you go and make a scene in front of the neighbours," he replied.

"I am not going to make a scene, Papa."

"Tell me something. What do you think will happen there?" he asked, rising from his seat. "Do you think Rana Ji will let you say whatever you want and then walk out of there with that girl? Do you honestly think that he will let you shame him in front of the whole world?"

"I'm not going to 'shame' him, Papa," I said; my lower lip was quivering as I had no answers to his questions. "Neera and I have made up our mind. It doesn't matter what Rana Uncle does, we have to do what we think is best for us."

"These kids, they understand what is good for them!" my mother replied, sarcastically.

"Ma, please, we have decided."

"Prachur, let's say you manage to walk out of there with that girl. Then what?" my father asked. "Where do you intend to take her?

She's not coming into this house."

"Fine!" I retorted. "If you can't support me in this, what can I do? I have no option but to go to Chandigarh with her. I don't care! I will take up a job, I will beg, I will do whatever I have to, but I will not let someone dictate my life."

"Dictate!" my mother yelled. Her eyes were streaming with tears. "Did you forget all that we have done for you? How can you even think of deserting your family?"

"I don't want to be separated from you guys," I said, melting at the sight of motherly tears, "but you are not giving me any other option."

"No one is going anywhere," said Innaya. She had come down on hearing the commotion. "Calm down, Prachur."

"He went to meet Neera last night. Did you know about this?" my father asked Innaya.

"No, of course not," she replied. "Prachur, you idiot! I told you to stay away. Did you take my car again, you overgrown child?"

I did not say anything and silence followed.

"Son, please let's talk first before you go out and do something stupid," implored my mother.

"Yes, Prachur. Sit and talk," said Innaya, politely.

I took a seat on the sofa. Innaya sat by my side, and my parents opposite to me.

"You're emotional right now," began my father in a calm voice. "You are not thinking clearly. If you walk out of that door, you will end up doing something that you will always regret. How can you have a child, tell me? You and that girl are not even married. You have no job and no plans for your future. And, worst of all, you're young - you'll be twenty two next month. How will you take care of a child when you are one yourself, Prachur? We're your parents; we know what's best for you. You have to calm down and think. Are we your enemies? No, Son, we're not. This is a step that you must take after you are married and well settled. Not now."

"Your father is right," said my mother. "We like that girl. We don't have a problem with her, you know that, but the situation is what it is. Rana Sahab doesn't want you to meet Neera. What can we do now? You are too stupid to understand the consequences of your act. Do you even know what kind of things people will say?"

"I don't care what people think. Why should I?" I replied. My tone was mellow.

"We have to care about what people think," my mother said, softly. "We live in a society, Son. We have to follow norms and rules set by our culture. How will we live as outcasts? You remember that daughter of Diwakar Ji, who eloped with a boy of a lower caste? Now, he can't even say 'hello' to people or make eye contact."

My parents were educated but they believed in keeping the social classes separate when it came to marriages. Equality is a joke in this nation; we are as far away from it as we could be. Making laws prohibiting discrimination achieves no purpose, we need to raise the next generation better.

Although I despised - or rather, I was ashamed of - the fact that my parents still believed in this outdated custom, I refrained from engaging in a debate; I had a more personal issue that needed resolution.

"I don't care what people will think of me. I can't imagine my life without Neera. I can't!" I said.

"Son, I know you want to be with her," said my mother, seating herself beside me and holding my arm. "Maybe you can talk to her about getting rid of this thing, and then we can think of what to do. No one knows about this yet. We can pretend that this never happened and go on as we all were, a few days ago."

I freed my arm from her grasp.

"Say something. You are his father," my mother said looking at my father.

"Your mother is right," he said, looking away from me. "Do what she says."

"No," I replied.

"No?" asked my mother.

"We want to have this baby, period. You are my parents, my family, I don't ever want to hurt you, but you need to understand that I must seek my own happiness. If I agree to go through an abortion, I will never forgive myself. Neera feels the same way. The question is whether you'll be with us through this or not?"

"The boy has gone insane, Tara," snapped my father. "There is no way we can change his mind. He can go and do what he wants. I don't care."

"What if I have a way out of this?" I asked.

"What plan could you possibly have?" my mother questioned.

"What if Neera and I were to get married soon - by soon I mean, a few weeks at the most? That would let us do what we want and you can say 'hello' to people with your head held high."

My mother did not appreciate that I ridiculed her concerns.

"People will understand what happened if you get married in haste," said my father, grimly.

"Yeah, but still, what is better for you guys, that Neera and I elope or that we get married here?"

"Look at him, he is blackmailing us. 'Either let us marry or we will elope,' he says. This is not why we took so much pain in raising you!" wailed my mother.

"I am not blackmailing you, Ma. I am suggesting the best way out of this situation. This way both you and I get what we want - you get *your* pride, I get my love."

"Prachur, do you remember that we thought that you were too young to get engaged to her? How could you think that we'll be OK with this? This is not your age to get married. Make something of your life before you go take up all that responsibility, silly boy," my father said. At least, he met my gaze this time.

"I understand that, Papa. I will take up a job. Please, I will do anything. I can work with you, or I can find something else to do. But, please, think about this proposition. Please!" I said, meekly.

Innaya looked at me doubtfully but seeing the determination on my face she knew that it was time to speak in my favour.

"Papa, sounds like this useless piggy has actually thought of something that is logical."

"Do you think he's right, Innu?" my father asked.

"Yes, I do," Innaya replied, firmly.

My parents looked at each other and my father walked out of the room.

"Let us think," said my mother, before she followed my father.

Innaya turned to me and said, "I can't believe this just happened."

"Neither do I!"

She punched my arm and said, "Never take my car without telling me!"

+++

"Let's go, brother," Innaya said.

I was sitting on the sofa ever since I had the last bout of conversation with my family. My parents had mused together and had decided that they wanted to meet Neera's parents; we were all going to walk to her home.

I followed my parents and Innaya walked beside me. The road was empty, and occasionally a car would pass by us, making us cover our faces to avoid inhaling dust. No one spoke. My parents were obviously apprehensive about discussing the issue at hand in public. I could hear my heart beating louder with every step I took.

When I was a kid, our family would often take long walks in the evenings. We found that time fit for bonding. At that time I believed my parents were proud of me because I had never been a nuisance to them; but while walking to Neera's home, I sensed the distance that had crept between us. I knew that I would never be able to mend this broken trust. Things were bound to change.

Maybe this is what growing up is, I thought; no wonder people despise it.

What was to come of this visit? I meditated. Either the Ranas would agree to let Neera be with me, or, she and I would have to choose a destiny that did not involve our families. I had not called Riayat and confirmed the job offer with his father; he was supposed to repeat the Economics course and we would only start working after he finished. Even if that job offer was still on the table, what was I supposed to do for two months?

By and by, we reached the home of the Rana family. My father rang the bell, while I stood riddled with fear and guilt. The former emotion was explainable, but I could not comprehend why I was feeling guilty. How could they make me feel ashamed of making love to the girl of my dreams? I believed in what I was doing, but if it was the right thing to do, then should I not feel calm? Understanding oneself is more complicated than anything else, or so I had discovered over the years.

Mrs Rana opened the door and was taken aback seeing our whole family on her porch, unannounced. Social conventions of hospitality forced her to ask us, politely, to grace her house with our presence, although I was sure that she muttered the word 'mongrel' when she saw me.

We walked into their living room, and sat on the sofas. The room had signs of the devotion the Ranas had in the immortal being referred to as God. The walls were full of pictures of Hindu Gods and scenes from the *Ramayana* and *Mahabharata.* Every evening their family would pray before they had dinner. My mother absolutely adored the example set by the Ranas and had time and again tried to inculcate these values in our family gatherings, but to no avail — I was much too stubborn to be made to pray to a figment of someone's imagination.

The room was carpeted and vases adorned its corners. This setting gave it a very hospitable look, which was deceiving to say the least.

Mr Rana entered the room and took a seat next to my father. He was followed by Neera. She stood next to her father, with her eyes fixated on me, and her hands held together.

"What brings you here?" Mr Rana asked.

"Rana Sahab, we talked to Prachur this morning. There's something we need to discuss with you," said my father, slowly.

"About what?" Mr Rana replied, although I assumed that he knew why we were there.

"He..." my father paused, and after thinking for a while, said, "Our son, here, wants to marry your daughter."

"I won't allow it," Mr Rana said, with a straight face.

"Rana Ji, you need to understand our reasons," began my father.

"Thakur Sahab, I don't know what your son has done to our daughter," interrupted Mr Rana. "She is bent upon having this child. Please," he said, folding his hands, "I beg of you to let us do what we think suits us. For goodness' sake, let us be in peace. I am sure you understand that we have a daughter; and as a girl, she will suffer shame no matter what your suggestion is."

"Rana Ji, you are getting emotional," said my father. "Please, try to understand me. We think that if these two get married soon, people will not talk so much."

"No, Thakur Sahab," replied Mrs Rana. "People will know. How can your younger son get married before your daughter? It is customary for the girl to marry first, even if she is younger. People will know why we are marrying these two in haste."

"I agree with you, Mrs Rana," said my mother, "but, they will talk more if they somehow find out what happened."

"I am aware of that," said Mr Rana. "If someone finds out that our daughter went and did something so shameful, no one will associate with us. Who will marry her after that? I have all these concerns as well, but she got herself into this and she will bear all the consequences. I don't want to see that child come into this world."

"Papa, I will never be happy!" blurted Neera. "You can't make me do something that I'll hate, can you?"

"Hate? You stupid girl!" shouted Mrs Rana. "If you had any shame, you would have never shown your face at our door."

"Aunty, please, calm down," I said. I had to start standing up for my future companion someday.

"How dare..." she retorted, angrily.

"I dare because I can't see you hurt Neera anymore!" I said.

"Shut up, Prachur!" exclaimed my mother. "You shouldn't talk to Mrs Rana in this way. It's so impolite."

"Enough is enough, Ma! Just because I respect them doesn't give them the right to say anything they want, to me or to Neera. I am tired of listening to everyone constantly disrespecting us."

"You have done something very stupid, Prachur. You deserve this disrespect. Stop being a little brat," said my father, sternly.

"I know, Papa, but I can't sit and listen to the same conversation, again and again," I replied passionately. Innaya squeezed my arm to indicate that I must refrain from further pouring my heart out, but she did not understand the severity of the pain I felt seeing Neera so miserable.

I turned towards our hosts and continued, "Here's the thing, Mr and Mrs Rana. I love your daughter and she loves me. No one, not even your God, can change what has already happened. I am suggesting that she and I get married and we can have this child. This is what *we* want. I don't want to listen to how we have shamed you, or how the idiots that live around you won't talk to you in the same way ever again. I honestly don't care! All I care about is Neera's happiness and her future. I will die trying to make her happy. I will get a job and I will do everything in my power to give us financial stability so that she never has to give up her dreams — she will be an administrator, just like she wants. Nothing will change as far as you should be concerned. Please, ask her once whether she wants to be with me. You can't overlook your daughter's happiness; that'll be irresponsible."

"You were always a bad influence on our daughter!" yelled Mr Rana. "I should have forced her to end this 'friendship' a long time ago. If you think that after facing all this insult I'll let you marry my daughter then you are mistaken, young man. How dare you talk to me this way? Thakur Ji, this is why you came here? So that your boy can humiliate me in my own home? No more of this. I am not going to endure this anymore."

"Rana Ji, please calm down. He's just a boy. He doesn't know what he's doing. I apologise for him," said my father, placidly.

"No Thakur Ji, No! I am not listening to this anymore." He got up from his seat and said, "Thank you for coming."

My mother got up and cried out, "Rana Ji, please, I can't see my son in pain. Please, let them do their will. Let them marry. We can bear what society throws at us, but how can we intentionally sentence our children to be unhappy? I beg of you Mrs Rana, please help Rana Ji calm down."

Mrs Rana did nothing and Mr Rana stood fuming.

"Is this your last decision, Uncle?" I asked, calmly.

"Yes, you swine," he shouted back.

"Fine, then," I walked up to Neera, took her hand, and said, "She's coming with me." Neera followed me towards the door, as she wiped her tears from her face.

"How dare you!" said Mrs Rana, grabbing Neera's other hand. "She's our daughter. She'll stay with us."

"Prachur, let go of her," said my father. "Son, don't make things worse."

"Look at him!" barked Mr Rana, reaching for his telephone. "I am calling the police."

"Call them! Call the freaking president of this goddamn nation. I don't give a crap!" I yelled back. "We're above eighteen and we can make our own choices."

"I am going to tell them that you are trying to kidnap our daughter!" said Mr Rana. "I am giving you a last chance. Let her go and return to your home."

My mother moved next to me and whispered, "Prachur, my Son, let her go. We can talk and convince Rana Ji to agree. This action will not lead to anything good."

"Ma, he's never going to agree," I said. I looked at Neera, and asked, "Are you sure you want to spend your life with me at any cost?"

She nodded and smiled; I needed nothing more. She freed herself from her mother and together we walked away. As we reached the door, Innaya said, "Prachur, please, don't do this. Not now! Not like this. If you do this people are going to say so many things about Neera. About *your* Neera. Please, for her. Calm down. Wait for a few minutes. Let me talk to them. If nothing changes, then you can do what you want."

I saw Neera nod in approval of Innaya's suggestion, and we stood at the door.

"Excellent!" said Mr Rana. His face was black with anger. "Thakur Ji, your son openly tries to take my daughter forcibly from my home and you don't say anything."

"What am I supposed to say, Rana Ji?" my father enquired, gloomily. "Kids make their own decisions these days. This generation has zero respect for their family's name. What can I do?"

"We don't want to listen to all this," said Mrs Rana, shaking out of her stupor. "We want to kill that child and we don't want to marry our daughter to your son. That's our decision."

"Aunty, please," said Innaya. "Look at them. Look how badly they want this. Please, think about their future. Stop being selfish for a few moments, I beg of you."

"No, no more of this," said Mr Rana, sinking back into the sofa. "If she wants to leave, she can." His eyes were wet with tears, which he quickly wiped away.

"Papa, I don't want to make you sad," Neera wailed. "Please, understand what we want. Please! Please!"

"No, your father is right," snapped Mrs Rana. "Choose, right here - us or him? I don't want to hear anything more. If you want to go with him, you may. Make your decision."

Neera wiped her tears, and moved towards her mother, who receded coldly. "Ma, don't make me do this," she whispered. Her parents had made their opinion very clear; they did not stir.

Neera sniffled, held my hand, and said, firmly, "Let's go!"

CHAPTER XI

Neera and I found ourselves walking on an empty road, laid out amidst the forest, to a local bus stop about half a kilometre from my parents' home. She was holding my hand tightly and we could hear nothing but the sound of our steps. I felt as if the whole world had perished and she and I were the only occupants of this planet.

I grew nostalgic, remembering all the beautiful memories Neera and I had accumulated walking through that stretch, but this particular train of thought was suddenly checked.

What am I doing? I asked myself. This was an event that I was always going to look back to; I must savour it. Living in the present was something I wanted to learn, desperately.I looked at Neera and found her looking back at me. Her lips, painted crimson, matched her shirt. Her shoulder-length hair was tied in a pony tail. Usually, her eyes would be lined with *kajal*, but it had been washed away by her tears and was giving her red cheeks a black tinge, sharply contrasting with her fair skin. She had tried to wipe it off, but the *kajal* seemed adamant and she ended up smearing it all over.

We smiled. No words had been spoken since we left her house, as they would have meant nothing; our actions had sketched a future, which appeared bleak, but we were certain we could retouch it with happiness and love.

"I was thinking that we could go to Mudit's place," I said, as we neared the bus stop.

"It's in Gurgaon. That's so far away. Why can't we go to Yashika's place? She lives in Ambala," replied Neera.

"Because, I don't want to be accused of hot-blooded murder, Darling! If I spend more than a few hours in her company, you know exactly what will happen."

"It's too bad that Pranay has gone back to Andhra. I wish he was in Chandigarh," she said, gloomily.

"Yeah, that would have been perfect. I don't want to bother Riayat, otherwise he lives there too," I replied. "Anyway, Mudit's place is the best option, in my opinion. His parents would find this whole thing surprising, but they love me. I am sure they'll let us stay there for a few days. In that time, I can find a job."

She nodded and we walked silently before she turned to me and said, slowly, "Isn't it better that I take a job? I know how much you hate the idea of working. Won't it be better if you dedicate yourself to writing? It'll be so amazing to see you do what you're really meant to do."

"No, Darling," I said, firmly. "I meant everything I said to your father. The only thing you're going to do is study for your prelims. Riayat spoke to me about working with his father and I will take up that offer. It's no problem."

"But, you'll not be happy, Prachur. I care about your happiness as well."

"I'll be fine. Don't worry about me," I replied, kissing her cheek.

"And suppose you get a job, then what?" she enquired, looking at me with wide eyes.

"I don't know. After a guy gets a job, the usual thing to do is to get married. So, I guess, I will try to find a suitable girl for myself."

She let go of my hand.

"I am kidding, Darling," I laughed, as I took back her hand.

"Be serious, please," she implored.

"OK. I'll be serious. After I get a job, we can get married, my Love."

"Wow! This is not how I expected it to happen. I mean, aren't you supposed to take me to a romantic place and propose to me? What am I supposed to tell people when they'll ask me the story of how we got married? That my boyfriend said, 'After I get a job, we can get married'? It's so bland. I used to believe that you'll ask me in a grand way, Prachur Thakur. I was so wrong!"

"The actual proposal will come later," I replied, smiling. "I am just telling you my plans."

"Oh, then that's OK," she replied, cheerfully. Suddenly she checked her smile and said, "I hope we didn't hurt our parents too much."

"They'll come around. I am sure when their tempers fall, they'll realise that they made a mistake."

"What if they don't? It'll be awful to get married alone."

"I am sure Innaya will be there."

"Yeah, thank God for that!" she exclaimed.

"I know you wanted a wedding with all our friends and family. I am sorry things turned out this way."

"All I want is to marry you, Prachur. Everything else is just icing on the cake. What can we do? They chose this. If only they could understand."

"You're right," I said, as I kissed her on the cheek, again. "Nothing else matters to me, but to spend my life with you."

Concerned though I was, I felt immensely lucky. I started seeing this turn of events as a new adventure in my life. I realised that I possessed something that only protagonists of romantic novels were blessed with — a person willing to stand by them at all times. I had found such a person early in my life and her presence made me serene. I felt determined to fight for a better future, for us, for our baby. What could I complain about?

"Wipe that black thing off your face. People might think that you cried because of me," I joked.

"'Help! Help! This guy is bothering me,' I would say," she said, chuckling. "That could be fun, don't you think?"

"Even if you say that jokingly they will beat the life out of me.

There are so many people in this town with nothing to do, other than become part of a lynch mob."

She laughed and on hearing a car coming from behind us, we turned around. It was Innaya's car, and we could see my mother sitting in the seat beside her, while my father occupied the passenger seat.

"What now?" I mused aloud.

Innaya stopped the car with a screech, came out, and exclaimed, "Guys, stop, please!"

I shook my head and asked, "Innu, what do you want?"

"We want to talk, please. Stop acting like a kid," she replied.

"I don't think there is anything left for us to say," I said.

"Don't leave like this, Son!" whined my mother.

"Ma, I don't *want* to leave. How many times do I need to say this? *I have* to leave because we don't have any other option."

"Prachur," said my mother, "come back to your home."

My father stepped out of the car and said, calmly, "Yes, Son. At least talk to us before you leave forever."

"I am not going to leave forever, Papa. Just till things settle down. Don't worry, we can fend for ourselves."

"Prachur, stop being so obstinate," said Innaya, firmly. "Listen to what they have to say, please."

I looked at Neera and she was looking at the ground. I reluctantly nodded my assent.

"Come, get in the car, Son. And you too, Neera," said my mother.

Innaya climbed into the passenger seat with Neera and me, while my father sat in the driver's seat, beside my mother.

"Things shouldn't have gone this way," said he, with a sigh. "Rana Ji is obviously angry; but, what's done is done. Prachur, you're our son. If you want to get what you want by being stubborn, and hurting your parents, what can we do? Everyone's going to know soon that Neera left her home for you. We have no other option but to support you."

"Prachur, if you're crazy enough to leave your family for a girl, obviously, you have pretty much made up your mind to be with her," said my mother. "You chose her over us, that is the reality. I am just your mother, what right do I have to advise you?" She paused. "But, now, please stop this nonsense of running away. Come back home. We will get you married."

"Are you sure?" I enquired of my parents. "I mean, we don't want you to do something half-heartedly and then repent your decision."

"Like I said, we don't have any other choice," said my father, grimly. "At least, our son will live with us if we allow you guys to do your bidding."

It was not the way in which I would have wanted him to vocalise his affirmation, but at that moment, I was willing to accept anything. All of us sat in silence.

Finally, I said, "We don't want anything huge, I am talking about the celebrations."

"We can marry you in a temple," replied my mother. "Afterwards, we can throw a reception party."

"The temple part's fine. You don't need to do anything more," I said.

"We have to," my father said. "We only have one son."

"Thanks, Pa, I guess. Thanks, Ma," I said, meekly.

"Thanks, Uncle. Thanks, Aunty," Neera said.

My parents nodded.

"Nothing for me? No gratitude, no praise, nothing?" Innaya enquired.

"Thanks, Innu Di," Neera said, kissing Innaya on the cheek. Innaya hugged Neera and whispered, "Welcome to the family."

My father drove us back to our home, and as we were walking towards the door, Neera asked Innaya, under her breath, "What about my parents? Will they come to our wedding? Are they really mad?"

Innaya chose not to reply and gestured that she will deliver the answer at a time that is more suited for a long discussion.

I turned around to see Neera walk in through the door, holding Innaya's hand. Things are never perfect, but leastways, Neera was with me and nothing stood between us, for now.

+++

I had expectations that the first night Neera spent at my parents' home would be exciting, but I was mistaken. My parents kept their distance all night. Following dinner, which was unusually quiet, Neera slept in the guest room with Innaya and they did not allow me to join their discussion.

"I am fun too", I pleaded, as they shut the door, after which I reluctantly dragged myself to sleep in my room.

The next day Innaya and I planned to go clothes shopping with Neera, something that she was in dire need of, owing to the unexpected departure from her home. We rode to Mall Road in Innaya's car.

After a few painful hours of scuttling around from one store to another, I grew increasingly fatigued and suggested we have an early lunch. Thankfully, the proposal was unanimously accepted and we went to a small bakery called 'The Muffin House', a place that Innaya usually described as "heaven". It was a small double-storey establishment. The wooden walls, along with the small tables arranged to effectively utilise the available space always made me feel claustrophobic. We walked to one of the empty tables on the ground floor and sat around it.

Banalities were exchanged before Neera asked what she had been meaning to ask since the previous night, "What happened after we left, Innu Di? I wanted to ask this last night but I thought the best place would be away from your home, where your parents might not overhear us."

"I don't know how much I should tell you," replied Innaya, pausing occasionally. "Don't freak out, OK? Your parents were upset. They said that they had lost their will to live. My parents consoled them for a few minutes before we left to get you guys."

"Is there no hope of them supporting me?" enquired Neera, trying to hold back her tears.

"I don't know," said Innaya.

"Should I go back and talk to them?" Neera asked.

"No, that is not a good idea. My parents will talk to them."

Neera covered her eyes with her hands and Innaya embraced her. I preferred to remain quiet, gently patting her arm.

"I don't know how things got so bad!" cried Neera, in a broken voice. "I was sure this news will be a surprise to them, but their reaction was so unexpected. I don't know what to do. I feel so selfish."

"You're not selfish, Neera," Innaya comforted her. "Life's just unpredictable. All you did was take a path that will lead you to your happiness. Please, calm down, Honey. We can only look forward now."

"I can't even go back to my own home. I can't believe my own parents hate me."

"I know, Sweety, but please don't think that they hate you. They're just confused. You need to give them time. Also, my mother will visit yours today evening. She'll make everything better, I know."

I knew that Innaya was saying something that she did not believe. Seeing someone you care about break down is one of the greatest pains that a human being can feel. Neera was devastated and there was nothing that Innaya or I could do. The sole way in front of us was to wait, patiently, for things to improve on their own.

After Neera stopped sobbing, she said, "This is even worse than the time I was caught with Prachur's cigarettes in school. I thought nothing could be worse than the way my parents treated me back then."

When we were in the eleventh grade, a surprise inspection was conducted in our school. I was not in the classroom at the time, and my friend, Subhag, had suggested to Neera that the best way to save me from suspension was to keep the cigarettes in Neera's own bag, as she would never be suspected; but, everyone was searched and Neera was suspended for three days. Her parents were informed and by the time I found out what had happened, Neera had borne the brunt of her parents' wrath. My confession managed to make things slightly better for her, but since that day, her parents had started looking at me as a drug addict.

"Yeah, sorry about that time," I said, awkwardly.

"You can only make her sad, Prachur," snapped Innaya. "She deserves so much better."

"Yeah, but now she's stuck with me," I replied. "And that is how you get a girl for life, ladies and gentlemen!"

Neera beamed, but her eyes were still full to the brim. "As we said yesterday, we don't want anything special," she said, to change the subject. "A small ceremony in a temple would be fine — with you and our parents. I would prefer if no one else joined us."

"My parents want to throw a huge reception," replied Innaya. "I am guessing that they want everything to seem normal, and for that, they want to do everything that normally people do before weddings, like issuing invitations."

"What good would that do?" I meditated aloud.

"That'll make your parents feel better, you no-good monkey. Just go with it," said Innaya, sharply.

I nodded.

"We are going to try everything to make sure that your parents are there, Neera," Innaya mumbled. "Anyway, on a happier note, are you guys not going to invite your friends to the wedding?"

"Perhaps," I replied.

"No, not to the wedding," Neera said, firmly. "I don't know if I'd be able to answer their questions. Maybe, we can invite them to the reception."

"Did you think about a job or anything, Prachur?" asked Innaya.

"Yeah, I am going to talk to Papa about it soon."

+++

At night, I sat at my laptop taking another swing at the third chapter of my book.

"He was alone, waiting for his train..."

The events that I encountered over the last two days had made me realise that I needed a job, and I needed it fast.

Slumping on the chair, I started ruminating, "If I could just finish this chapter, I can submit it. Maybe some publisher will accept it, and all my problems would be solved. If that doesn't happen, I could try to get a job. So many people do it, I can too. I can't stay with Mama and Papa all my life."

I checked my email, and saw an update from the Placement Department of our college that there were some vacancies in the field of knowledge processing.

"What the hell is that?" I wondered. "Well, beggars can't be choosers."

I did not even have a CV. Therefore, I started working on it. My college had a set form for me to fill in my details.

"What skills do I have?" I thought. "Think, Prachur. You must be good at something. Never mind, what else do I need to fill?"

I quickly submitted the form.

Strangely, I wanted my application to be rejected. I hated the idea of leading a disciplined life.

"Where was I? Oh yeah. . ."

And I went back to my book.

CHAPTER XII

It is quite strange, this scheme concocted by our species - every human born on this planet must toil, unconditionally, to work towards an idea that most of us do not understand. They call it taking up a job; I call it a waste of precious time.

Suppose I had all the money in the world; would I still try to find a job? Never! So of course, I would have to work unwillingly. Not that my family ever prodded me to earn my living, yet I knew that I could not live on their money forever.

I admit that modern occupations are necessary to sustain an economy, undoubtedly, but most of them are not satisfying - maybe because we humans are not meant to reach our aim, but only to wonder about our place in this charade. As soon as we are born, we must start wondering, and eventually we must die — this is life for us; nothing else.

We cannot be happy being 'something', we need to work towards it. How uncertain; how menial...

I had always thought that whether I became a doctor, a writer, a bus driver, a good or a bad person, my actions would produce negligible effect on this grand Universe. What good are our actions? We are insignificant - with so many planets in the Universe, does it even matter whether life exists on ours or not? Not that I was at ease with this thought; but it often kept me occupied. I had managed to find a temporary solution to it: I started to give meaning to my place in a smaller subset of the Universe - lie to myself about my importance. I was important to my family, to Neera - that is why I must live. That is why I must find work.

+++

On a quiet Wednesday morning in August, I encountered my father sitting in his study, and talking on the phone. He was wearing his reading glasses and was scribbling something in the small notebook, which he always carried with him. Dressed in a neatly ironed grey shirt, he was about to leave for work. I knocked on the door, and he indicated that I come in and take a seat, which is what I did.

The drapes were wide open and the room was sufficiently bright with sunlight. Stacks of papers stood tall on his desk. A book case on my right held books related to a variety of topics; they had been my companions for numerous hours during my childhood.

"What can I do for you, Son?" he asked, as he kept his mobile phone on the table.

"Nothing much, Papa. I wanted to speak to you about taking up a job."

He nodded and said, "Yeah, it's about time. With matters moving the way they are, at least you are trying to be a little responsible. What exactly do you want to talk about?"

"I wanted to tell you what I was planning. I can seek a job in my field. That would involve going through a lot of lengthy interviews. I applied for one yesterday. It's easier to get a job through the Campus Placement Programme of our college - I am eligible for it as a pass out - but that will only begin in November. So I was hoping that I could find something to do with you, if I don't get the one I applied for. Or you can suggest something else that I could do."

"That is a good idea. You'll get a better job through your campus placement, no doubt. You should do what suits you. My door is always open for you, if you want to engage in the printing business.

But I can talk to Verma Ji and you can think of working for him in his engineering consultancy."

"I don't think I am good enough to work there," I joked. "My friend Riayat's father has a warehouse in Chandigarh's Industrial Area and Riayat offered me a job there. I could also look into that. I don't know how much that'll pay but I am sure that I will enjoy Riayat's company."

"If you ask me, I would prefer that you stay in Shimla with us till November. You can work for me. I think that'll give you a little idea of how to run a business and it'll prove beneficial if you ever decide to get an MBA or if you ever decide to take over my work."

I expressed my agreement.

He continued, "If you do choose to work with me, you can start any time you want - next week, the week after that, whenever you feel ready. Just tell me a few days in advance so that I can inform my manager that you'll be joining us."

"Sure, Papa," I replied. "If you want me to stay with you guys till November, I can. I will prefer staying in Shimla, myself. I love this place."

"That's good to hear, Son. Do anything you want," he said, smiling.

"Thank you!"

I intended to leave the room, but before I had left my chair, he said, "We should talk about the other part of your life as well." I slumped back into my seat. "When do you intend to marry her?"

"Anytime that suits you," I replied.

"I was thinking next week."

"Oh!" I said, taken aback by the promptness of his plans.

"What do you think about next week?"

"I guess it's OK. I don't see anything wrong with it."

"Good. We can have the reception party one week after that. Your mother and I will go out today to get the invitations printed so that we can distribute them over the next few days. We must invite a whole lot of people to your reception."

Probably, my face betrayed my apprehensions and my father asked, "Why do you look so shocked?"

"It's all happening so fast," I replied.

"Get ready to see your life fly by you, Son. Before you know it, you will be having this conversation with your own children."

I had no words to say in return. What else did I expect? Those things seemed distant, but I realised that they were staring me in the face. I composed myself and after a brief pause, said, "I know that this has been tough for you and Ma. I am sorry for that." I had caused them heartache, and I repented my action, at least to a certain extent.

"Don't worry. Forget the past now. If we keep talking about it, we will only deepen our wounds. Your mother and I just want you to be happy, Prachur." I smiled, and he went on, "As your father, I must tell you that you are entering a very sacred bond. I know right now you feel the warmth that love provides and that makes you think that you are ready to be married. Let me warn you - this is not a joke! You cannot be a child anymore, Prachur. Responsibility awaits you on the other side of this ceremony and I want you to expect compromises. The last thing I want to see is you repenting your decision and later telling me that you guys want to split up. If you must take her hand, make sure that you hold it till your last breath. Divorce is not an option later, OK?"

"I understand that, Papa. I have thought this through and this is what I want. This is not an impulsive decision."

"Good to know that," he said, plainly. "I suppose a father is also supposed to talk about some other private matter at this point, but looking at the circumstances, I am sure that we don't need that conversation."

I snickered.

"Financial stability must be your only goal now, Prachur. Your mother and I have no problem taking care of your monetary needs, but you will have a child soon. You and Neera must learn to provide for your kid. I remember the first time you told me that you don't want a job; you were in your second year, I suppose. Things will be different from now on, Son. I don't want life to catch you off guard."

I nodded.

"What about your friends? How many of them are you going to invite?"

"Neera and I don't want to invite anyone to the wedding. Maybe we can invite them to the reception, but we're not sure."

"Whatever you prefer."

"And what about our relatives, Papa? Will you invite them?"

"It's better that we invite everyone only to the reception. The wedding can be a small family affair."

"And, one more thing, Papa," I said, hesitatingly. "What about Neera's parents? Will they come to the wedding?"

"No, I don't think so, Son."

"If you talk to them..."

"I don't think there is any chance," he interrupted. "I talked to Rana Ji this morning. He was saddened by the news of you and Neera getting married. Prachur, some things are just not meant to be. Tell Neera that we tried but there is no way."

"So, they'll never speak to their daughter?"

He shook his head.

"Neera's going to be devastated," I said, grimly. How absurd can people be!

"I know, Son, but you guys have to think about your new life now. Her relationship with the Ranas will only be fixed with time. There is nothing that we can do as of now. I even suggested to them that they should come to the reception just so that people won't ask questions, but they're adamant. What you did was horrific to them. They can't accept it; at least not now, Son. Tell Neera to be patient."

"I will tell her."

"Go on now. I'll tell your mother about your agreement to our plans, and after she returns from work, she and I will take care of the invitations. We have to go personally to some people. They all were expecting this news but I am sure everyone would be surprised because of the haste. Anyhow, we have to do what must be done."

I thanked him and walked back to my room. Neera was sitting on my bed, waiting for me to return. We talked for hours but I refrained from telling her that her parents would not join us at our wedding.

+++

In the afternoon after I had the conversation with my father about my job plans, I drove Neera to the Glenn, a place near Annadale Ground. She held my hand, as we descended down a sloping path. We were walking to a spot located about a hundred feet below the road.

When we reached our destination overlooking a valley, I took a look around. The view was mesmerising. It was a desolate place, and the only sound I perceived was a distant honk of a train's horn. We sat on a rock protruding out of the ground, with our backs towards the sun.

"Your mother spoke to me about our honeymoon yesterday," Neera began. "She suggested that we could go to any place, in India or outside. I thought I would talk to you about it. Anyway, I don't want to put any financial burden on your parents, you know. So where do you think we should go?"

"Any place you want, Darling."

"My Love, I was thinking that we are planning a trip to McLo in a month and a half, anyway. What if we treat that as our honeymoon?"

"Really?" I questioned.

"Yeah," she muttered. "I mean, we could wait till we earn money to take a trip ourselves. I want your parents to spend as little as they can. Your mother assured me that money's not an issue, but since things are happening so prematurely, maybe we can try to rein in our budget for the marriage."

"Are you sure? You always told me that you wanted to visit some place romantic. Company of our nosey friends is the least romantic thing imaginable to me."

She nodded and said, "I know. But things have turned out such that we must adjust. I am not saying that we tell everyone about this. We can tell your parents that we don't want to go anywhere, and when we visit McLo, we can take a separate room and in our time alone, enjoy each other's company."

"I am fine with anything you want, Neera."

"I say then, McLo is our honeymoon destination."

"Great, I agree then."

During our car ride I had informed her about the fact that her parents would be absent from our wedding. "That's expected," was her reaction.

"Do you think that we should go talk to your parents ourselves?" I asked, carefully.

"No, Innu Di went yesterday. They're not interested, Prachur."

"Neera, I know. But look, hasn't there been enough of this indirect transmission of information? We can go and talk today."

"No. We've asked them plenty of times," she said, grimly. "I can call them tonight maybe. If they agree to talk to me then it's fine. The bottom line is that they don't want to accept their daughter's happiness. I am tired of letting people think for me. We made a decision, and I am willing to do whatever it takes for me to give birth to my child. Please, can we talk about something else? I don't want to talk about this subject anymore. It'll just make me unhappy."

I nodded and she took out a plastic water bottle from my bag. As she finished taking a sip of water, I enquired, "Do you remember the time when I asked you out, here? It has been so many years since then."

"You did not ask me out!" exclaimed she. "I had to lead you to it. You were so shy. That's why I named you 'Shyny'!"

"I wasn't shy!"

"Yes, you were. I remember what you said, word by word." She laughed and mocked me, "You said, 'Neera, I want to say. . . I wanted to ask . . . I mean, I was thinking . . .'"

"I do not remember it happening like that," I lied.

"I do!" she said, jubilantly. "You were so cute! I loved it."

"Anyhow, let's just agree that it was a beautiful moment, OK?"

"The funniest part was that you just gave up the plan. If I had not led you to it, you would've never done it. Thank God, I knew what you wanted to say - I saw it in your eyes."

"You could always see through me."

"Yes, I could and I can. And I know why we're here."

"Why, may I ask?"

She smiled and looked at me.

"What?"

"Do it, Shyny," she said.

"Do what? I have no idea what you're talking about."

"OK!" she said, getting up.

I held her hand, and prodded her to sit down.

"I think I will have to lead you to this one too, right?" she asked, her eyes gleaming. "No problem. I know you're going to ask me to marry you. I know you'll tell me how much you love me and that you'll love me no matter what. Then you'll say how you will always keep me happy and never make me sad. Isn't this what you wanted to say?"

"Not really," I replied, with a plain face. I wrapped my arm around her waist and continued, "You're wrong on so many levels. Firstly, I don't love you. I only like you and that too at moments you're not a pain in my bum. Secondly, even if I did love you, I can never love you 'no matter what'. I know Indian girls are beautiful before they get married but as soon as they have their first kid — boom — fat, like a melon. Thirdly, I don't think, if we get married, I would always keep you happy. I mean, married people fight. We'll fight a lot, no doubt. We might even come close to hating each other."

"This has to be the most romantic proposal ever!" she giggled.

I gently caressed her face and said, "Darling, the only thing I can promise is that even if we do end up having a few terrible moments together, you'll always know that there is a person who cares about you, as a friend and as a husband. I'll make sure that every night we will sleep holding each other lovingly, even if it is right after a fight."

"We will make a world with dreams, sweetheart," she said, softly.

"You make me so happy," I said before we kissed.

"I have something for you," I said. "Yesterday, when I went out with Innaya, I bought something."

I took out a magenta ring box out of my pocket and opened it. It held a gold ring, donning a small diamond.

She smiled and I slid the ring onto her finger.

"We'll have countless beautiful moments all through our lives, Darling."

"I know we will," she replied, and we embraced.

When we arrived back home, Innaya greeted us cheerfully. She was aware of the motive of my outing with Neera, and she held both of us in her arms.

Maybe better times were coming.

+++

Monkeys playing hide and seek with each other knocked our satellite dish and my mother could not enjoy the afternoon news. Rising to the occasion, I climbed out to the fourth floor balcony to fix it.

"Stupid monkeys," I mumbled. "Is this OK, Ma?" I shouted.

"Yes," my mother replied, with her head sticking out of a window, two floors below me.

I wiped my brow and descended down the stairs only to find Neera bursting in through the door, crying. She was followed by Innaya.

"What happened?" I asked, bewildered.

She darted past me.

"We ran into Savitri Aunty," Innaya said, seriously.

"Neera's aunt? I don't think she's so ugly that she'd make Neera cry like that."

"No, you joker."

"What happened then?"

"We met her outside Cafe Coffee Day on Mall road. It wasn't pretty. First she ignored Neera, but when Neera went on to talk to her, she made a scene. She was so mean, I tell you. I almost killed her."

"What did she say?"

"She told Neera what the town's saying about you guys. People somehow found out that Neera ran away from her home."

"Who the hell cares? So many idiots in the world; we can't care for everyone's opinion."

"Neera does. It was humiliating for her. Go talk to her."

I nodded and walked to the room that Neera had locked herself in.

CHAPTER XIII

"Yukti will not be coming to the reception," I said, taking a seat next to Neera.

She was sitting in the balcony on the top floor of my parents' home. We could look down the valley, part of which was barren.

"Why? When did she tell you?"

"I just got off the phone with her. She thinks it is better that she stays with her brother. He's detoxing, you see. She says that we shall meet during the trip to McLeodganj anyway."

"Whatever she prefers," she replied, dryly.

"What?"

"Nothing. I don't know for sure, but I think she likes you."

I laughed, "No, she doesn't."

"I think she does. She's so strange. I like her, that's not a problem... you know what, forget it. Was she shocked at the news?"

"Yeah, she was. I did not tell her about the pregnancy part, but she was surprised with the rest of it. She asked me how come our parents approved of this, and I just told her that everyone is OK with it. Also, Mudit's going to be here a few days before the reception. He told me today. Pranay will come the night before the reception."

"Yashika will also come a few days before the reception, not that you asked."

Pandit Ram Lal Sharma, our family priest, determined the eleventh day of August, as auspicious enough for Neera and me to tie the knot. The aforementioned conversation took place one day before our wedding. Being the only occupants of the house at that moment, I had suggested on numerous occasions that such is a time suited for love making, but Neera had deemed that we must refrain from physical intimacy until our wedding night.

The sky was covered with clouds and we were sure that it would rain on the day of the ceremony - rain of course was considered a good omen. Earlier in the week, we had made a few calls inviting our friends to the reception, which was set to be on the eighteenth of August.

The next day, we were going to be a married couple, sworn in front of God to be together until eternity. I was contented that my future partner was sitting next to me and she was jolly. I would have preferred her parents to join us, but a call to them made by Neera a few days ago, had sealed all hopes we ever had. They hung up without even listening to her pleas. Following that, we gave up trying.

My parents had got the wedding invitations printed, and the previous few days had seen many acquaintances come to the house to enquire into the matter. "They want to get married before they start their careers. You know how kids are!" was the explanation given by my parents, but they failed to account for the absence of the Rana family from the arrangements. Doubtlessly, the town was abuzz with speculations, but nevertheless, my parents had managed to keep their head high and Innaya had been a huge assistance to them, skilfully dodging repeated enquiries into the matter.

Neera and I had been busy shopping and we had managed to restrict our expenditure. We were greeted and congratulated by people whenever we travelled to the Mall Road, which we found a matter of great joy.

"Should I take up your last name?" Neera had asked me, on one of our excursions.

"Yeah, if you prefer, Dear. Maybe you can keep both the surnames. Yours and mine."

"Mrs Neera Rana Thakur sounds weird, doesn't it?"

"I don't know. Sounds fine to me," I had replied. "You could invent a surname. Like, amalgamation of the two. Something like Rantha or Thakna."

She laughed and enquired, "What are you, a ten year old child?"

Occasionally, we would run into Neera's parents, but they avoided our gazes on every instance. Neera was hurt to see the cold eyes of her mother, one day when they ran into each other at a bakery. What could I do? I felt helpless. I was glad that Innaya had mostly kept Neera's mind occupied all through the turmoil, and almost everything seemed to go according to our plans.

The behaviour of my parents towards us had changed remarkably. Both Neera and I felt that she had been accepted as a part of the family. This relieved me of a huge chunk of my guilt and I had started feeling like myself. Our family dinners were now punctuated with laughter and every person in the house acted as if there had never been any emotional crisis in the preceding days. This environment had assisted Neera in attaining what I perceived as an emotion close to happiness.

I had decided to start work one day after our marriage. My father had called his manager, and informed him of the same. I knew what lay ahead of me — a married life and the immense weight of responsibilities, but I was not the least bit afraid. This observation stupefied me as I was a person who was apprehensive of change.

In a few days, I will be a working man, I thought, as I sat alongside Neera, the day before our wedding. I will be like every other human being who toils all day, just for survival. This is not something I wanted to do, so of course, I will feel lost. I must keep my head strong. I am not doing this for happiness. I am doing this for Neera and for our baby. When things settle down, I can indulge in my passion. Time to become an adult, Prachur Thakur!

I felt Neera had sensed my thoughts and I found her looking at me.

"What?" I asked.

"What are you thinking so deeply about?"

"Nothing, Darling!"

"Prachur, I would hate it if you end up being miserable after we are married, just because you were adamant about taking a job."

"I'm OK. I will not be miserable. We must do things that are necessary. Anyway, how could I let you work? Even if we forget about your IAS preps, the fact remains that you are going to have a baby soon."

"I know that. Just let me work for a few months. In the meantime, you can work on a book or a bunch of short stories. Please, think about this, Prachur."

"No, forget it. I don't want to chase something crazy."

"It's not crazy. You do write well; you know that. And the best part is that you love doing it. Please give yourself a chance, Darling. I believe in you so much. I know you are meant to do brilliant things."

"You have always believed in me, and I have no idea why. But, look Neera, isn't it better that you spend the next year studying and I spend it working? I mean, I am still young and if I ever wanted to pursue writing, I can do it one or two years later, or I could do it part time."

"I don't know. I want you to be happy and I know you'll not be happy at your father's printing press. You are telling everyone that you want to work there, but I know you, Prachur. I know that you are going to be unhappy after you spend two days in there."

"I'll be fine," I said, hugging her and kissing her forehead. "I don't want to talk about this, anymore. Forget this topic. Let me at least go and work for a few days."

She nodded in agreement, reluctantly.

As the evening approached, my parents and Innaya returned after their last round of distribution of invitations. We heard them opening the main door.

"Everything's done, I suppose," I heard my father say. "I don't think we need anything more for tomorrow."

My mother replied in the affirmative. Innaya walked to us and took a seat beside me.

"We leave tomorrow morning at eleven, Prachur," Innaya told me.

I smiled back at her.

"Nervous?" she asked.

"Not really," I answered. "I am never nervous. I have nerves of steel, Bro."

She turned to Neera, "And you?"

"A little. I have to spend my life with *him,*" she answered, pointing at me, and they giggled like school girls.

I got up shaking my head and started walking back to my room. "I am not going to take this," said I.

"Get used to insults, Sister," Innaya shouted as I descended down the stairs. "You're going to get a lot of them."

I heard them laugh again.

+++

On the morning of the eleventh of August, I felt my stomach clench, as I wiped my face with a brown towel — probably nervousness was causing this particular symptom, although I did not want to accept it at the time.

"You are going to get married today", I said to myself. "You're fine. Yes, you are. You're going to marry Neera. In a few months, you'll be a father. Oh my God! Are you ready? Of course, not! What are you saying? You are ready! Take a deep breath. Yes, that's good. Now, calm down and remember what Neera means to you."

A violet *sherwani* with a chequered pattern was lying on the bed. It had black lace around the neck and was accompanied by a pair of black pyjamas. My mother and Innaya had helped me pick it up. I did not care for the colour, but they thought I looked good in it.

"Come in," I said, on hearing a knock at the door soon after I had finished dressing up.

"Ready?" Innaya enquired, as she peeked inside.

"Yeah," I said, softly. "I don't think I have an option to back down, anyway," I joked.

"At least comb your hair today, please. You look like you've just woken up and wet your hair."

"Na, I prefer it like this."

She walked to me, and started combing my hair.

"No! Go away," I said, gently pushing her.

She sighed and walked out the door, with me following her. On coming out of my room, I saw that the door of Innaya's room was shut, and she noticed that I was looking at it.

"Neera's getting dressed, you pervert!"

"Pervert? Really? She's going to be my wife. Plus, I am not trying to look through the keyhole or something."

"She doesn't want you to see her just yet. She wants you to look at her only at the moment she is called to fulfil the marriage customs. Girls care about things being romantic and stuff, you know?"

"How would *you* be aware of what girls care about? Is it because you are in love with one?"

We were not homophobic, but since we grew up learning to laugh at people with different sexual preferences from ours, remnants of that sense of humour still prevailed in our mind. In our nation, making fun of someone by suggesting that they are in love with a human being of their own sex is definitely acceptable, but joke about religious customs, and hell may befall you. Queers have no feelings but religious nut jobs do, apparently.

As we walked out of the house I saw my parents sitting in their car, waiting for me.

"And you'll drive Neera there, for real?" I asked Innaya.

"Yeah, she wants it this way."

I climbed inside the car and my father pulled it out of the parking.

"How're you feeling, Prachur?" he asked.

"OK, I guess."

"My little boy is growing up!" my mother said.

"Calm down, Ma. There's no need to get so emotional."

"Am I not supposed to feel anything on the day my boy's getting married?" she cried out. I saw my father smiling in the rear view mirror of the car.

I preferred not to answer and my mother continued, "You will start distancing yourself from your parents now! You'll forget your family. I don't want you to get busy with your life and work, Prachur. I don't care if you sit at home doing nothing for the rest of your life. I just want you to live with us."

"Stop treating him like a kid, now. He has grown into a man," my father said.

"When have I ever treated him like a child?"

"You do it all the time, Ma."

"I treat you like my son. Is that illegal?"

I did not reply and just smiled. My father asked, "So, you want to start work from tomorrow, Prachur? Are you sure you don't want to take some time to savour your married life?"

"Na, I am sure it is better that I start early. This way I will have something to do all day and I won't feel useless. I want to keep my mind occupied."

I saw my father nod.

"Don't talk about working. Not now," my mother said. "Enjoy yourself, Son."

"What about Neera's parents?" I enquired as the car flew through Vikasnagar.

"They are not in town; left yesterday for a few days. I don't think the timing's a coincidence," replied my father.

Their loss, I said to myself. They are losing an amazing daughter like Neera. I cannot teach them the value of what they were going to give up.

Within an hour we reached our destination. My father stopped the car on the side of the road, and I read a sign board which said, "Shiva Temple, Waknaghat". It was a temple that my parents frequented. To the right of the sign was a narrow pathway through the mountain side. I bent down to pass under a low arch, which led to a winding path downhill towards a garden, surrounded by a dense deodar forest. A white temple, with a sloping roof stood in the centre of it.

Pandit Sharma Ji stood outside, and waved to my father on seeing us. He was proud of his heritage and had donned a traditional Himachali cap. A *tilak* divided his forehead into two equal halves. His white *kurta pyjama* was spotless, though I could not say the same about his character. I had heard some things that I cannot mention here, for I do not want to engage in gossip.

"How are you, young man?" he enquired.

"I am fine, Uncle. Thank you."

"Ready for the occasion, eh?"

I nodded timidly and ran my hand through my hair, following which I felt a chill going down my spine which I attributed to the cool breeze.

"He's shy," said my mother.

"I am not shy", I wanted to say. How was I supposed to be candid at that moment? If I said too much, I would be called "shameless" by the same people. Life is so confusing in this country.

"When can we start, Pandit Ji?" asked my father.

"As soon as the bride arrives," Pandit Sharma answered.

My father called Innaya, who did not answer. "She'll be here any minute now," he said.

My parents and Pandit Sharma Ji engaged in dialogue, and it got to a point I was afraid of.

"Who will be giving away the bride?" Sharma Ji asked my father.

My parents looked at each other and my mother replied, hesitatingly, "I can do it."

Pandit Sharma Ji nodded, contemplatively. "That could work," he finally said.

I looked around to avoid his gaze. Soon, I heard him take his leave and disappear behind the temple building. We waited in silence.

Never, during the time I was growing up, was the topic of my or Innaya's marriage discussed at home. My parents believed that we must complete our education before such an issue was even considered. Obviously, the current predicament was as far as it could have been from what my parents could have ever pictured. Still, they were supportive at the moment and I saw no reason for this compassion to wobble in the future. When the time comes, I have to support my kids in whatever they do, I told myself.

By and by, Innaya walked in through the arch towards us.

"Where's Neera?" my mother enquired.

"In the car," Innaya replied.

Eventually, I was called to the back of the temple and I walked on a concrete pathway till I saw the *mandap*. It was a pavilion without walls, with its green roof supported by pillars. Its marble floor had a square space in the centre, which was used to light the ceremonial fire during weddings or *havans*.

My parents followed me while Innaya went back to the car, to keep Neera company. Pandit Sharma Ji beckoned for me to sit beside him, which is what I did, after taking my *jutti* off. He sat reciting hymns in Sanskrit, which obviously I did not comprehend, although he stopped off and on to explain the meaning of certain things to me. I simply smiled and nodded my head, and readily followed his instructions when I was told to throw certain things into the fire.

I do not believe in God, and I have never considered myself a

Hindu. The concept of God as an immortal being with infinite wisdom and omnipotence is difficult, maybe even impossible, to prove or disprove. But the idea that this being demands sacrifices and gets angry at our mistakes is self-contradictory. Subjectively loving God and being thankful for your life and happiness is one thing, but blindly following an organised religion and looking at everyone who does not embrace your views as a heretic is something I consider imprudent. God cannot order you to harm anyone; that idea is against the logic of infinite goodness. Granted that I saw religious people as uneducated, but I would never go as far as to do any harm, through my actions, to any human being. So theoretically, their God will have more reasons to be pleased with me than someone who commits atrocities in the name of religion and belief in a Supreme Being.

The only reason I sat enduring the smoke and putting rice into a fire that day, was because I loved Neera too much to object to any ceremony that might bind us together till the end of time. I must admit that the idea of the institution of marriage is romantic, even to a cynic - with or without the concept of God. Neera was the only reason I was wearing an uncomfortable formal attire; she wanted the event to resemble what she had, as she claimed, always pictured in her mind. Love made me a hypocrite on several occasions.

All this while, my parents were looking at me. I felt my cheeks reddening, so I fixated on the fire, to take my mind off the embarrassment.

"Call the bride, please, Thakur Ji," said Pandit Sharma Ji.

My mother phoned Innaya. Moments passed before I heard footsteps behind me. Innaya walked in and sat next to my mother, who had taken a seat opposite to me. I heard Neera sit next to me, to my left, and her leg brushed against mine. I could smell her perfume.

Should I look at her? I wondered. I am supposed to do it, right? What am I shy about? She is going to be my wife, soon. And of course, she wants me to look at her and admire her. Why else would she insist on travelling alone and wait all this while in the car?

For the first few minutes, no words could coax me to turn and look at Neera amidst the stares of my parents, but finally, lust beat any concerns of civility and I could not resist throwing a swift glance at her. I could not see much, as her face was covered partially with her translucent red veil. She was aware that I was looking at her as I inferred that she was smiling and was looking at the floor. Her traditional sari, which was partially red, as is customary, was black in various places. The choice of this colour was for me, I knew - black was my favourite colour. How thoughtful was she! I felt her move closer to me, as Pandit Sharma Ji's chants saturated the atmosphere.

I was amazed at her will to seek happiness. She could find pleasant moments, and savour them, even during the worst day of her life. Leastways, I had a lifetime to learn this particular skill from her.

The ceremony went on and I could not help but feel thankful to whoever invented the tradition in which her hand, painted with henna, was placed in mine. I clasped it tightly and saw her look at me.

Minutes later, we were circling the ceremonial fire, with the God of fire, *Agni* bearing witness to this spectacle. I stared down all the while. "Stop looking at me!" I wanted to say to my parents and Innaya.

Finally, I looked into Neera's eyes, while I put the *mangalsutra* around her neck.

If a guy like me can get as perfect a woman as Neera, maybe God is real, I thought. Who knows?

Henceforth, she was mine, forever. Or so I thought...

CHAPTER XIV

I sat up in my bed and stretched. It was seven in the morning, but the room was dark as the drapes were closed. The place beside me was empty. Neera and I had slept in a bedroom on the ground floor of our house; I was no longer a resident of my old room, as it was "only suited for bachelors", according to my mother. She had spent a whole day preparing this room for me to start my married life in. The room was larger than my old one, had an attached bathroom, and small tables on both sides of the bed. After much deliberation, Neera had settled to sleep on the right side, and I was cosily tucked in on the left.

I fell back and pulled the white quilt over my head. The room still smelled of her and it made me smile. Slumber overpowered me, and when I roused again, I saw the clock and ascertained that it was eight in the morning.

My heart was full of desire to see Neera, but I was too apprehensive to venture out of the room. What if I were to run into my parents? A boy must not be so shy, I had been told all my life, but shy I was anyway.

Following a hot shower, I dressed up in a black formal shirt, which had been gifted to me by Neera, and a pair of light blue jeans. When I saw myself in the mirror of the dressing table, I felt ready to work. I ruffled my hair, took a deep breath, and walked out of the door.

I made my way to the living room, before I encountered any other life form. Innaya was sitting at the dining table, sipping coffee, and occasionally taking bites off a lonely French toasted bread on her plate. She grinned when she saw me, and I halted.

"How're you?" she asked. Her smile was bound only by the boundaries of her face; if it could do its bidding, it would have jumped out and filled up the entire room.

"I am fine. How're you?"

"Fine? Just fine?"

"Yes."

"Neera told me she is great."

I felt my cheek warming when I heard her name.

"OK," I replied, trying to keep a straight face.

Innaya broke into laughter. She enquired, "Do you want to know where she is?"

"Yeah, sure."

She was laughing so hard that she could hardly breathe. "You're like a little girl, Prachur!"

"Could you drop this and tell me where she is?"

"There she is!" exclaimed Innaya, pointing behind me.

My heart stopped. I felt Neera walk past me and she looked at me, her face beaming with happiness. Her curls were open and wet, and when she brushed her hair back over her ears, I saw the red *sindoor* which marked our bond. She was wearing a green top with round neck and her wrists were decorated with red bangles.

How beautiful is the female form! After I die, I must complement God - if I find one - on creating something so perfect, I reminded myself, as I had done on numerous occasions on seeing Neera.

"Hi, Good morning," Neera said, kissing me gently on my cheek.

"Hi!" My voice cracked as I spoke.

"I must get out of here. I don't want to be the third wheel," Innaya said without showing any intent of leaving.

"No, Sweety. Please, stay," Neera said, as she placed another piece of toast in Innaya's plate.

"This girl has been assisting our mother in the kitchen, all morning."

"And Ma let her?"

"She protested, but Neera is very adamant."

Neera smiled. "What will you have, honey?" she asked me.

"Yes, honey. What would you like to eat, honey?" Innaya asked.

"I will take it myself. Thanks, Darling."

"No. Please, tell me. What do you want?"

My mother entered with two plates.

"Sit, *Beta,*" she said to Neera. "Have something to eat."

"I can eat later, Mummy," replied Neera.

"No no, I insist that you do it now."

Neera yielded after my mother pleaded a few more times and took a seat beside me. I concentrated hard on my breakfast and after I finished drinking tea, I bid goodbye to my mother and Innaya. Neera glanced at me as I was leaving and her gaze went back to her own plate.

"I see that you are dressed. Are you leaving for work, Prachur?" my father asked me. I met him on my way back to my room.

"Yes, Papa," I replied. "I'll leave in an hour."

"Just go and meet Chauhan Ji. He'll tell you everything you need to know."

I nodded and walked to my bedroom and sat down on the bed. Minutes fleeted by before my heart leaped with joy and I felt that it would come out of my mouth when Neera entered the room and closed the door behind her.

I stood up and hugged her. Her heart was so close to mine that I could read her thoughts; how glad was I after finding out that she was feeling the same as me! I whispered, "Oh, Neera! I love you so much." Our lips met.

"I don't want to go," I said, holding her tightly.

"Then stay here," she said, passionately, under her breath.

We fell on the bed, with me on top of her. I just wanted time to stand still.

Sadly, my phone rang. It was Mr Chauhan calling.

"Damn it!" I said, as I looked at my phone. "I *have* to answer it."

She nodded as she stroked my face.

"Good morning, Uncle. How are you? I am going to be there in half an hour. Yes, Uncle. I am not sure when Papa will come, but probably after lunch. OK, Uncle. I'll call you when I get there. Bye."

I tossed the phone away, and went back to my wife's lips.

+++

"I have to go," I said, reluctantly walking towards the door.

Neera was sitting, leaning against the backboard of the bed, putting her tee shirt on.

"Come here," she said, invitingly, as I was unbolting the door.

I could not resist and walked back to her, even though I was already late.

Ten minutes later, I was driving past Kasumpati in my mother's car. My destination was the Industrial Area in Shoghi. The drive was slow and the scenic landscapes were inadequate to take my mind off Neera. Her face was engraved in my thoughts.

I slowly drove up a road drifting from the highway towards a plain hilltop and parked the car next to a two-storeyed building with cream coloured walls, my father's office. A large board on the wall of the top floor bore the name 'Tara Publications Pvt. Ltd'. There was a warehouse next to the office building, which was painted in maroon and had blue doors.

I entered the office through a glass door. A quick glance at Mr Chauhan's office told me that he was not there, so I slumped on the sofa near the reception.

I smiled at the receptionist, Karuna, who was a twenty-eight year old married woman. She had been working for my father for many years and I had found her quite cordial during my visits.

"How're you, Prachur?" asked she.

"I'm fine, thank you! How about you?"

"I am good, too. Congratulations on your wedding. The reception is on the eighteenth, right?"

"Yes, Ma'am. Thank you for your wishes."

"Are you waiting for someone? For your father?"

"I am waiting for Ravindar Uncle, actually."

"He's gone out to the warehouse. Maybe you can go there to meet him."

"Will he be gone for long?"

"He could be."

I nodded, got up from the sofa, and after taking my leave, walked out of the door. I was nearing the entrance of the warehouse, when I saw Mr Chauhan walking towards me. He was a thin man, in his late-fifties. I had been told that he was bald by choice. His sunken eyes and poorly kept beard made him appear stern, but he was actually quite a gentle soul.

"Good morning, Prachur, my man," he exclaimed, as he extended his hand. "Congratulations on your wedding. I am looking forward to the reception."

"Good morning, Uncle. Thank you."

"Let's go into my office."

We walked together to his office and he settled in his chair. His desk was laden with stacks of files in dark green covers. He spent a few minutes clearing his desk, then turned his attention towards me.

"So, Prachur... Are you ready to start working here?"

"Yes, I am, Uncle."

"Good. Good. Have you thought what you would like to work on?"

"Not exactly. I'm fine with wherever you think I'll fit well."

"You have not been here for a long time. Much has changed since then. So, let me show you what we do exactly. Afterwards, you can make your choice. Follow me."

He led me to a hallway, with white walls, which opened into an open space with cubicles.

"This is our Editorial Division. We have separate teams for Hindi and English. If you want to join this, you can start under one of our editors, and make your way up."

I nodded, and followed him to a staircase, which led us to the Accounts Section. I had no interest in learning tax rules and adding numbers for the rest of my life. I had no educational qualification for working in this branch of the enterprise either. That is why, our visit was a short one, and finally he led me to the warehouse.

"Well, you know what we do here," he said. "Printing is done over there," he shouted over the noise of numerous printing machines working at full capacity. "The binding is done over there, and the storage is done at the back side over there, and in the attic. Our warehouse manager sits over in that office."

So much expansion has occurred over the past few years, I thought.

Finally, we returned to his office and he asked, as he settled in his seat, "Which department do you think you want to become a part of, Prachur? If you ask me, I recommend that you take the position of Assistant Manager, and I could train you so that you are fit to handle all the responsibilities that your father does right now. As you know, he is busy these days in setting up the new printing press in Baddi. When that becomes operational we will need someone to oversee things over there as well. It's better for you to get a hang of these things so that you can handle them yourself."

"Whatever you prefer, Uncle. Although, I could also assist in the editing section."

"Yes, Yes. Take any role you want, Son. I will introduce you to

Mrs Bhatia this afternoon. She'll guide you in finding a way to help in the editorial section. As far as learning to handle the business is concerned, you can spend an hour a day with me and I will tell you all about the financial structure and the daily activities over here. Apart from that, you can settle down in your father's office, till we make some permanent arrangements."

"I wouldn't mind a cubicle, Uncle. I noticed that there were some vacant ones."

He nodded to indicate his assent - "As you wish, Prachur."

The following hour was spent with him teaching me some basics of how the business functioned, which he did with enthusiasm, but I did not particularly enjoy learning about the business model or about the plans of expansion over the following years.

I had never developed a desire to make money, like most of my peers, probably because I grew in a middle class home. I was never excessively pampered, nor did I ever face shortage. It was no wonder that I did not look at money as an important commodity in life.

My parents had always advocated keeping happiness as one's sole goal. My father was not a businessman for earning money; he started it because he wanted to create jobs. My mother was a lecturer in a college because she loved teaching. Innaya was pursuing Liberal Arts - even though it is usually regarded as a sign of mental retardation in our society, which has more respect for people pursuing professional trades - because she wished to work towards improving the plight of women in India. How could I work just to make money, even though it sounds practical, after being raised in such an environment? I knew I had the freedom to chase whatever destiny I wanted, with the full support of my parents. The grim fact was that I had no idea what that terminus was.

After I was let go by Mr Chauhan, I found my way to the office canteen where I sipped tea while I devoured delicious paneer *paranthas* prepared by my mother. Since I was supposed to report back at three, I had a good hour left to spend, which I spent walking.

By five minutes to three, I was sitting on the sofa at the reception waiting for Mr Chauhan. He led me to Mrs Bhatia's office, which was on one side of the cubicles.

She was a thin woman, wearing a pair of khaki pants and a shirt. Her glasses were hanging from her neck and she was staring lazily out of the window, as Mr Chauhan and I entered the room.

After an extensive discussion, which I shall skip, I walked out of her room carrying a file with seemingly hundreds of pages inside it, which I was supposed to edit and submit in four days.

+++

At around six in the evening, I decided to call it a day, and returned home. My parents were out, so I hurried into my bedroom only to find Neera sitting at the study table. She turned around when she heard me walk in.

"How're you, honey?" she asked. "How was your first day?"

"Boring," I said, sitting on the bed.

"Really? What did you do?"

"Nothing much. I spent the afternoon proofreading some articles that are going to be published next month. I got a cubicle to sit in, so that's nice. Papa wasn't there today. He went to Baddi, and he'll come back late in the night. Ravindar Uncle taught me a few things about the business, though, to be honest, I don't remember much now. I think I will learn as I spend more time there."

"Are you happy?" she asked, hesitatingly.

"I am OK."

"OK is not happy."

"Darling, please. I know why I am doing what I am doing. Forget this. Tell me how was your day?"

"Good. I prepared some food, and mostly studied. I realised that

I have much to prepare. At least, I have my notes from the coaching classes. Do you wish to eat something, my Love?"

"Na, I don't feel like eating."

She nodded. I knew she was sceptical about the prospects of my vocation. To her, my happiness was the only concern. She would take up a job and prepare for IAS exams at the same time, if it meant that I would be happy; but I had realised that I must fulfil my duty. It was not a sacrifice, it was a necessity. How long could I keep avoiding things that must be done?

I took the work, that had been handed to me by Mrs Bhatia, out of my bag and said, "I should get at least fifty pages done by tonight. I won't disturb you, honey."

I started reading and Neera stared at me for a few minutes, before she turned back to her books, her face carrying a concerned look.

She was only worried about my happiness, but I had other apprehensions. The events and turmoil that had led up to our wedding had distracted me from the fact that Neera was pregnant. Now that finally things were settling down, I had a free mind to feel anxious about being a father.

CHAPTER XV

"Are you sure she knows where the new bus stand is?" I asked Neera.

"Yes, she has been here before, you know? I'm sure she'll find her way."

It was a calm and rather cold Saturday evening. Neera and I were waiting for Yashika near the bus station at Tutikandi in my mother's car. She was visiting Shimla to attend our marriage reception, which was due to take place the next day.

"How come you guys came all the way here to receive Yashika, but told me to take a bus this morning?" queried Mudit.

How could I forget to mention that he was in the car as well? He had arrived in the morning and had made me question my decision to invite him numerous times.

He continued, "Tell me, honestly, why do you guys give this preferential treatment to her? Don't you hate her, Prachur?"

"Yes, I do," I replied. "But there is this girl who lives in our house, and she insisted."

"Sounds like this girl's super annoying."

"She is. She is."

Neera shot a sharp look at me as I smiled. Thankfully, her phone rang and she answered.

"Hi, Yashi. Yes, we're waiting outside. Where are you? OK, I'm coming, stay there."

She left, leaving me alone with Mudit in the back seat. Sadly, Yashika's face appeared in my field of view soon and it made me cringe. Neera slowly slid into the seat next to me, while Yashika sat beside Mudit.

"Hello," Mudit said, ecstatically.

He was always enthusiastic. Maybe he was on drugs.

I have to ask him whether my inference was correct, and if it was, I must ask him for a dose, I told myself.

"Hi," Yashika droned.

I drove the car slowly back up the path towards the old bus stand.

"How's your work, Mudit?" she asked, as we reached Khalini. "I must join mine soon and I want to know what it's like."

"It's fine. They were not very happy with me taking a leave for a few days so soon, but you know how good I am at talking my way out of situations."

"Yeah, talking your way out of your job, maybe," snapped Yashika.

Mudit chuckled and continued, "My working hours are long, but I enjoy it. Not much to do, really. I sit around pretending to do stuff and following the advice of our seniors in college, I don't really exceed anyone's expectations. Mediocre, that is how I will define my work, and that is how I intend to keep it."

"Is it like you expected it would be in college?" It was Neera making this enquiry.

"I didn't really think about what will happen after college. I was too busy living the carefree life, I guess."

"And for how long will you keep this job?" asked Neera.

"I have been told by a lot of my colleagues to work for two-three years and then try for an MBA, but honestly, I am done studying. I don't think I can prepare for an exam like CAT and then spend years studying again. Besides, there would be quite a good amount of growth if I keep working at this place. I'll be OK with that for some time. Let's see what happens after that. Anyways, how's your preparation for IAS coming along?"

"It's good. I am studying a little these days, but I need to work harder. I qualified Prelims last time, so this time I am concentrating more on the Mains."

"You'll do it this time, for sure," I said.

"Yeah, totally," Mudit agreed quickly.

"And what about you, Prachur?" Yashika enquired. "Neera tells me that you are working with your father. So, you finally figured out what you want to do in life?"

"Yeah, I suppose," I replied. I did not want to discuss my apprehensions with her.

My job was a necessity, nothing else. I did not enjoy it, I was not proud of it.

Writing was what I loved. They say that if you make your hobby your career, you will never have to work; but is that true? I had always enjoyed writing but I would often get tired of it too.

Rainer Maria Rilke in his letters to Fraz Xaver Kappus tells the latter to ask himself: *"Must I write?"* and recommends that if the answer is, *"I must,"* only then one must dedicate one's life to writing.

If I ask myself this question, I think the answer would be, *"Meh, maybe."* Sometimes I would write a poem every week, sometimes once every month - I was not consistent. And, of course, I could not get past the first line of the third chapter of my book. Was writing actually what I wanted to do? Or did I just tell myself that it was, so I could feel I had a purpose, however murky its image might be, in my mind? This question had time and again resurfaced during my meditations, and on such occasions, I found it best to lie to myself.

My thoughts were stopped short by Yashika's snort. She was laughing about something that Mudit had said.

Our group had nothing more than general banalities to discuss before we reached home.

My parents were ecstatic meeting my friends. During my college years, I had avoided inviting my friends over and Mudit was the only one who had frequented my home - except, Neera, of course. I was not discourteous; but since my parents had an image of me never enjoying a puff or a sip of alcohol - save for occasions on which I had been caught red handed - I did not want to risk a friend stupidly spilling the beans.

Dinner went placidly, as my father and Innaya joked with my friends about me. Neera refrained from contributing, but did not hold back her laughter. By and by, all of us, except my parents, retired to a guest room, which was large enough to accommodate me and my entourage, on the second floor of the house. One side of the room had a table, with reclining chairs surrounding it, which we all proceeded to occupy.

"I am adequately prepared for this night!" Mudit exclaimed, as he took out two bottles of Jack Daniels out of his bag.

"Wow, alcohol. So refreshing," Yashika said, rolling her eyes.

"I hope your sis is OK with us drinking here," Mudit said, looking directly at Innaya.

"No problem, just don't make a lot of noise," she replied, with a smile.

The night went on and Innaya went to sleep around midnight, citing tiredness as her reason to evade the remaining of our 'fun' gathering.

"Did you hear anything about your submission to *Panorama*, Prachur?" Mudit asked.

"No, not yet."

"Hasn't it been very long?"

I knew that the silence on the part of the magazine meant that my poem had probably been rejected, but I was not ready to accept that fact.

"Yeah, it has been. All I can do is wait, right? Can we talk about something else?"

"OK, I have a question. Why did you get married in such a hurry?" Yashika asked.

Finally, the question everyone wanted an answer to was out! I looked at Neera and she looked unfazed.

"We felt everything was just right. That's why we said, 'Let's do it!'" she replied.

"Yeah, that is not it. I know why they're doing it," interjected Mudit.

"Why, then?" enquired Yashika.

"Isn't it obvious?"

"No, tell me. What do you know that my best friend failed to mention to me."

"I am sure Neera's pregnant," Mudit said, placidly.

"What! No way!" said Yashika, her face streaked with shock and pity.

"She's grown so fat. What else could be the reason?"

"I am not fat!" exclaimed Neera. "Am I fat?" she asked me. I mouthed the word "No" to console her. "This is not it, Mudit," she said.

"Oh yeah. OK. Maybe I am wrong. Yashika, do you want to put a wager on it? I say Neera has a baby around May next year."

"Yeah. I'll take that bet. How much? Five thousand rupees?"

"That sounds like a small sum. What about ten thousand?" I said. I wanted Yashika to lose. This was my version of match fixing.

"I am really tempted to take that amount of money from you, Mudit," Yashika ruminated aloud. "But when I think about it, how could he land a girl like Neera. Of course, there is something up, but then she was always nuts about him." She paused for a while and responded, "I'll take that bet." They shook hands to commemorate their agreement.

"You're wrong, Mudit," said Neera, trying to sound apathetic. "You can place all the bets you want. I am telling you the truth."

"Oh yeah? If I am wrong, here, drink this," Mudit said, pouring Neera a drink.

"She is giving up drinking, Man," I snapped. "Cut it out."

He beamed at me and went back to sipping his bourbon. Thankfully, Yashika felt that we need not drag the "Neera is going to have a baby soon" conversation for long and was kind enough to shift the flow to a more acceptable topic.

"It would've been great if Pranay was here," said Mudit, finishing his drink. "He would support me and say that Neera, indeed, has put on a lot of weight."

Tomorrow is not coming any time soon, I sighed.

+++

"Congratulations, Son," said Mr Garg to me.

He was a man in his forties and had his hair cut short. His wife with cat like eyes and a short stature, was standing alongside him.

"Thank you, Uncle."

"Beta, I can't help but wonder, why your parents are not here?" asked Mrs Garg.

Neera looked at me. Mrs Garg was certainly not the first one to ask this question. Mr Garg probably realised the faux pas that his wife committed and quickly led her off the stage.

Neera whispered to me, "It's better you sit here. I was ambushed by Jhamta Aunty on my way back from the restroom. She was asking me why we hurried so much. What was I supposed to say? Oh, I wish people would stop interfering in our business! Your parents were right; even if we're married, people will understand the haste when they find out that I am pregnant. I think everyone somehow knows the reality of the situation."

Neera and I were sitting on a stage, on one side of a spacious party hall. Our reception had been dreary and we had spent most of the time being greeted by people we barely recognised. My parents looked jubilant, but what they felt inside their hearts, I did not know.

The hotel was posh and I knew that they had spent a huge amount of money, although they would not tell me the exact amount.

Why do people come to these things, anyway? I asked myself. I understand that as a society we like to rejoice in each other's happiness, but what is the point of sitting for hours, staring at a couple sitting on a podium? I had always found marriage ceremonies bland, and therefore I felt pity for the people attending mine. Leastways, the snacks were delicious.

"What can we do, darling," I replied. "Let them think what they want. You know we're not doing anything wrong. Mama and Papa wanted this reception. All we can do is to endure it. The only thing we should concern ourselves with from now on is to grow into responsible parents."

"You'll be an excellent father, my Love" she said, affectionately.

"Thanks, and you an excellent mother."

"Everything else's perfect," Neera said. "I just wish my parents were here. I would have felt better."

"I know, Dear. But what can we do? Perhaps they will forget this whole business with time. I am sure that they won't be away from you for long. We can try to visit them after a while. Time will heal your bond. I have no doubt about this."

She nodded, and smiled at me.

Mudit had spent the last two hours making a fool of himself on the dance floor. At least, Pranay had been docile, and my parents had formed a good impression of Yashika. Riayat and Yukti had missed the reception.

"Look, at that idiot," I said, pointing at Mudit. He was dancing with Yashika, who did not look very comfortable.

Neera snickered and said, "Yashika is going to kick him, in a minute or two."

"I hope she does. He has been drunk since last night. My mother was telling me this morning how she blames Mudit for my drinking, howsoever little I might be doing."

Neera laughed and we were joined by our parents.

"People are very intrusive, Papa," I said to my father.

"I know, Son," he replied. "Just two more hours, then no one will talk about this."

I nodded. Mudit smiled at me and walked to us.

"Hello, Uncle," he slurred. "Congrats."

"This is the tenth time you've congratulated us, Beta," my mother interjected.

"Your son is going to be a father soon," Mudit stated, loudly. "Did you know about this? Is that why you're marrying them in such a hurry?"

Crazy person! Papa looked at me and I shook my head to indicate that I have not told Mudit anything.

"No, Son. They wanted to get married, it was their choice," my father replied.

"I believe you, I believe you," he said, winking. "Then, why are Neera's parents not here yet?"

My parents left us with Mudit, and went on to attend to other guests.

"Go dance with Yashika, Mudit," I snapped.

He gladly went to the dance floor.

"This guy can't hold his liquor," I said, shaking my head. "I hope Yashika beats the hell out of him."

"And you can hold yours, my Love? Remember the time when you and he stood on the top floor of the Department of Architecture building in the college and peed while standing in front of a floodlight. So many people swore that they saw your shadows being cast all over the football ground. I was so embarrassed!"

"I was not the one who peed, OK?" I said, under my breath. "It was just Mudit. I was the one who fell over from that roof to the roof of the bus; I was the 'Ninja-roll guy'. I've told you a million times.

Why don't you believe me?"

Neera laughed and asked, "How is it that every time you defend yourself, you find it better to be the guy who fell from the roof?"

"I don't know. I find it better somehow. How did we get here? Oh right! Forget Mudit's drunkenness. Let's talk about something else."

She pressed her lips together in a failed effort to contain her laughter and nodded.

"On a brighter note, something good happened this morning, as well," I began. "Papa offered me a drink to celebrate. Can you imagine? He has never done this. I have finally become a man, I feel, at least in my parents' opinion. I feel oddly prepared for the future, my wife."

"I feel prepared too, my husband. Whatever happens, we will face it together, right?"

I nodded. My joy was short lived as I saw a few more relatives climbing the small staircase leading towards us.

God, please, let this day be done, I prayed.

CHAPTER XVI

Neera, Innaya, and I were wandering around the Lower Bazaar of Mall Road, searching for *Golgappas*. Neera had voiced her desire for them and Innaya had vowed to find the same for her. I had protested, since I was not a particularly ardent fan of road side food, and we had come to an agreement of finding some of agreeable quality, which we can prepare at home.

"Give it up," I exasperated. "We're never going to find them. I'm tired. Let's go back home."

"Wait, we still have shops to ask," Innaya replied. "I can't believe that we can't find *golgappas* in this city. All we have is this 'thing' to mix in water, and I am sure it tastes awful".

"Let's forget buying them, and go and have some at the stalls near the Library," Neera suggested.

"No. They're not clean. Can't we go to *The Great Indian Place*? They have a stall too."

"Roadside *golgappas* taste way better," Neera retorted. "I want the ones they sell near the library."

After much reluctance, I yielded and we set on foot towards the Ridge.

"So tell me again, do you think food tastes much better when you know that it might give you Hepatitis? Is that why you want to trust roadside vendors?"

Neera did not reply. Innaya just shook her head.

"Spicy and full of filth, that is how we prefer eatables in this country."

As we were climbing the gentle slope leading from Scandal Point to the State Library, I saw Mrs Rana walking in our direction; she was probably returning from her job. Knowing that it was inevitable that Neera would see her soon, although she was engaged in a conversation with Innaya, I decided to give her a warning.

I poked Neera, and whispered in her ear, "Don't freak out, please. Your mother is coming up ahead."

She looked straight ahead and froze in her steps. Even though Mrs and Mr Rana had not spoken to us since the day Neera and I had walked out of their house, she had a hopeful look on her face.

It was painful to watch Mrs Rana walk past us, with Neera following her with her big eyes.

"Ma," Neera said, but Mrs Rana was too stubborn to melt.

Neera carried a sullen look on her face for the rest of the day, and until dinner, she barely spoke.

On our way back home, Innaya said to me, "I will try to fix this, Prachur. I can't see Neera like this. She wanted to talk to her mother so much... How crazy of Aunty not to reply."

I nodded my assent but said, "I don't want Neera to be put through any more pain."

"Don't worry," she replied. "I will go talk to them myself. Neera will not know about it unless it goes well."

+++

The room was dark and I was staring at the beige ceiling. Neera's head was resting on my chest and I was gently stroking her waist. Her breath was regular and her warm leg was resting on mine. She had drifted off into slumber mid-conversation.

"You're awfully quiet, Prachur," she mumbled. "Are you asleep?"

"No, I'm not, but you slept for a while. That's why I was not saying anything."

"OK," she replied, drawing herself closer to me. "Say something. I want to hear you."

"Say what?"

"Anything. Tell me that you're happy."

"I am happy, Darling. I've always been happy with you."

I could discern her smile. "Is something troubling you?"

"Nothing in particular, Dear. I feel that everything's settled now — I am doing fine at the job and you are getting time to study. All's good I guess, but I think we must start taking this baby thing seriously."

"It'll be fine," she said, slowly. "We'll figure it out."

"Will we?"

"Yes, Darling."

I kissed her head. "You're so positive all the time. I love it so much. You're right. My parents are here with us. We can think our way around this."

I felt her nod and heard her mutter something indistinct.

"What, dear?" I whispered.

On receiving no reply, I thought it best to leave her alone with her dreams.

The last few days, since our wedding reception, had been merry, for the most part. I struggled at work and would often procrastinate, but overall the days had been tolerable on account of the fact that I had a perfect wife. To me, the days felt longer.

"I am doing it for Neera and the baby," I would tell myself every day. "We can live for others."

Do not for one moment think that I considered what I was doing as sacrifice; I only wanted to give myself a reason to tolerate what seemed like, an aimless life. I had often felt that we have an innate desire to look for a goal and when we achieve it we wonder what to search for next. That is why, in my opinion, people who begin a quest that has no terminus, such as the search for God or knowledge, are the happiest. They always have something to look forward to; they never have to say, "I got what I wanted. Now what?" Since I lacked a goal, I had to explain to myself why I must keep living.

I started thinking about the past and I could hardly believe that Neera and I were married. If my parents had not agreed to our nuptial, life would certainly have been tough for us at this very moment. Saying that I was thankful for this act of theirs would be an understatement. Their action was the only reason that I did not have to worry about a vocation. It was because of them that I could focus on finding happiness, rather than being hassled about where to earn the bread for the next day.

Anyway, now that the world knew that Neera and I were married, my mind was, for the most part, occupied with the anxiety of becoming a father soon.

I must read books on this subject, I thought. After all I cannot be the first guy in his early twenties to become a father. Someone would have gone through the same ordeal, prevailed, and written a vast account on the subject. Reading that will help me, I am sure.

Parenting is undoubtedly a daunting task, but somehow I felt that I had learnt a few things from my parents while I grew up - things that a parent must do, and maybe equally importantly, things a parent should not do. Of course, this did not soothe my nerve to any degree, whatsoever.

I looked at Neera's sleeping figure, and admired her beauty. I was stupefied by how peacefully she slept. No one could tell by looking at her that the very same day she had had an agonising encounter with her mother.

As for the trip to McLeodganj, which we had planned with our gang, it had been put on hold. Yukti had expressed her doubts regarding her availability to Mudit, and Yashika found herself too occupied with her new job during the first day.

"We must go," Mudit had said to me on the phone, the previous day. “I desperately need a break from work.”

I had assured him that I will do everything in my power to make sure we all come through with our promise. It was supposed to be my honeymoon, after all!

“We will be fine, Dear; we will be,” I whispered into the darkness, before sleep took over me.

+++

The next day when I returned from work, tired and irritated, I found Neera lying on the bed. She was sobbing.

“What is it, Dear?” I enquired.

“I met my mother again, today, in Kasumpati market.”

“And?”

“She ignored me.”

“I’m so sorry,” I said, kissing her forehead.

“I want to move out, Prachur,” she muttered. “I don’t care where we go, but I can’t live here. I can’t tolerate running into my parents every day.”

I did not answer.

“We can rent a house.”

“Do you really want this, Neera? Can’t you just compromise a little bit?”

“No,” she whined.

“I’ll see what I can do,” I sighed. “Let me talk to my parents.”

CHAPTER XVII

A week or more passed without any significant development. Innaya had failed to help Neera's parents accept our relationship, so nothing had changed on that account. I had been doing a fine job, according to Mr Chauhan, and was learning the basics of running the business very quickly. My father had been busy with the new establishment at Baddi, and he had often mentioned to me that he would prefer that I continue working with him, than start a new job. Neera had been studying hard and was usually buried in her books during most days.

She had been bugging me to move out, but I was resisting. Every time she asked me, I would tell her that I would talk to my parents soon.

During one of our dinners together, she pushed me to talk to my parents; but all we ended up doing was discuss her pregnancy. It was decided that the time had come for Neera and me to reveal her pregnancy, first to a doctor, then to the world via our nosey relatives. Following this discourse, I fixed an appointment with Dr Ruchir. I can skip the formal title, as he was my cousin, and his family had been quite close to mine.

One rainy morning, Neera and I woke up early and drove to Kufri, where my cousin owned a small hospital. By and by, we found ourselves outside Ruchir's office, waiting for our turn. A poster of a baby with big black eyes stared at me. "That baby's so cute," Neera said, gleaming. I nodded, but in the deepest fathoms of my heart, I was praying, "Please, do not stare so viciously at me, humongous baby."

"Welcome, guys. Come in," Ruchir said, standing at the door of his office. Neera and I gladly accepted his offer and walked into the room.

A man in his mid-thirties, he had a sharp nose - a characteristic shared by each member of our family on my mother's side - on which he wore square glasses, to complement his square face.

"Tara Aunty called me yesterday. Is it true? Are you pregnant, Neera?"

"I think, yes," she replied.

"Congratulations, then. When did you have your last period?"

Lying to a doctor is not something we intended to do. Therefore, Neera and I had decided, in a private conversation the previous night, that we would be truthful with Ruchir.

Neera looked at me, and then replied, plainly, "Around sixth May."

Ruchir looked at her and then at me. "May?" he asked.

"Yes, May," I replied. He looked interested, and therefore I continued, "We don't want to lie to you. I hope you can keep a secret."

He smiled and proceeded with questions pertaining to Neera's general health. Neera had been nauseated lately, and he was glad to prescribe medicines for the same.

The way he skipped over the part of us conceiving a baby out of wedlock, made us comfortable. The dread and nervousness I had in my mind, about the consequences of relaying the truth to him, was now vanishing. Now that I think of it, I should never have been concerned in the first place. Ruchir had always been a practical person, dedicated to his job, and bent upon helping people. The fee at the hospital, which was jointly owned by him and his wife, was meagre, and ready discounts were available to people who needed financial support. Many a times during my childhood, I had talked to him and wondered how he could be so lucid about his calling. Having known him all my life, I was aware that he was not one among those who *think* they have a purpose, but never ever stop and question this belief. He was a contented guy by choice, not by chance. What would I not give for a similar state of mind?

'Grass is always greener on the other side', they say; maybe that was the reason I saw his life brimming with fulfilment.

"There's the baby," he said, pointing at a black spot on a grainy background.

I saw Neera smile and felt her hand clutching mine. She was lying on an ultrasound table with green padding, her eyes fixated on a screen to her right. I was aware that as a father, I must feel jubilant on such an occasion; but that 'thing' in the picture did not look human to me. Therefore, I wondered whether I was looking at the correct place. Ruchir saw me squinting at the screen, and he pointed at the 'baby' again.

"It's too early. You will see more when you visit the next time," he clarified. "Anyway, I must tell you that you came very late for your first check-up. I don't want you to do this again. For the first two trimesters I want you to visit once every month, OK?"

"And is there any way we can find out the sex of the baby. I know it is 'illegal', but I'm just curious."

"You're right, Prachur; it is illegal," he said, sternly. "Don't expect me to tell you. I am your brother, but I am a doctor first and I am bound by law."

"It's a law alright, a law for cretins," I muttered. "But what if we really want to know?"

"I don't want to know," Neera said, looking at me.

Ruchir chose not to answer me and went on to explain precautions that we were supposed to take as new parents. "And Neera, keep checking your weight every month. You should gain about one kilo by the end of your first trimester. Since you conceived in May, the expected due date for you guys will be around mid-February, thirteenth to be specific." He stopped, as if to search for appropriate words for expressing his idea, and said, "If you want to keep this pre-marital thing a secret, you can tell people that you conceived this month, August that is, and then later we can say that you had the child prematurely. I'm sure that will relieve people of any doubts."

"I am always ready to deceive people," I said, without thinking.

Neera was placid by the time we left Ruchir's office while I resolved to study more about parenting, because I felt ignorant.

"This parent gig is complex," I mused aloud. "Why could we not have adopted a dog?"

✦✦✦

"I can't believe that you want to know the sex of the baby!" Neera exclaimed, as we walked outside the hospital premises. "Why do you want to find out?"

"I like to know stuff, you know that. I don't like secrets. If someone says to me, 'I have something to tell you' and then doesn't follow through, I feel like murdering that person. How can I survive not knowing such a key thing for so many months? Also, aren't I supposed to read more about this baby thing? I think, if I know whether it's a boy or a girl, I will be more prepared when our baby's born."

"But, it's illegal."

"So is homosexuality in our country. Laws are for idiots, people who can't separate right from wrong. I think sex determination is legal in every other country in the world. Maybe everyone else is wrong, and only we are a special snowflake."

"People in other countries don't kill the baby if they know it's a girl."

"Yeah, maybe. But blatantly restraining everyone because morons exist, is a very bad thing as well. For example, let's say that terrorists take over a building, and they have hostages. One of the solutions is to bomb the hell out of that place, killing everyone. That is technically an answer, but is it the optimal one? I honestly don't know how to stop female foeticide, except by educating our population, but I know the current stance is not the best option. Since I do not have an alternative, I am not saying that the government should scrap this law, just that you shouldn't expect me to follow it."

She was not convinced, but decided to resort to a different argument and said, "I don't want to know till the day the baby is born, but if you know, you will reveal it."

"I can keep a secret. I'll avoid pronouns. I will refer to our baby as an 'it'. I will do everything to make sure that you don't find out."

"You will tell me by mistake. I can't allow that!"

"I wouldn't."

"No," she said. "Anyway, Ruchir Bhaiya will never tell you."

"He just might; I will beg, I will cry. I will bribe, I will try." She was not amused with my rhymes, and I asked, "So, there is no way to make you change your mind?"

She shook her head.

On our way back to Shimla, she turned to me and said, "You have to give up cigarettes and drinking, you know?"

"Darling, I don't do it around you anyway. I make sure that you are not exposed to the smoke, so what difference does it make?"

"Ruchir Bhaiya said explicitly that *if* we smoke and drink, we must stop it."

"I can try to quit after we return from McLo. If I do it now, I will start again with Mudit on the trip. I promise when we get back, I will give up both the things."

She did not believe me, for obvious reasons, and I spent the rest of the day declaring my sincerity to give up my vices. After she reluctantly agreed to my proposal, I finally got to smoke my first cigarette of the day.

✦✦✦

The next morning, after Neera nagged me for an hour, she and I went to talk to our parents about moving out.

"Ma, Pa, Neera thinks we should move out," I hesitated.

"Move out?" my mother replied. "Why? Did we do something to bother you, honey?"

"No, Ma. You did not," Neera smiled, and went on to narrate her reasons.

After hearing the whole story, my father nodded and looked at my mother.

"We want you to stay with us," my mother said, hugging Neera. "Don't leave us alone now. If anyone should change place, it should be your mother. She's the one avoiding you."

"Ma, I don't want to leave you alone. You guys have given us so much support and love. I want some change. It's very difficult for me to live here. I run into my parents every third day."

My father looking at me, asked, "How about you?"

"I'm fine with whatever she wants, Papa."

"Where do you want to go? Do you guys want to move out of Shimla?" he asked.

"No, Papa, just out of the neighbourhood," Neera answered. "We were talking and if we could find a place near your office in Shoghi, that would be very nice."

My father nodded. "I will look into this."

"No, don't look for anything," my mother injected. "I want them to stay with me."

"Tara, Neera doesn't want to stay here, you need to understand her reason."

My mother was not convinced.

"Don't worry you two, I'll do something about this," my father reassured.

Neera thanked them both, and as we were climbing the stairs back to our room, said to me, "Thanks for throwing me under the bus, you ass."

"What? When did I do that?"

"When you said, 'Neera thinks we should move out.'"

"I don't think my parents would look so much into that. Don't worry."

"Now they might think I'm trying to steal their son from them. I'm sure your mom does. You're so insensitive, Prachur," she cried.

CHAPTER XVIII

"This looks like a cheap place," Yashika whined. "Why can't we stop at some place fancy?"

"Oh my God! You're not going to find an expensive place out here on a highway," Mudit yelled. "I swear if you don't keep your mouth..."

"Calm down, Mudit," Pranay pleaded.

"But - but - she is going to drive me insane!" Mudit said exasperatedly, under his breath. "Does she ever stop talking?"

"I know how that feels, Bro," I comforted him.

Neera was standing with her hand in mine. We were staring at a dust-laden roadside restaurant - better known as a *dhaba* - with a thatched roof. The blue tables under the open sky were sticky with only God knows what, and flies were having the time of their lives feasting on the remnants of food on the ground. Plastic chairs, which surrounded the table, were in shambles and I knew from their very look that a person must take precautions when taking a seat on them. The open kitchen, which was not adequate to serve more than one variety of cuisine, made people lower their expectations and rein-in their desires.

I took out a pack of cigarettes from my pocket, lit one, and passed another to Mudit.

"Let him smoke and die," Yashika said, as she led Neera away from me. "You come with me."

"What will you have, Prachur?" Neera asked.

"Order anything for me, Darling. Some tea, perhaps."

She nodded and said, turning to Yashika, “I want something to drink, I am thirsty.”

By this time, the rest of the party, consisting of Yukti, Pranay, and Taara, had occupied one of the five tables.

“Yukti has been awfully silent throughout the trip, don’t you think so, Mudit?” I enquired.

“Yeah. Maybe her mind’s occupied with something. I won’t lie, I overheard something strange about her brother - something about drugs, I shouldn’t say. I think she is worried about him, although I can’t be sure. Even convincing her for this trip was a huge task; I called her every day for like a week before she agreed. She has been quite strange ever since college finished. She barely answers my calls.”

I voiced my agreement and on finishing our cigarettes, he and I walked towards the rest of the gathering.

“How far is it now?” Pranay asked me. “I don’t think I can take any more of these winding roads.”

“We passed Una a few minutes ago. I think it’ll take us three hours to reach Dharamshala and it’s like half an hour, more or less, from there to McLo.”

His face fell.

Meanwhile, Neera gazed at me, questioningly. She and I had decided to break the news of her pregnancy to our friends during the course of this trip. “You must do it, I can’t,” I had told her, before we began our journey. She wanted me to give her some sign to indicate that I was fine with the revelation being made in that setting. I shrugged and, as the conversation arrived to a standstill and everyone sat silently sipping their tea or coffee, Neera hesitated, “We have something to tell you”. Everyone looked at her curiously. “We’re pregnant!”

“Told ya,” said Mudit, extending his open palm towards Yashika. “My money, please.”

“Dammit, Neera! How could you do this to me?” exclaimed

Yashika, her face turning red. "I don't have the money right now, Mudit. I'll give it to you later. Don't worry, you peasant."

"Are you serious, Neera?" asked Yukti.

"Yes, I am!"

"Congrats," said Pranay, bewildered with the news.

Taara just stared at Neera in disbelief.

"Told you she was fat!" Mudit declared. She is fatter now. I'm all knowing. I see everything."

"Could you guys not have waited?" asked Yukti. "It's too soon, don't you think?"

"I think the timing's fine," replied Neera.

"Am I going to be an uncle?" exclaimed Mudit. "I am old. You guys made sure that I feel old from now on."

"Thanks, man. I love the words you chose to congratulate us," I said, sarcastically.

Following subsistence of our passions, all of us climbed back in the car. I took the driver's seat and Mudit sat next to me. Soon, the car was flying down a cramped road that the government had wrongly labelled as a National Highway. Silence prevailed; probably everyone was trying to digest the new piece of information that had been disseminated.

The lack of noise offered me an opportunity to reflect upon my life. My father had found us a small two-room apartment in Shoghi, and Neera and I were supposed to move after we returned from the trip.

"What about your preparations?" I heard Yashika ask Neera.

"I am studying every day. My personal life will not interfere with it in anyway."

"Are you sure?" enquired Mudit. "Seems like a lot of responsibility to me."

"We'll be fine," Neera said, placidly.

"Would you not be due around your prelims?" Yashika asked.

"I don't really know, maybe. But, here's the thing - my personal life is as important to me as the other parts. The prelims might coincide with the baby, but I would not mind. I can always take the exam next time."

Neera's determination quelled all the possible enquiries brewing in the minds of our companions.

"Dharamshala, 110 KM," a road sign said.

I sighed and asked Mudit to light up a cigarette, as I rolled my window down.

+++

The morning after we reached McLeodganj, I was lying on the bed, dressed in a white collared shirt, looking blankly at the television. The spacious room had maroon drapes and green walls. I would not describe it as a honeymoon suite, but, Neera and I worked hard the previous night to make it into one. Our luggage was lying on an arm chair, on one side of the room, and the wall opposite to that had a small television mounted on a bracket. The bathroom walls had water stains, but on the bright side, the dilapidated white electric geyser functioned and we had an abundance of hot water — which, believe you me, sometimes in a hill state is all you ask for.

"Get up, lazy," Neera said, as she combed her beautiful hair. "Go and wait outside. If you keep watching TV, we will spend the whole day here."

She walked towards me and I pulled her in an embrace. "Why can't we stay here?"

"Because everyone's waiting for us. Come on now, let's go, Darling."

She and I walked out of our room, where we were joined by the rest of our group. We had planned a hike to Bhakshunath Waterfall, a place located around two kilometres away.

The September morning was cosily cold and a light breeze was blowing. We had to climb a steep path to our destination, a journey I knew I would despise. Right I was, and half way to the top I was panting.

"What the hell, man! You are from Shimla. How can you be so out of breath?" teased Mudit.

I had no answer. I muttered a few profanities - at Mudit or the mountainous terrain, I knew not.

"How's married life, Prachur?" enquired Pranay.

"It's good."

"Good, as in all of it, or just some parts? Don't you guys fight or something?"

"Not really. I mean, nothing worse than when we were in college. Our fights are short lived, I would say."

Of course, Neera and I had our bad moments. Before we got married, we had decided that we would never go to bed without resolving a fight, if we were to have one; but, when we actually had our first fight, Neera had not spoken to me for two days. I had to apologise numerous times to her before she became amiable with me. I was not going to share all the details of my marriage with my friends — not leastways when I was sober, for I did not want to be labelled as a 'whiny husband'.

"And Neera is fitting in well at your home?"

"Yeah, my parents love her. My mother and sis simply adore spending time with her, so the environment at home is pretty calm."

"Listen," began Pranay, in a voice that was barely audible. "I wanted to ask this when I was at your reception, but I didn't because I thought it would be inappropriate. Don't get mad, OK? Why were Neera's parents not present at the reception? You don't have to answer, if you don't want to."

I contemplated for a while before I answered, "It's this whole issue. Very long story, actually. I will tell you sometime else."

Since it was Pranay interrogating me, my reply put an end to the questions. If it were Mudit, he would have tortured me for the whole day.

"You *have* to tell us later; you must promise," Mudit insisted.

"I will," I promised, with no intention to stay true to my word.

"Also, I must ask, are you sure you are prepared to have a baby?" asked Mudit, as we were walking up a very steep road, with deodar trees on both sides.

"Yeah, I guess," I panted.

"You guess or are you sure?"

"I am sure."

"Are you ready to take care of a little human being that cries and leaks all the time?"

"I am, OK?"

"I believe you," he said, sarcastically.

Neera was walking with Yashika, Yukti, and Taara behind us and I could hear them laugh occasionally. At least, she was having a better time dealing with all this.

The rest of the outing went by peacefully, and Neera and I enjoyed our time. The sun had set by the hour we started our journey back to the hotel, and I descended with my arm wrapped around her waist, which I felt was growing everyday with my baby inside her.

+++

On reaching the hotel, I fell asleep as soon as I hit the bed.

The following day was genial, and we visited various tourist spots around the place, including Dal Lake and Norbulinka. On returning, I was exhausted and wanted to sleep, but Mudit insisted that since that was our last day at McLeodganj, we must drink together.

During the course of our drinking session, I noticed that Yukti was aloof, and was standing in the balcony. I walked to her and said,

"Yukti, you have spoken like seven lines in total to me during the course of our trip. What's the matter? Are you worried about your brother? How's he, by the way? Is he getting better?"

"He's fine. We made him join some support groups, and now he's well. I am very sure that he hasn't smoked ever since I got back home. I think he'll be healthy in a month or two at best. My joining date has been delayed, and now I have time to spend with him till he gets out of it completely. So, I am not really that worried about him."

"That's great! Then why are you so sullen?"

"Nothing, specifically."

"You won't tell me yet? I think you need more alcohol. I'll grab you a drink."

She smiled and I returned in a few moments, with her glass containing Vodka mixed with Limca.

"Now, what is it that is troubling you?" I asked.

"I am telling you, it's nothing specific. Things are moving so fast, you know. I realised this over the course of the last few weeks. I mean, Neera and you got married and are having a kid. So many things are going on and this bums me out."

I nodded, to show that I understood her affliction, although I did not. Our rhetoric went on late into the night and in the course of it, she said to me, "Can I tell you something? You have to promise me that it'll stay between us."

"Yeah, sure."

She giggled, "I kind of had a crush on you in college. I don't know why I am telling you this. I think I'm drunk. Don't yap to Neera, OK?"

"No, I won't," I replied. "I had no idea. When was this?"

"I know you have no idea. You're so naive. It was in the first year. Then I found out that you had been with Neera for a long time, so I stopped."

"That's funny. Why didn't you tell me earlier?"

"Why? Would you have left Neera for me?"

"No, not that. I just like to know things."

"Yeah, that's what I thought," she said, grimly. "Now you're going to have a kid, and I am still at the same place."

"You're a precious girl, Yukti. I am sure..."

She raised her hand to indicate that it is better that I stop. "I am not asking for your pity or any kind words, OK? Save it!"

She walked out of the room, with my eyes following her.

"What's up with her?" wondered Pranay, out loud.

I shrugged and pleaded ignorance.

+++

"Why pack a box so well that it can't be opened?" I snapped. "How the hell am I supposed to open it?"

Neera and I were unpacking our belongings at the new apartment. It had two rooms, a bathroom, a small balcony outside one of the rooms and white-washed walls. The whole place barely got sunlight due to trees all around. The view, of course was mesmerising, except that there was an abundance of langurs.

"Open it with a knife, sweetheart," Neera replied. She was lying on the bed, tired from hauling the boxes up two floors.

"The box that I am trying to open has the knife inside it. See, it says 'Kitchen Utilities.'"

"Oh, here use this pen."

It took us another four hours to make the place look like home. We had no sofas, no dining table. Only one bed, two study tables and chairs. "We could buy the furniture with time," Neera had suggested.

"I'm glad we got this place, Prachur," she said, as I finally managed to retrieve the knife from the box. "Finally, I feel comfortable."

I nodded.

We heard a knock at the door, and I opened the door to find our new landlady, Mrs Jamwal, standing with a huge grin on her face.

She was a woman who even though had seen more than three-score years, could never accept her age. She was cheeky and appeared to be kind, but then I am not a good judge of character. She held a plate of *barfis* in her hands.

"Namaste, Aunty," I said, with a smile as big as her.

"Hello, *Beta*. I thought I would welcome you guys. Your father told me that you'd be moving in today."

Neera led Mrs Jamwal into the house.

"I don't understand why you have to move here. Shimla is a much better place. Even the local market is quite far away," Mrs Jamwal said, eating her own *barfis*.

"This place is closer to my work, Aunty," said I.

"Doesn't your father travel to the same place from Shimla?"

"Yes, but then I despise driving for so long every day."

She agreed, while looking at Neera.

During the one hour she was there, I tried to keep myself awake. Needless to say, Neera was a good hostess — she was good at everything. She was what completed me, maybe I was meant to end up with her.

After Mrs Jamwal left, Neera and I retired to the bed and recollected the memories from our trip. Even though Yukti had been indifferent to me, I characterised the trip as 'enjoyable'.

I fell asleep with the realisation that we were back to reality and I would have to drag myself to work every day.

+++

The next morning, I received a text from Yukti. It said:

"Sorry for the outburst."

"No problem," I replied.

"How's Neera?"

"Good. How're you?"

"OK. I feel like Neera's angry with me."

"No, she isn't. Don't be silly."

"I believe you."

"Neera and I moved to our own place."

"Really? Wow, that's nice."

"Yes :)"

I heard Neera walk into the room. I could not understand why my reflex was to put my phone back into my pocket — I was not doing anything wrong. Anyhow, I was not quick enough.

"Who are you talking to, Prachur?" she asked, laying my pressed shirt on the bed.

"Yukti."

"That's why you were hiding the phone."

"No, what? I wasn't doing anything like that."

"OK. I believe you," she said, squinting at me. "Here's your shirt, I pressed it for you."

"Thanks," I said, before she left the room.

CHAPTER XIX

The first few days that Neera and I spent at our new home were hectic. We lacked several items that we required for daily use, and this meant that we had to take a trip to the market nearby every second day. When I say 'nearby' in a hilly town, I mean at least five kilometres. Innaya had been very generous and had lent her car to me, till we could decide on buying one.

Neera and I used to split duties. I did not know how to cook, so Neera would do it, while I washed the dishes. We would clean the house together, and we found a laundry nearby.

Neera was not pleased with me because I had not stayed true to my word of ceasing to smoke and drink. With the work being insufferable, I would drink every evening, in the confines of our living room. She did not appreciate this behaviour, and we would often have minor arguments over it. In my defence, I had tried to quit, but failed on all those five or six occasions.

"Bloody hell, I don't want to go today, Neera," I would say, every morning, when she woke me up. I had to reach work by nine, so she would wake me up at eight thirty. "I can skip one day. My father owns the damned place."

No words would compel Neera to stop, and eventually I would jump out of the bed.

Every time someone would tell me to do something at work, I would say, "Sure, why not." And as soon as they would leave I would add, "Why don't I lick your ass while I am at this? Idiot."

I was disrespectful, I know, but I was frustrated.

I would reach home by six, wanting to drive the car off a cliff, but would find Neera waiting for me, with a warm cup of tea.

She was my reason to live. My reason to endure life.

I did not feel completely unhappy because she and I had a bunch of things to look forward to. During my free hours, I would read literature related to parenting. We would amuse ourselves by trying to come up with baby names, both for a boy and a girl, but hitherto had not settled on any.

I had completely given up working on my book, and its idea was getting murkier in my mind with every passing day.

By the end of September, time had come for our second visit to Ruchir. As for the sex determination fiasco, I had managed to convince Neera to let me find that out.

"If Ruchir Bhaiya tells you the gender, which I am sure he'll not, but *if* he does, keep it to yourself. And by that I mean don't tell your parents or Innu Di, because if they know, I will know it," Neera had said to me during one of our dialogues.

"I will not tell you, Darling," I had said. "I promise."

"If you tell me, even by mistake, I will leave you."

"Leave me?"

"Yes I will. That will be the end of our marriage."

"Message received," I had replied, stupefied by her resolve.

How can people stand not knowing? So much depends on it - the name, the clothes you buy, the books you need to read. What surprises me more is that a person who wants to know is considered a minion of the Devil. Since I was not exceptionally rich, I could not travel outside India to find out, what I considered as my right; therefore, I was obliged to try to break the law within this country. Could we not think of a better alternative?

Returning to the story, we visited Ruchir on the day of appointment.

"Everything looks fine, here," said he, while examining Neera. "Any discomfort?"

Neera's waist had grown in size, slightly, although I would never accept this, while I was in my senses. She had not been having emotional swings, which was a blessing to me.

"May I ask you a question?" I asked Ruchir. "Not that I am asking the gender, but as a doctor can't you see it?"

"I'm not allowed to tell you," he said, plainly.

"I won't tell anyone. Do you think I will go announcing to the world that you told me?"

"It's not about that. It is not legal, and that too for a reason."

"I know it's illegal. But let me ask you, do you think that if I knew that it was a girl I would consider, even for a second, to abort the baby, just because of the gender?"

"I'm sure you will not, Prachur, but you should understand that it's a very big problem in our country. Even today, when women give birth to a girl in my hospital, I can see that they are disappointed. I have seen mothers being apathetic to their own baby girl. It makes me sick. You need to understand that we need to restrain these people. India is full of people who'd gladly kill a foetus if they knew that it's a girl."

"OK, I give you that, but isn't right and wrong subjective? You can't judge me with the same standard as those people. Look, you're my brother and I don't want to force you into doing something that you don't think is right; but if you are convinced that giving me this information will not result in any harm to the baby, you should not let a few words on a piece of paper written by some people - who probably had no idea of the implication of what they were doing - stop you. I won't press this matter anymore."

"I thought Neera doesn't want to know," he said, looking at Neera.

"She doesn't. We've decided that if I were to run into this information 'accidentally', I will not tell her or anyone, for that matter."

He nodded and proceeded with other medical procedures. Finally, as the examination concluded, Neera and I bade our well wishes to him and walked outside the office.

"Prachur, hold on," he said, as Neera was out of an earshot.

"What is it?" I asked. I knew what he wanted to talk about, but I decided to play unknowing.

He paused for a moment and said, "Nothing special. I just forgot to tell you that the ovaries look fine, as well."

I thanked him and walked out of the office with a huge grin on my face.

"You know, don't you?" Neera asked, looking defeated, as I entered the car, and slipped into the driver's seat.

"Not necessarily. What makes you think so?"

She shook her head and I drove us back to Shoghi.

In about four months, I was going to hold a little baby girl in my arms - my angel! I took Neera's hand and kissed it.

"If you tell me, I swear I will leave you," she warned. "I will raise this baby myself."

"I won't," I said. "Don't worry, my Love. Don't tell Mama and Papa that I know. They'll pester me to tell them and then you'll find out eventually."

As I took the turn towards our house, she, who had been staring at me for quite a while, said, "God dammit! I can't stand it now that you know. I hate you! I hate you!"

I burst out laughing as she shoved me away. "I'm so happy," I whispered.

+++

A week had passed since our visit to Ruchir. Mrs Bhatia - the editor at my father's firm - had kept me burdened with tasks and she cared not that my father owned the place. She was highly critical of my work and on numerous occasions was downright insulting, especially when I would miss deadlines. She had a strange habit of piling more work on my desk, after I had missed a deadline.

I spent all my day at work, sitting alone and day dreaming in my 'cubicle of depression'.

Often I would work late into the night. Do I even need to say that I was not excited about these developments?

On one such night, I was sitting at the table in my bedroom, sipping the heavenly nectar sold by Jack Daniels. The room was dark except the part lit by a table lamp. The window of the room was open and the air outside was calm and pleasant. Moths wanted to enter but a wire mesh on the window prevented them from doing so.

"Could you please not do that?" Neera pleaded. "You've been working and drinking for so long now. Come to bed, please."

"I'm sorry, is the light bothering you?" I asked. "I can work in the living room."

"No, the light is fine. Just stop drinking."

"This is the last one for tonight, I promise."

She was lying on the bed with her back towards me. I quickly emptied my glass, switched the table lamp off, and slipped into the bed, next to her.

"You reek of cigarettes and alcohol," she remarked, as I was kissing her neck.

"I'm sorry. You know I get bored while correcting all those pages. Besides, I did not smoke since I got back from work."

"What if Mama and Papa find out? What then, Prachur? They have no idea that their son is killing his liver every night." I ignored her rhetorical question, and she continued, sitting up, "You told me weeks ago that you'll quit everything, but I don't see any signs of you even trying. I know your life's tough, Prachur, but you can't slowly torture yourself for it. How do you think I feel watching you every day like this? Do you think I can ignore watching the love of my life being miserable? Stop this nonsense, please, if not for yourself, then for me."

"Neera, I think you're overreacting. I drink occasionally, and I smoke only at work. I would never smoke around you; I know that it's bad for the baby."

"An alcoholic father is not good for our child, either."

"I don't drink that much."

"Prachur, I've known you for a long time, so don't tell me that I can't see the difference. In college, you'd drink once every three days, maybe; now you do it every day. And I know that you are smoking at least one pack a day, and the fact that you smoke it all during the few breaks you get during your work makes me feel no better." I did not answer, and my silence provoked her further. "I thought you'd mature, Prachur. I was wrong."

"What do you want from me? I am working all day, can't I just take one or two sips before I sleep?"

"You're impossible," she snapped.

"And you're being unreasonable."

"I'm being unreasonable? Prachur, you know what you drinking your life away makes me think? It makes me feel like I have brought you to this. I feel like you will destroy your life and mine, as well; and worst of all, the life of our baby."

"Neera, stop this. You're saying as if I am a drunk and I engage in domestic violence or some other crazy thing like that."

"No, but you've been quite distant from me lately, emotionally. That is equally bad for me! It's been a week since we made love. If you are so miserable at your job, leave it and try writing. I'll support you in anything; but I can't allow you to drink every day like this."

"Baby, first of all this has nothing to do with you. I'm sorry that I made you feel that I was being distant. It'll never happen again. As for the writing proposition, leave that thought."

"Fine! Just tell me, will you stop drinking and smoking from tomorrow or not?"

I answered, after a pause, "I can try."

"No. No trying anymore. Will you or will you not quit?"

"I don't know. I can only promise that I will try."

She lay back on the bed, and closed her eyes.

"Neera?" I said, slowly.

"I'm tired. I need to sleep," she cried out.

She had sacrificed a lot, physically and emotionally, for me and for our marriage. I felt like a selfish wretch. Since she had started pressing for me to change, I had often been tempted to lie to her. Obviously, I knew it was not the right thing, thus I had never gone down that path.

Quitting smoking seemed like a possibility to me, but every time I thought of giving up alcohol, a certain dread filled my heart. How could I feel sane without alcohol? I was a weak-willed person; moderation was not an option for me - either I had to stop altogether or I should continue consuming it.

I must quit both — smoking and drinking, I thought, finally, after a bout of argument with myself. It seems impossible right now, but you will get over it. You are doing this for Neera and the baby; like everything else.

+++

When my parents visited Neera and my new apartment for the first time, the timing could not have been worse. Neera and I had had a fight in the morning, and we were in a bad mood when the bell rang.

"Ma, Pa," Neera said, opening the door. "What a surprise! Where's Innu Di?"

"She's parking the car, sweetheart," my mother replied.

My parents entered the living room, and hugged me.

"So this is where you've been putting up?" my mother said.

"Kuldeep, I asked you to find something nice for them. This is so small."

"I know Mrs Jamwal. She's a nice lady. She'll take care of our kids," my father replied.

By this time, Innaya had joined us. I hugged her. She and I had been talking regularly on the phone, but lately she had been more of a sister to Neera than me.

"So many dirty dishes in the kitchen sink," my mother pointed.

"It's Prachur's duty to clean them, Ma," Neera smiled. "And you know how lazy he is."

"I'll do it tonight," I droned.

"Don't forget to do it. Look at this, how dirty this study table is! Is this also Prachur's job?"

Neera nodded.

"This place is not good enough for an expecting mother," my mother said, looking at the bathroom.

"It's fine," my father reiterated. "Don't overthink stuff, Tara."

"I'm not overthinking. Neera, you need to move back to our home soon."

"We'll think about it, Ma," I said.

"Don't think. Just move back," she said, absentmindedly, while fiddling with a jammed cupboard.

CHAPTER XX

Awaiting a baby requires a massive amount of shopping for utilities, such as clothes, which if your wife does not know the gender of the baby, is twice the work. While out on one of our excursions, on a cold December afternoon, Neera asked me, as she stood holding an orange baby sleep suit, "Does this look fine to you?"

"It's orange. Is that a unisex colour? What if we have a girl? Would she look OK in orange?"

"Why do you always object when you think that the colour won't suit a girl? Don't you dare give me any hints!"

"Darling, if I were to object every time you choose a girlish colour, you will think that I am trying to tell you that we're going to have a boy. What can I do? I am just saying that we must buy clothes that are useful whether we have a girl or a boy." I saw my mother walking towards us, "My mom's coming. Buy this if you want."

I still had not told my parents that I knew the sex of our baby.

"Look at what I found," my mother said, spreading a white baby suit with floral pattern on the glass counter of the shop.

"It's lovely, Ma!" cheered Neera.

"Buy plenty of those. Kids tend to spoil them a lot," my mother chuckled.

"Prachur has been training very hard to learn how to change diapers, Ma. I am sure we won't require a lot of them."

"I like this one," my mother said, pointing at a green suit. "Come on now, we still need to buy a bassinet."

"Isn't it too early for that, Ma?" I enquired.

"No, we must be prepared. We have to make sure that we don't do anything in a hurry, even if the baby is born prematurely. Better be prepared, than hurry when things actually happen."

After these words, we went on to buy a wooden bassinet with plenty of padding.

"Car seat, now!" said my mother.

"Calm down, Ma," I said, before she glared at me and beckoned for us to follow her, which is what we did.

She had been very enthusiastic and had been helping us shop for all the basic utilities, although at times her behaviour could have been easily classified as tyrannical. After a long day, we reached home around the time for dinner, which I ate while trying to stay awake.

As soon as I slumped on the bed, Neera asked, "Do you remember we decided that today's going to be the first day for us to try and wake up in the middle of the night to prepare for the time when the baby cries?"

"Oh my God! Neera, your due date is months away. What is wrong with everyone in this family?"

"Prachur, you promised."

"Please, I'm very tired today. Can't we do this tomorrow?"

"No, I am setting the alarm. You promised that you'll share the work with me. Today is the day we try. I'm not hearing another word."

I pleaded, but I could not move her to take pity on me owing to my dreariness. Around One a.m. in the morning, her phone's alarm went off. I opened my eyes and tried to be sneaky and disable the alarm before Neera woke up; but, alas, she awoke before I could even sit up!

"Get up, Prachur."

"I'm up. See? I passed the test. Now let me sleep."

"No! Go to the crib and put the diaper on that doll. We talked about this," she murmured in her sleep.

"What does it matter, anyway?" I mumbled, as I got out of the bed.

One of my assertions, that human beings can sleep while standing up, was proved correct, as I drifted into slumber even before I tore open the bag of diapers, but Neera was well aware of this being a possibility. Thus, she kept asking, repeatedly, "Are you done yet?"

Finally, following a visual inspection of my work, she allowed me to go back to sleep. I might have felt comfortable in bed, after I was set free of my paternal duties for that particular night, but the apprehension that I would have to repeat these actions filled my heart.

Not that I think this is an advice that I need to share, for it is axiomatic; but I must do so for the sake of posterity - setting decoy alarms to simulate a baby crying at night makes one cranky and promotes hostility in a marriage; never do it.

+++

I remember the day I got a response from *Panorama*. I was sitting on a newly purchased bean bag in the living room of our apartment, sipping tea, and going through the newspaper.

"It's from *Panorama*," Neera said, placing a white envelope on my lap. "Open and read it, please."

It said, "We regret to inform you..."

I needed to read no further. I passed the letter to Neera and, of course, she was hysterical. She tried her best to lift my spirits, to no avail.

"I am destined for mediocrity", I said.

"Oh Prachur, don't let one letter make you sad," she said, hugging me.

"I am not sad, and don't think that only one rejection is making me say this. Look Neera, for two years now I have been trying to work on my book, and I haven't done anything. What good is writing for me anyway? Success in it is so improbable. Writing was just a hobby for me, anyway. Forget this. I need to get to work."

"Prachur..." I heard her say as I went into the bathroom to take a shower.

+++

Neera was lying with her head on her study table, trying to catch a nap. It was a habit of hers. Often during her study sessions she would doze off, especially when she felt overwhelmed.

"Neera," I whispered, "go and sleep on the bed. Should I carry you? You'd be more comfortable."

"No," she replied, her speech muffled. "I can't sleep for long. Just two minutes."

"You know what you need? A break. Come let's go out and get some fresh air and a drink."

"No," she said.

I dragged her out of her chair to the car. Twenty minutes later, we were sitting inside a Barista.

"You have to stop stressing yourself out so much. You're seven months pregnant now, you look like a paper weight...."

"I look like what?" she interrupted.

"You look very beautiful, but a little stressed out. You need to take a few breaks once in a while. Do you maybe want to take a trip?"

"No trips, Prachur," she said, with a heavy voice.

"You don't even want to know where I think we should go?"

"OK, tell me, where do you want to go?"

"To either Delhi or Agra."

"We've been there and you hated those places."

"I know, but we'll go there, take the torture, come back and relax back at our home. It would be like realising 'there's no place like home.'"

She shook her head and said, "My *Mains* this year were awful. Awful. I have to start working for the next try."

"Neera, you gave that test like ten days ago, and plus the results have not come yet. How do you know you won't clear it this time?"

"I know, OK?" I did not reply, and she added after finishing her mango smoothie, "I'm so stressed. I can't anymore. I just can't."

"You don't have to work so hard, Neera. You're intentionally putting yourself in a bad position. Take your mind off this for some days. Please."

"No."

"Well, there's nothing that I can do then, you crazy girl."

We drove back home in silence.

When I found Neera lying on the table again, I said to her, "Do you maybe want to move back to Shimla till the time you have the kid? I know you don't really want to run into your mother everyday but please, my mother will be there to help you. She'll like it too. Please think about it."

+++

Time flew and even before we realised it, it was mid-February. I would not describe the preceding months - that is, the period from December to February - as utopian. Neera and I had been having numerous confrontations, whether it was about my drinking, which I had not given up; or smoking, which I claimed to have quit but continued to indulge in during work and lie to Neera about it, howsoever unsuccessfully. Some of our fights had gone out of control and on such occasions, my mother had to intervene to negotiate a truce. What baffled me the most was the realisation that I, who was once a man who hated the sight of tears in the eyes of this beautiful creation of God, was hardly affected by them anymore - I had lost that Prachur, that integral part of me.

The readers to this memoir might think that I was in the wrong to treat a woman - who was going through a very trying experience for me - so badly and this would be an astute judgement, which I should have made myself, but I was nothing if not a common fool; how could I realise my mistakes in time and make amends? Our kind acts only when all is lost.

My work was no help to my temper; I felt as if I had been reduced to slavery. Although, I understood that I should be thankful for what I had, for few people possess that, but I knew no satisfaction.

Is this my purpose? Only to correct history books? I would ask myself. Contemplating these questions presented me with another difficulty. Do we even need a purpose, or a calling? If say, I had a purpose, would I be able to affect this vast universe with my actions? Would I feel contented? Would I have to achieve my goals to feel happy?

Sensing my worries, Neera used to persuade me to keep on writing.

"Do it for me, my Love," she would say, every night. "Please, write something. I want to read what you write."

I would smile and ask, "What's the point?"

On the lighter side of things, I had been able to conceal the gender of our baby from Neera. Innaya had managed to extract this information out of me, but she was a good secret keeper.

Neera and I had moved back to Shimla, to our parents' house, and Neera found my mother's presence comforting.

During this time, Neera's mother visited her once, in January, and she could not hold her tears back, when Neera and she conversed. All this became possible due to Innaya's constant efforts; she would visit the Ranas every week, and compel them to see their daughter. Mr Rana had been unmoved, but his wife had yielded.

"I feel so much better," Neera had cried after her mother left, with her head resting on my shoulder. "I feel like things will improve with time. Mama said that she'll visit me again, next week. I'm happy! Things seemed so grim before, now I see Shimla in such a different light."

"Are you thinking to move back to Shimla, permanently?" I had enquired.

"I don't know, maybe. I have a feeling that my father will come to meet me soon. I just know it, although Ma was clear that he'll not. I was thinking maybe we can delay moving back a bit more. Is that OK? I'm sorry I am being so indecisive. I think, I just don't want to give up my hopes. In my heart I still believe that we will be a complete family - your family and mine, all living together happily."

Hitherto, Mr Rana never showed up and Neera still hoped that he will visit once the baby was born.

As for the name of the baby, we had settled for Aadhya if it were a girl, and Manogya if it were a boy; and I already knew the winner.

+++

On the thirteenth day of February, I was holding a frail human being in my arms. Her skin was shrivelled up and although her eyes had been shut for most of her life, I had noticed that she had her mother's eyes. My heart was pounding, and I was sure that the baby could hear it. How small was she! Was I ever this small? Worried that I might drop my daughter, I placed her, gently, back into Neera's arms.

"Hello Aadhya, I'm your father," I said. "I also contributed to your creation, howsoever small it might have been. Thank goodness that she doesn't have my nose!"

Neera laughed, and looked contented. I wanted to kiss her, but did not because she was lying on a hospital bed with my whole family surrounding her. The baby had been delivered at Ruchir's hospital and the room was filled with flowers and balloons, courtesy Innaya and my parents.

"What use are balloons to a new born?" I wondered aloud. "I mean, flowers she might smell, but balloons?"

"Your daddy is no fun, little one," said Innaya to Aadhya, imitating a baby voice.

My mother was vocal, reiterating her advices to Neera. "You must teach her good habits, else she will keep you up all night. When Prachur was little, I got him onto a very strict schedule, and he would sleep at eight every night. He was a good child. So was Innaya, for the most part."

"Don't lose the baby," interrupted Innaya, seriously. "That would be my advice to you guys. Don't go out and forget her somewhere."

Looking around the room, I was joyous to see the cheer our baby had brought to our family. It was satisfying to see everyone smiling and laughing. If Neera and I had murdered this angel, how would we be so happy at this moment? Our family would consist of two parents and one son who loathed them. Let this story be a lesson to every couple that seeks to abort a baby only because of fear of society's reaction - you might be killing your own happiness.

Things had been moving so quickly during the third trimester of Neera's pregnancy that I could barely remember them all in order. Nevertheless, I had learnt quite a lot about myself over that course.

One of the most recent discoveries I had made about myself was that I did not have nerves of steel — I had been light headed during Aadhya's birth, though I did not admit it! I would simply reply, "I'm fine," whenever I was asked about my state.

While I was immersed in my thoughts, Innaya's phone rang and she left the room, only to return and murmur, as she peeked through the half opened door, "Neera, someone is here to see you." And along came Mrs Rana.

"Ma!" Neera exclaimed.

Mrs Rana hugged her. What followed was shedding of tears, and exchange of good will.

"The baby's beautiful," Mrs Rana, cried out. "Let me hold her!"

"You wanted her dead," I wanted to say, but I am a man with common sense. Additionally, I had been raised to appreciate change in people, especially when it is for the better.

"Where's Papa? Is he coming? Won't he see me today?" asked Neera.

Mrs Rana shook her head in disappointment, and said, "You know he still loves you."

I stood on the side of the bed, trying to act sane, while Neera and her mom chatted. When it was time for her to leave, she gestured that I follow her. Her gait was slow and she barely spoke to my parents on her way out.

As I closed the room's door, she began, "Prachur, I know lately things have been a little dicey between us. Maybe you think of me and my husband as bad or selfish people, and I have no control over that; but, if you need anything, never hesitate to ask me. I would be happy to become a part of my daughter's life. I regret that I have lost so much time. I know that your parents are not very comfortable having me around you and Neera, but the only thing I want is to see my grandchild a few times a week. I hope you can allow and arrange that much for me."

"Of course," I replied. "Ma," I added hesitatingly.

She smiled, and as she turned to walk away, I blurted out, "Ma, is there no way you can get Papa to meet Neera? It would mean the world to her. I know that he doesn't want to, but please, could you talk to him just once?"

"I will, Son. I can't make any promises, but I will try to convince him."

After I walked back to the private hospital room, I sunk into an arm chair. Finally, I had some time to assimilate that I was a parent now, and I knew that my life would be different from the last few months. I had read ample material, though I could not recall any of it.

"What should I do if I fail at this parenting gig?" I asked myself, with a sense of panic. "You have people to help you. Calm down, you nitwit."

+++

Fourteenth of February was the day that Aadhya first graced our home in Shimla with her presence. My mother carried her to my bedroom. It had been a few hours but I was not yet over my fear of handling a fragile newborn.

Why are babies so delicate? I wondered.

Her arms were very little, and her fingers were no bigger than a doll's. I watched over her, as she lay peacefully in her bassinet. She would occasionally open her mouth as if she wanted to convey some information, but I did not understand her.

No matter what I do hereafter, she is going to be my proudest creation, I told myself.

Neera was led to the bed by Innaya.

"Rest, my child," my mother said, kissing her on the forehead. "I'll take care of Aadhya."

Neera smiled and in a few moments she was asleep. We quietly moved out and seated ourselves in the living room.

I was unaware of the precedent that I was supposed to follow now that I was a father. Would there be any difference in how my parents treated me? Would they consider me as a man? I had these doubts because in my experience, my marriage had not changed my parent's behaviour completely - they still treated me like a child, on most occasions.

Why was I so inept at social interactions? I thought.

If I were not, I would have known what to say because my family sat looking at me. Thankfully, Innaya broke the silence.

"She's so sweet. Like a little marshmallow," she said. "I want to steal her and keep her for myself."

"She *is* very sweet!" my mother replied. "Prachur, from now on, don't you dare make Neera sad. Take care of her and your child. You've got to be responsible - you're a father now. You must act like one."

"I will, Ma. Don't worry," I said.

"That's good to hear," my mother said.

"It was nice of Mrs Rana to show up," my father said, as if he was talking to himself. "I called Rana Ji, after she left, and although he sounded concerned about Neera's health, I don't think he will come to see her."

"I bet if he sees Aadhya he'll just melt," Innaya pointed out.

"Yes, maybe I can talk him into coming to see her," my father stated. "Let me try."

"Prachur, take a few days off work," my mother, who seemed oblivious to the ongoing conversation, blurted out. "I don't want you to get busy with work. Help your wife out. She's just a kid. I want you to try to make her life easier. Do you understand?"

"I do, Ma," I replied.

She nodded in agreement.

+++

The next few days were not difficult. What I learnt, mostly, was that babies are not fun. They hardly do anything except sleep, cry, eat, and convert the things they eat to faeces, which, contrary to what I believed, does not smell better than an adult's. I had taken leave from my job, and all I did the whole day was to check on Aadhya every few minutes. I had started putting on weight, while Neera tried to lose hers, as Innaya would often point out.

Our baby girl would cry every night, and I tried to keep my promise of helping Neera as much as I could, but since I was a deep sleeper, Neera would always wake up before me on hearing Aadhya's wails. Then, she would wake me up and I would get out of bed eagerly, because although I suffered sleepless nights, I could always get up late in the mornings.

"I could be a great house husband," I would tell Neera, on numerous occasions, usually while displaying my prowess at being a father.

I felt I was in utopia, but little did I know that this feeling was about to change eventually. What I could not understand at the time was that doing the same while also working would be difficult. The first eight or nine weeks seemed to breeze by, what came after would be relevant to this story — therefore, I must again skip forward four months, to, mid of June.

Before I move on, I must mention that Mr Rana did not visit to see Aadhya during this time. Some people can be stone hearted.

CHAPTER XXI

I stood leaning against my mother's car; puffing on a cigarette, which was probably the last one that I was going to have for the day; and speaking to Yukti on the phone.

"How's your brother?" I asked.

"Better, actually. Way better."

"That's good to hear. It has been so long since you spoke to me; there's just so much catching up to do."

"Sorry for not speaking to you guys. I have been very busy lately, with the job and constant travelling to my home to check on my brother. Also, you didn't message me anyway."

"Yeah, Neera doesn't like it much when I talk to you."

"Really? Why?"

"Yeah. I don't want to talk about that."

"So, tell me, how does being a father feel?" she asked, after a while.

"It's tough, I'd say. Aadhya's about four months old now and she cries all the time. I mean, *all the time*. It's been impossible to get her on a cycle; she is mostly a nocturnal being, you know? Neera has to stay awake at nights, because I need to work in the morning. I try to help, but honestly I am tired after working all day. The worst part is that I can't say this because then I sound like a bad father; this is the first time I'm saying this aloud. Anyway, my parents are of great help, but they live in Shimla, so they can't really take care of Neera or Aadhya. She's putting up fine, at the moment, at least, but she has hinted to me several times that her studies are being affected. She hasn't really said that I am not contributing enough, but I feel her growing impatient with me every day."

Yukti had no solution to my problems; she only told me to stay positive, which is what I had expected from her. Besides, I was not expecting any advice, I only needed to vent out my frustration. Innaya had been siding with Neera on every issue lately, and thus opening up to her was not an option anymore.

After bidding her goodbye, I looked around. The night was dark, and the highway to Shimla was swarming with traffic.

"Another cigarette would be mighty fine", I said to myself.

Neera had stopped criticising me for smoking, and would only shoot a disappointed look at me, which, honestly, I hated more than an argument. She had approached Innaya regarding this subject, who, acting like a responsible sister-in-law, had taken it upon herself to lecture me to quit every single day.

"See, you need to stop smoking," Innaya or Neera would say every time I coughed. Coughing had taken the status of being a 'vice' for me. "Can a man not be sick, now?" I would reply.

What they did not grasp was that quitting smoking was impossible for me - it was the only thing that relieved my anxiety. I had restricted my consumption of alcohol to Neera's strict limit of two drinks every day, which she insisted that I lower to one. "I would go insane", I had warned her, to no effect.

As for the other members of my family, my father was satisfied with my progress at work, and my mother was busy in her job. Innaya was on her way to finishing her master's degree and was looking forward to pursuing an MPhil.

I had lost my drive for writing, which I attributed to my work, but the truth was that the rejection of my poetry by *Panorama* had dampened my spirits.

Tired of standing alone in the darkness, I drove back home and saw Neera cooking dinner. Rather than joining her, I walked to the bedroom to find Aadhya lying calmly in her bassinet. I went to her and saw her bright smile. How peaceful was she! She had her mother's lips and a 'shyny' forehead. After picking her up and walking around the room for a while, I fell back on the bed.

Half an hour must have passed before Neera walked in through the door, picked up our wailing daughter from her bassinet, and started breast-feeding her. I looked at her, expecting her to start a conversation, even if it involved nagging me; but her silence broke me.

"Neera," I began, as she put Aadhya back into the bassinet.

"Shh," she replied. "She's finally sleeping. Please don't wake her up."

"I'm sorry," I whispered. "How was your day?"

"Fine."

"Just fine?"

On not receiving a response, I sighed. We went on to have dinner in silence. I washed the dishes, after which I joined her in bed; she had her back towards me.

"Neera, are you OK?" I enquired.

She did not reply, so I held her, and kissed her neck.

"Not today, Prachur," she said, sounding half asleep. "I'm very tired. Aadhya kept me busy all day."

"I'm sorry, Baby, but I can't even remember the last time we did anything physical. Don't you think our marriage is losing its intimacy?"

"I don't know anything about that. I'm tired. Let me sleep, please."

"Tell me what am I doing wrong?" I said, flustered. "You've been so rude to me lately. I work ten hours every day, for us, and yet, when I return you behave as if I'm not contributing at all. Even worse, you never say this to me directly. All you do is make sad faces and nag."

"So you want me to say things directly?" she exclaimed. "Prachur, you need to help out at home as well. You barely help around here.

I can't take this anymore. All day, I'm alone with her. I can't catch a break for even a few minutes. We're kids ourselves, how am I supposed to care for a child? This empty house makes me feel lonely during the day — no one is here to hold me, no one to tell me that things will get better. You come back at night, drink, and sleep. I feel like I lost my family, my career, and you don't even care. When was the last time you offered to take her for a walk, even around the neighbourhood? I hate this! This is not how we pictured it."

Meanwhile Aadhya woke up from her slumber and started crying.

"Great!" she said, getting out of bed and picking Aadhya up. "Now she's up."

"Please, keep your voice down; I understand you, OK? Tell me, what more would you have me do?"

"Do I need to tell you everything? I'm stressed as it is," she whispered.

"Calm down, God! You're acting as if you are the only one sacrificing your life for our marriage and Aadhya. I'm working at a job that I don't want to do, what more do you want from me? If I want a few hours to myself, after toiling for the whole day, what is wrong with that?"

"How selfish could you be!"

"Selfish?"

"Yes, Prachur. Selfish."

"Neera, stop being so judgemental," I said, losing my patience. "I am trying my best, OK? Don't forget before all this happened, I had told you that having a baby was not a good idea."

"What?"

"We were not ready."

"So, you're saying this is my fault? That I put you in this situation?"

"No."

"What's stopping you, Prachur? You are free to leave anytime you want. You want to get out of this? Just say so. I won't object."

I sighed, "You know that's not what I meant."

"What did you mean, then? Enlighten me."

"Just that we knew we would both be bad at this parenting thing, all along. You need to stop acting like I'm the only one who's screwing up."

She stared at me and murmured, "I can't talk about this right now, I have to put her to sleep."

"Look, we can work things out. We can find a way out of this. Right?"

She did not reply, and bobbed around the room with Aadhya in her arms.

"Neera?"

Silence.

"Now isn't this just perfect!" I snapped. "You can leave an argument whenever you want. If I do that, you don't talk to me for days."

I slid out of bed, picked up a box of cigarettes, and walked out of the apartment door, slamming it behind me. As I was descending the stairs to go towards the ground floor, I met Mrs Jamwal standing at her door.

I ignored her, but she mumbled, as I walked past her, "Everything OK?"

+++

After I was contented with the quantity of nicotine in my blood stream, I casually called Innaya's cell phone. She answered and I could not figure out how to tell her about the fight. I knew that I must start the conversation, however awkward it would be, but Neera had apparently already called her.

"What the hell, Prachur? Did you have a fight with Neera again?"

"She called you, did she not?" I asked her.

"Yeah, she did," she hesitated. "That was something. Sounded like the worst one you had."

"It was."

She fell silent.

I continued, "So, what do you think? You obviously will support her; you always do that."

"Prachur, you act like a jerk. What else could I do if not take her side?"

"I am a jerk? She wants me to work all day, not to drink, not to smoke, not to be alone, and, on top of that, pay her all my attention all day. I can't do everything, I am not God. If I were, I would know, right?"

"How could you be so insensitive? She loves you so much and you ignore her every day. Are you even aware how badly she feels about the growing distance between you? You've to act responsibly, Prachur. She's not just your girlfriend anymore. She's your wife and you have a kid together. How can you still act like a boy just out of college? If you don't change, you will lose her, I'm telling you."

"I am not acting like a boy. You expect me to change so quickly. And you ask this as if I am not doing enough, already. I've given up so much of my identity for her and Aadhya. I'm tired of everyone blaming me for everything that goes wrong in this marriage - today it's you, yesterday it was Ma. Why do you guys never blame her? Why am I your scapegoat, every time? Did you ever tell her that I need some space as well, and maybe some independence? She's acting like my granny, telling me to come home on time! What is this? I swear I'll go crazy like this."

"You're angry with her for no reason. She's not the one who's acting like a baby..."

Frustrated, I started pacing around on the road.

"I have to go," I said, finally, controlling my anger.

She snapped, "Good! Run away from this conversation; yes,

that sounds like a good option. Is this what you want to do in your marriage as well? What did you call me for, if not for hearing my point of view?"

I replied, passionately, "No, I don't plan to walk out on Neera, but how can I continue talking to you if you're bent upon thinking that I'm the bad guy? I need you to be my sister for a while and listen to what I want to say."

She promised to hear me calmly, and following that I whined, "You need to understand that I'm trying my best to be a good husband and a father, but if you treat me like everything I do is an abomination, how am I supposed to feel anything but terrible? I don't know what to do, I don't know how to solve all these things. Just let me have a little peace when I am at home."

I heard her sigh.

"Say something," I requested.

"I don't know what to say."

Silence followed and a few moments later, I droned, "Anyway, Papa told me that I need to go to Delhi next week, to negotiate with our distributor over there. That trip will take my mind off this problem, and I am sure when I return, I will feel better. I need some time off from these complications."

"There's no sense left in you, Prachur," she retorted. "You're talking about running away from a woman from whom, a few months ago, you were inseparable. What can I say? Do what you feel is right. I'll not interfere anymore."

+++

When I returned to my apartment, I saw that Neera was sleeping. Lying down beside her, I took out my phone out of my pyjamas, and texted Yukti.

"Had another fight with Neera."

I waited for her reply, but gave up after half an hour. Just as I put my phone down, I heard it buzz.

"Sorry," she had replied. "What about?"

"What do you think? About responsibilities."

"Hmmm..."

"I hate these fights."

"Understand."

"Are you OK?"

"Yeah, I am. Just not interested in talking about her."

"Oh...OK. I might come to Delhi next week."

"Great! You can stay at my place :)"

"I don't think Neera would like that."

"How could she be so cruel to me?" I began thinking. "I'm doing all that I can. And how peacefully she sleeps. She knows I can't sleep when I'm angry. I can bet that like me, she's also thinking that the best course would have been to not have a baby. What am I saying? Aadhya is my angel. I love her. Anyway, what could we do now? We're stuck. OK, 'stuck' might not be the right word — 'Bound', maybe. I don't know. Semantics are not important...Neera needs to understand my position."

+++

The next day, I was washing the dishes when Neera entered the kitchen and said, "My mother wants us to visit my home."

She had not talked to me since our last fight and her demeanour was cold. I felt as if I was sharing the apartment with a stranger.

I nodded, disinterestedly, and saw her walk out.

That evening, she and I drove to Shimla, to her parents' house. Aadhya was cosily tucked into a warm baby suit. Neera was holding her gently on her lap during the ride to Shimla. No one spoke, because Aadhya could not and Neera and I chose not to.

Mrs Rana welcomed us into her living room with a genial smile.

Neera hugged her and said, "I missed you, Ma."

I touched her feet and soon we found ourselves sipping some poorly brewed tea.

"Where's Papa?" Neera asked.

"He's not back from Mall Road yet."

"Does he know we're coming?"

"No, Beta, he doesn't."

Neera sighed, "I was hoping to see him today."

"He'll be back soon, Dear. I want him to see you guys here. I'm sure everything'll be fine."

An ambush, how ingenious! I thought. Not that she has anything to lose. The only person in the room her husband would kill is me.

"Prachur beta, you look lost in thought," Mrs Rana said to me. "Are you OK?"

I smiled, "Yes, Ma. Of course."

It was strange for me to see how distant Neera was acting. She was literally sitting on the other end of the sofa that we occupied. I was sure that her mother would have sensed the tension between us - any idiot would have, it was that apparent.

I felt uneasy, but I wanted to act responsibly, so I sat looking at pictures on the wall, and occasionally listening to Neera and her mother talk.

We heard a car pull into the driveway, which we all knew was Mr Rana's. Neera got up and walked to the door, with Mrs Rana following her. I chose to stay on the sofa with Aadhya.

"Neera!" I heard Mr Rana exclaim. Neera's sobs followed soon.

They were having a family moment on their driveway. I was sitting, trying to act sane, waiting to die by Mr Rana's hands.

He saw me the minute he stepped into the living room. His steps froze.

"What is this?" he asked his wife.

"Prachur and Aadhya are here too," Mrs Rana said, slowly. She was looking at her husband hopefully, waiting for him to accept me.

Rather he said, "I don't want him and his bastard child here. Get them out!"

"Message received," I droned, as I picked up Aadhya.

"Prachur, where are you going?" Neera said.

"Back to Shoghi. He called my angel a bastard. He can go fuc-," I took a huge breath. "I'm leaving."

Neera's defeated look and Mrs Rana's constant imploring could not stop me.

I started the car engine and saw Neera walk towards me.

"You're not leaving like this, Prachur. Come back inside," she whined.

"Neera, how could you stay after hearing him say something like that to our daughter? He's an asshole. He's always been one."

"Prachur, don't call him that. This is my one chance to get my family back together. Don't ruin it for me."

"He's not worth your time, Neera."

"You have your family with you, Prachur. I don't. I have to get them back. He's angry now, that's why he said what he did. He's not a bad person. Don't do anything stupid. Come inside. Please, don't be selfish."

"I'm not being selfish!" I retorted, fuming. "Why do you always keep saying this? He's inconsiderate. He never cared about Aadhya or you."

"I thought you never wanted to have Aadhya in the first place."

"Neera, you know I did not say that last night."

"Well, what you said was pretty close to it."

I slammed my hand on the steering wheel.

"Stop making it worse, Prachur," she said. "Come inside."

"No, I am leaving. Are you coming or not?"

"No, I am not," she snapped, taking Aadhya from the back seat.

"She's staying with me."

"Neera!" I yelled, as I saw her walk into the house.

CHAPTER XXII

I was scuttling around in my bedroom, packing a bag to leave for New Delhi.

"Prachur, could you please change Aadhya?" Neera asked from the kitchen.

"Can't you do it? I have to leave in like twenty minutes."

"No, I'm in the kitchen, washing some dishes."

I jammed a pair of jeans in my bag and walked to the living room. Aadhya's bassinet was standing near a newly bought sofa. She was dressed in a yellow baby suit and was sobbing profusely. I changed her, kissed her forehead, and picked her up.

"Stop crying, my little angel. Papa needs to leave."

After she calmed down following a quick walk around the room in my arms, I put her back into her bassinet, and went to the kitchen to see Neera.

"I'm leaving now," I said.

"OK," she replied, without looking at me.

"Are you still angry with me? It has been six-seven days since our fight," I asked.

"I'm not angry, Prachur. I am busy," she retorted.

Ever since she returned from her family's home, her behaviour towards me was becoming worse. I felt hatred towards her, but only for a moment, after which I felt guilty.

On seeing no window for receiving a goodbye kiss, I went back to the bedroom. Ten minutes later, I was driving to New Delhi.

+++

New Delhi is intolerably hot in the summers for someone travelling from Shimla. The dry air and scorching sun band together to roast anyone who dares to step in the city. 'India's Oven' is the most astute expression that could be used to describe India's northern plains.

I had always disliked large cities, probably because in my heart I was a small-town boy from the hills - I despised commotion and areas with high population density. My first visit to Delhi was enough to make me never question the fact that our country is habited by more than one billion people, and, additionally, never after that did I recover from the shock of knowing that this unorganised collection of houses, this poorly developed village, is deemed to be our nation's capital.

As for my visit, I was not looking forward to my meeting with Mr Dhiman. He was the primary distributor of the books published by my father. I was supposed to negotiate the terms of our business together for the forthcoming year, which is to say I was to have a cup of tea with him and sign a piece of paper. He and my father had been friends since college, and the only reason I agreed to take this needless trip was to take some time off from Neera and our life back home.

I must not give the impression that I was tired of my family; every person needs some time alone. The problem was that I did not realise before marrying Neera that such a union would imply that I would never get to be in solitude. I was a husband and a father now, and I could not be anything else.

The meeting went as I had hoped - without any particular incidents worth mentioning in this memoir. By evening, I was free and decided to check on my friends and meet them. On calling Mudit I learnt that he was on a work trip to Mumbai; finally, I called Yukti and we set up a meeting. I drove to her apartment in Green

Park, and parked my car a hundred metres from her building, albeit after a tedious search for space.

She opened the door with a grin and we embraced each other. Dressed in an emerald tee shirt and black shorts, she looked stunning and I told her so after we broke the hug. I had not seen her for a very long time and I had forgotten how dark and profound her eyes were.

Her apartment had a bedroom and a large living room with an open kitchen. You could guess that it had been a while since she started living there as the place looked well furnished. She even had cushions on her sofa set; if that is not a sign of a home, I do not know what is.

She invited me to take a seat on the sofa, probably to show off her cushions, and sat beside me. She looked as amiable as ever.

"What will you have to drink, Sir?" she asked, politely. "Would whiskey do?"

I nodded and she began pouring us drinks, and one after the other, they flowed and we chatted for long about her job, her life, and her family, before she asked, "How's everything else? Your job?"

"Fine, I guess. Can't complain. I am not writing anything these days."

She nodded, disinterestedly, and enquired "How's Neera? How're things between you guys?"

"She's nice," I replied, after gulping down alcohol from my glass. "Things between us are different; they're not like when we were in college. We fight a lot more these days. I never thought that I could actually get irritated with her."

"That's sad to hear."

"Normally, Neera's perfect, I'm not questioning that. It's just that long-term relationships are difficult. We've been together for so long, it feels like an eternity. When we used to fight before marriage, we got to go to our separate rooms in the hostel, and take some time off; but now, even if we have a horrendous fight, we need to share a bed. It's difficult to just wake up and act like nothing happened the previous night. How could I do that? Plus, the next day she acts sullen and that day is ruined as well. It is like a feedback loop of sadness."

"You deserve better. I'm sorry for saying this, that's what I feel."

I nodded, although in my heart I was aware that there was no woman as precious as Neera, and that I was lucky to have her. "Would we have something to eat, anytime soon?" I wondered aloud. "An empty stomach and alcohol do not agree with each other."

She snickered and went on to order some food, and droned, "What I was saying is that if I was the one who was with you, I would give you all the independence you need. I understand your nature. The problem, I think, between you and Neera is that she tries to make you into a person you're not. She's so straightened out, and she expects everyone to be like that. That's why she is so close to Yashika; they're like peas in a pod."

"That they are!" I burst out, laughing.

"Like I was saying, she wants to change you. I talked to her about this once or twice during college; did she tell you about it?" I shook my head, and she continued, "I told her that I felt that even though you tend to adjust to her demands, you'll eventually suffocate. She was not happy with that, obviously. And, I stand by what I had said, even today."

"I never thought about my situation like that," I replied, contemplatively.

Neera had always tried to fashion me into a better man. She pushed me to expand my horizons, and she cared not whether I wanted what she saw as my future. This irritated me often.

"I'm sure she talked you into this marriage and having a baby so early. She has a 'plan' and she doesn't want anyone to change that."

"No, that's something that was not really planned," I pointed out.

"OK, maybe, but still you need to talk to her about this. A person who loves you shouldn't try to change you, even if *they* feel it's for the better. I mean, you never try to change her. For me, it's funny to see couples struggle to create better versions of each other, in a way. I tried to do that once, remember that idiot, Jatin, I dated during the second year? I tried to force him into a commitment, even though I knew he was just with me for the physical aspect. I wasted so much of our time trying to get him into a long-time relationship, you know? At the end, it was just terrible for both of us. I have experience with this kind of stuff, that is why I'm warning you, like a friend — tell Neera to not put both of you into misery."

"I will tell her, for sure. While we're on the topic, are you seeing someone?"

"No, not at the moment."

"Oh, why is that?"

"I don't know, never found anyone, I guess. Every guy I like turns out to be otherwise occupied."

"That's sad to know and impossible to believe."

"Are you trying to flirt with me, Prachur Thakur? That is such a cheesy thing to say to a girl."

"No," I giggled. "I'm married, remember? Why would I flirt with anyone? I'm just saying that you are beautiful and funny. Those are all the qualities guys look for in a girl. I was stating a fact - a well-known fact."

She stared at me, and her face betrayed that she was anticipating me to say something more - but what, I knew not.

"What is it?" I questioned.

"Nothing, just looking at you."

"I feel shy when people look at me. Stop that!"

"You know how happy I feel when I see you smiling? I always wanted to see you happy, you know that, right?" she asked, with a broken voice.

"Yeah, I know..." I held her hand and smiled.

She leaned forward, and kissed me.

+++

What are you doing? I asked myself.

I was lying on my back, with Yukti on top of me. We had our lips locked and I could smell her sweet essence. Her chest was pressed firmly against mine and I could feel her heaving.

Realising the consequences of my actions, I broke the kiss, and without uttering a word, walked out of the door. I heard her calling after me, but I had no courage to face her.

The street outside was deserted, and I walked quickly to my car. It did not take me much time to realise that I had forgotten my keys and phone at Yukti's apartment. I could not get myself to walk back and decided that I would take a stroll to calm myself before I chose to do so.

For about an hour, I circled the residential block on foot. The forthcoming day was only a few hours away, and my anxiety was ascending with every passing second.

What have you done? I asked myself. You kissed Yukti. You cheated on Neera. Neera, the mother of your daughter! Oh my God!

Although I had the comfort of knowing that I did not initiate the kiss, I had not tried to stop it in the first place. Even on severely rattling my brain, I found no words to justify what I had done. I had cheated on Neera, plain and simple. Some may think that a kiss does not amount to cheating, but I thought it did. And I was sure that Neera too would definitely consider my act as cheating. The bottom line was that I, in all likeliness, had shaken the very foundation of our relationship.

How could I have done something so heinous? I wondered. I had an image of myself as a 'good guy', and I found the same wavering in my mind.

I was talking to myself, "Neera must never know. She will never forgive me. Never. But, how could I lie to her? If I don't tell her and

Yukti does, she'll be devastated. No, I must tell her myself. That way I can ease her into it, and explain myself while I am confessing; but, what would I explain? That I saw an opportunity to kiss a girl and I took it? No, that won't do. Neera had been acting crazy lately. We've been fighting a lot. Yes, she has been unreasonable. And think about the distance between us; I mean, it has been three weeks since we did anything physical. Maybe that's why I slipped. How awful I sound right now! No, this can't be it, I must think of something else. I was drunk, so maybe I can blame alcohol. Yes, that sounds good. Alcohol clouded my judgement. I would never hurt Neera if I were in my senses. So, it's settled - 'I was drunk', is my excuse. Now, when should I tell her? I must make sure that she's in a good mood. That's an unlikely situation now, isn't it? She's not been in a good mood for so long now. Anyway, what's the worst thing that could happen? She'll be very angry with me for a long time, but she loves me; she'll forgive me. Yes, she will. Would I have done so if she was the one who had done something like this? Probably not, but she's a better person than me. She loves me. At least she *loved* me, but does she still love me? I mean, she married me, maybe that's only why she's with me. I hope she still cares about me. Should I tell Innaya? No, I should not. This must stay between Neera and me. I hope Yukti can keep mum. If she tells Neera before me, I'll be in quite a lot of trouble. Why would she? I mean, she has just as much reason to be ashamed of it, as me. She won't tell, I'm sure. Should I ensure this by talking to her? No, that could be really awkward. But, she would be in as bad a state of mind as me. I should comfort her, right? Nope. Forget about her now. Just get your keys and drive off to the hotel."

Swiftly, I climbed the stairs to her apartment, and entered without knocking. She was sitting on the sofa with her head in her hands. I grabbed my car keys and my phone, and trotted to the door.

"Prachur, wait. We've to talk about this," she pleaded.

"No, we don't have to," I replied. "Forget that this ever happened."

"This meant nothing to you?"

"No, it did not. I am married. I was stupid for a moment and I lost myself. It's my fault. Don't feel bad about this. I need to go now. Bye."

She did not reply, and fixated on me as I left her apartment.

Even while driving back to my hotel room I was feeling increasingly giddy. I realised that things would never be the same between Neera and me.

There are some things in life that you can never go back from. You can pray, you can whine, but things will never be the way they used to be. This realisation made me feel depressed. I felt a need to cry to let out my emotions, but boys are not supposed to cry, are they?

CHAPTER XXIII

When I finally arrived back at my parents', two days after kissing Yukti, I felt no better than I did in Delhi. Neera had told me that she felt lonely at our apartment, so she had gone to our home in Shimla. She wanted to visit her family, but after arguing with me for a while, she yielded to not meeting them.

My family was assembled in the living room. Neera sat beside Innaya, and both of them were laughing their lungs out. My father was sitting with them, making jokes about someone from our neighbourhood, while my mother was holding Aadhya, who was watching, with wide eyes, every object that my mother pointed outside a window.

"Fascinating", I imagined her saying to herself. "How marvellous is a scooter!" I was not sure that a baby so young could think that much, but if I were her, this is what I would have been thinking.

I waved at them, as I passed, devastated to feel the happy atmosphere in the room.

Is this the serenity I might endanger? I asked myself. How could I have been so irresponsible?

That evening, I was sitting with my family on the balcony of the second floor of our house, when my father turned to my mother and said, "Neera's been so great with the kid, I'm surprised. She does everything by herself and never demands any help. I can't believe how she finds time to study. What a strong girl! I'm very happy for you, Son."

"Is everything fine, Prachur?" my mother enquired, when I did not reply to my father.

Probably, she had sensed that there was a tumult inside me. I had spent most of my time with them sitting glumly in my chair, staring blankly at the horizon. My face always betrayed my deepest emotions, especially to my mother.

"I'm fine, Ma," I replied, without enthusiasm.

"Is something troubling you? You can share anything with us," she reminded.

"No, Ma. Nothing's troubling me. My mind was just someplace else. What were you saying?"

"Your father said that Neera's a very strong girl."

"That she is, Ma. That she is."

"Did you guys have another fight?" my mother questioned, concernedly. "Your spirits are down."

"No, what? No! Who told you that?"

"Nobody did, Son," my father answered. "You seem lost ever since you arrived from Delhi. Is there something that we must know?"

During my drive back to Shimla from Delhi, I had planned to ask my parents for advice. Needless to say, I was not going to tell them the whole truth, just sections of it, and I was going to ask their opinion, indirectly.

After a bit of contemplation, I shrugged in reply to my father's question and told myself, "Today might not be the day to break the news."

My abstract answers to the questions that they asked thereof did not satisfy their curiosity and when we split before dinner, I told them that I was feeling under the weather and would like to eat in my room, in a desperate attempt to avoid more enquiries.

+++

"How're you feeling, Prachur?" Neera asked me, gently stroking my hair.

"Better, way better. What time is it?"

"It's about eleven," she whispered.

"Your behaviour is different."

"How?"

"You're nice with me today. You haven't been so in weeks."

"Maybe you didn't deserve it then, but being away from you for a few days reminded me of your importance in my life."

I nodded.

"Aadhya is sleeping in Innaya's room. I missed you so much," she said, before she kissed me. "Are you sleepy, Dear?"

"No, I'm not. Come lie beside me."

She crept in the bed next to me and asked, "How was your trip? Tell me about it. Did you have fun? I hope you did not smoke too much."

"I did not smoke much," I lied. "The meeting was a small affair. It was over before I knew it. In the evening I went to see Yukti."

"You did? Didn't you tell me that you were going to see Mudit?"

"I must've forgotten to call you after that. I was going to see Mudit, but he is in Mumbai for two weeks. So, I called Yukti and we met at her apartment."

"Her apartment? Did you sleep over? I sure hope you did not."

"No, I went back to my hotel room."

"That's good to know. I don't like the idea of you hanging out with her alone."

I feigned a smile.

"She hasn't talked to me for so long. What's more, when she was talking to me, she was so rude at times. You should really have told me that you were going to meet her. I would've told you not to."

"Sorry about that. I didn't think you'd mind."

She shook her head. "I trust *you*, I just don't trust her. I was so concerned that you'll go to Delhi and do something stupid." She laughed. "I'm so silly."

"Yeah, there is something that I must tell you."

"I'm listening," she said, with her head on my chest.

"Yukti and I were drinking and talking, and one thing led to the other, and," I hesitated. "Please, don't take this the wrong way, OK?"

"You're scaring me, Prachur. What is it?"

"Yukti and I, we kissed," I mumbled, hoping that she would not hear me.

"What!" she exclaimed, sitting up.

"Please, it did not mean anything. We were drinking and she leaned in."

"Oh my God! How dare you!" She could not contain her anger and started pacing around the room. "I knew it. I knew it! She's a bad person. So are you."

"She's not a bad person. I don't want you to think that it was her fault," I replied. "It was just a stupid thing we did. Could you please forgive me?"

"It wasn't her fault? That means that you wanted it too, right?" she asked, with tears streaming down her face.

"No, I did not. The situation..."

"Are you trying to justify your actions?"

"No, I'm not."

"So, you kissed her...knowing that you're married. She kissed you knowing that you're married to her friend."

"It wasn't like this."

"You rascal!" she exclaimed. "Never even in my dreams would I have anticipated you to do something like this. Horrible!"

I was taken aback by her tone. Neera was always soft spoken, relatively speaking, even when she was angry. I could say nothing. She sat down on the bed, and occasionally uttered, "This is not happening. How could you?"

"Neera, please, forgive me," I kept repeating.

"Get out of this room!" she said, determinedly, after a while.

"What?"

"Get out of this room, Prachur!" she reiterated, furiously, but in a low voice. "I don't want to make a scene. Leave now!"

"Where am I supposed to sleep?"

"I don't care where you sleep. Go and find a place."

"Won't you even give me a chance to explain my side?"

"You've done enough as it is. Now, I'm going to call Yukti and listen to what she has to say about this."

"No, don't call her," I pleaded. "It's so late into the night."

"Prachur," she said, attempting to reign in her volume, "I don't want to bother our family. I will do what I think is right. You've done what you wanted to do, now let me do what I want to."

"Neera," I began, but she interrupted me.

"I'm not hearing another word," she said, and turned away from me.

I walked out of the room with my head hung, and she bolted the door from inside.

+++

I had decided to occupy the guest room, and it was cold. My whole night was spent tossing around in bed. How could I sleep? My mind was cluttered with the fear of Yukti revealing the nature of our kiss.

Numerous times, I went and knocked on our bedroom door, but mostly Neera chose not to reply, except occasionally shouting, "I don't want to talk to you! Don't you understand that?"

My anxiety was at an all-time high. I was moving from one floor to the other, waiting for the morning to arrive. I had no courage to call Yukti and risk Neera knowing that I had done so. The lack of information was a torture. I felt a dire need to smoke, but thought it best to not offend Neera with my actions anymore.

I was wondering what Yukti was going to tell Neera. In what sense would she describe the scene? Would she be angry with Neera? Would they have an argument or would Neera only request for some information?

I did not want Yukti to come out as a bad person in this situation. I understood that only two people were involved and the fault had to be pinned on someone, and if she were to escape the blame, then my intentions would have to be doubted; but somehow, taking the fall for her seemed better to me.

I knew that Neera would be smouldering in that room, but the knowledge that she was a very level-headed girl, quelled, to some extent, the terror brought on by bad scenarios in my fantasies. I consoled myself that she would find a way to bring our relationship back on track, that is, if my anxiety did not give me a heart attack.

Amidst the crescendo of my worries, my phone vibrated in my pocket. With trembling hands I took it out and saw that I had received an e-mail from Yukti.

It was quite lengthy, but the crux of it said, "You told her that I kissed you? How pathetic could you be, Prachur? You were as guilty as I was!"

Rather than replying to this e-mail, to make Yukti feel better about herself, I marked it as 'Unread', and put my phone on the bed. I could not risk doing anything that could have possibly been against Neera's wishes.

"Good job, Prachur," I said aloud. "You managed to screw your marriage and make Yukti think you're a bad person. Brilliant!"

+++

The clock had struck seven, when Neera walked in through the door of the guest room. I was lying on the bed, with my arm over my face. As soon as I heard her, I sat up, startled. She sat beside me, but avoided eye contact.

"Neera," I began.

"Prachur, I talked to Yukti. I'm devastated by what she told me. How could you do this to me? We have a family together. How could you risk that for something so stupid? It's clear to me that you care about her, and you're confused about being with me."

"What! No, there's nothing in my heart for her. You need to believe me."

"Don't think that I haven't noticed the change in your behaviour. You have been drifting away from me, and into her arms."

"It's nothing like this. Please Neera, don't read into this situation more than what there is. Can't you let it go for this once."

"No, I can't stop imagining you with her. I tried to see past this, but I can't. You've crossed your limits, Prachur. I thought you'd never do something like this, but you disappointed me."

"Neera, I'm so sorry," I said, before she stopped me.

"Let me finish, please. I don't think I can live with what has happened. I need some time away from you."

"What're you saying?" I questioned, my voice betraying my fear.

"I called my mother, I'm going to my parents' house and I'm taking Aadhya with me," she replied, coldly.

"You can't do that. I'm sorry for what I've done, but please, you can't make me live apart from yourself and our baby."

"You drove us to this point, Prachur. Not me. You need to accept the consequences of what you've done. You can still see Aadhya whenever you want, but she's going to live with me."

I could not reply, and stared blankly at the floor. "Don't you think you're overreacting?" I blurted out, after a while.

I knew that her reaction was justified. What I had done was unforgivable, but at the moment, I only wanted to stop her from leaving, and for that purpose, I was ready to say anything.

"Really? You think I'm overreacting? Prachur, *you* were unfaithful to me."

"It was just a kiss. Please, I was not unfaithful to you."

"Just a kiss? What you don't understand is that you broke the sanctity of my trust. How will I ever trust you after this? Tell me!"

"Neera, please don't go. I'll do anything that you want. Just, please, don't leave. We'll make it work, somehow."

She looked away from me, and I sat down on the floor, almost at her feet.

"Please, I was stupid," I pleaded, with my head resting on her lap. "Don't kill me for it."

"I'm sorry, Prachur. This is how it must be," she replied, sulking. "It's as difficult for me as it is for you, but, at this time, I can't think of anything else that I could do. I've already packed a bag, and my mother's coming to pick me up in a few minutes. I don't have the courage to face your parents right now. I'll leave without talking to them."

I kept repeating, "Please don't leave me," until, by and by, we heard a car honk outside. Neera got up slowly and went into our bedroom. She returned, with a small bag hanging on one shoulder and Aadhya on the other arm.

Her face was streaked with reluctance and she had dread in her eyes. Maybe she was hoping that I would say something that would make her change her mind, but I had no such words. Our marriage was shattering and I was confounded.

"Don't go, please," I pleaded.

"I have to," she cried.

"You don't have to. We can figure a way out of this."

"No, Prachur," she spoke, with a broken voice. "I need some time away from you."

I stood, stupefied, looking at her as she walked out of the main door.

This is not happening, I kept telling myself. This is not possible. I must be dreaming.

But, a few minutes later, her mother's car disappeared, and with that my happiness.

CHAPTER XXIV

On the morning of 22 May, hours after Neera left, I was sitting in the living room alone, watching the television, when Innaya came and asked: "Where's Neera? I haven't seen her or Aadhya since morning."

"They're at her parents' house," I replied.

"That's so great!" she exclaimed. "I'm happy that Rana Uncle budged. It was about time. When Neera told me what happened when you visited him the last time, I was so shocked. And for the record, I agree with you - Rana uncle is an asshole. Glad that he called them to reconcile."

"They did not go there because of that reason."

"Then, why did she go?"

"We had a little fight."

"Really? What did you do?"

I shrugged to indicate that the exact reason for Neera's actions eluded me.

"That's strange. I'm sorry," she replied. "Surely it would have been your fault. Do you want me to talk to her?"

"No, I will do it myself."

"When will she be back?"

"No idea," I replied, without taking my mind off the television.

I wanted to dodge questions related to Neera. I had no other choice - how could I tell my family? Opening up to them would have wreaked havoc in my life. There was no way I could rephrase, "I cheated on my wife and now she has left me," in a way that would make them sympathetic towards me.

Innaya left and I spent hours on the couch, until the evening when I decided that I did not want to wait for time to heal my wounds, but rather take matters in my own hands. Determined to get my wife and baby back, I walked to the Rana's.

My mother-in-law answered the door.

"Hi, Ma. Could I talk to Neera?" I stuttered.

"Oh, she doesn't want to see you, Beta. I'm sorry. She wouldn't tell us what you did but she's very sad."

"Ma, please, I need to see her. I *have* to talk to her. Can't you ask her to see me even for one minute?"

"I don't think she'll agree, but I can try. Come on in."

We walked to the living room, where I sat on a sofa, while she went to talk to Neera. I picked up a magazine lying on the coffee table, which I did not actually read, because I could not concentrate with my blood rushing faster through my veins with every passing minute.

My mother-in-law returned alone, to my disappointment.

"I'm sorry; she wouldn't come down. She says that you can see Aadhya, though. Would you like to do that?"

"Of course, Ma," I said, slowly.

She went upstairs and came back with my daughter. I smiled and spent the next hour walking with Aadhya.

"What have I done, Aadhya!" I spoke to her, as we walked past my house. "I lost your mother. Thank goodness you're very young. Otherwise, you'd hate your father too. But, don't you worry. I won't let you grow up in a broken home. I'll do whatever your mother needs me to do to win her trust back. I will make everything right."

When I returned, I met Mr Rana outside his home. He was alighting from his car, and he appeared to be as shocked with the meeting as I was.

I hesitated, but since we needed to share the same path into his house, I uttered a short, “Hi.”

He did not say anything in reply, but nodded slightly. Awkwardly, we entered the front door together, with me walking behind him.

I was startled to see Neera sitting with her mother in the living room. The moment she saw me, she got up and walked up the stairs.

I wanted to call after her, but restrained myself and glanced at her father. He chose not to talk to me. Thank god for that!

Following a few clumsy minutes during which Mr Rana and I stared at each other and the ground, he left the room, to my relief.

“I must go home, Ma,” I said, handing Aadhya to her. “If you don’t mind me asking, how’re things between Neera and her father?”

“Things are better. Rana Ji has still not accepted Aadhya. But he will in time, don’t worry. Neera is enjoying her time with us, except she’s very upset with whatever happened between you two. She won’t tell me what that is, and I am sure that you won’t either. You need to make this right, Prachur. Whatever it is, just clear it up.”

“I will, Ma,” I said, determinedly.

“This little one is a gift from God,” she said, referring to Aadhya. “She has made our days wonderful. It’s so nice to say that I’m a grandmother. I am thankful to God for blessing our home with her. It would have been a terrible sin to kill her. Thank you for not letting me make you do that, Son. I would’ve never forgiven myself.”

I smiled and expressed my agreement with her. How I prayed for her not to ever find out about my actions!

After conversing with her for a while, I bid goodbye to Aadhya and walked to my house. Ignoring my parents, I headed straight to my room. A cigarette pack was lying on my table. I took out one.

This is the last one, I told myself, as I opened the window to smoke.

One more thing that I must mention regarding my visit to the Rana’s is that my phone was vibrating constantly — Yukti had been trying to reach me but I had been avoiding her calls for a while.

The sky was getting darker and cloudy. While blowing smoke against the wind, I was trying to think my way out of my predicament, but even after hours of meditation, I was sans any ideas.

+++

Days flew by, but Neera did not budge. She dodged my calls, and even when I approached her during one of her evening walks, she ignored me. During one of her excursions, I took hold of her hand, which only made her demeanour towards me worse. If only I could get her to return to our house, things would get better, I believed; but nothing I said, or did, changed her mind.

My family was obviously concerned, but since they did not know the reason for our separation, they could not help me in any way. I was bogged by their constant enquiries.

"Where's Neera? What happened between the two of you?" they would ask.

"Nothing happened. Just a small fight; she will be back soon."

The more I repeated this lie, the more I started believing it to be the truth. I would go to work every day, and started assuming that she will return to me.

But she did not.

Every day I kept losing some of the hope I had of getting Neera back. Finally, even two weeks after Neera walked out on me, I could not get her to budge. So, I decided to move back to my apartment in Shoghi.

"Have you gone crazy?" Innaya enquired, when I revealed this to my parents. "You shouldn't be alone now. Don't be stupid."

"That apartment is way closer to my office," I replied, without any enthusiasm. "I think I will have more motivation to go to work if I am living there."

"Don't go, Prachur," Innaya requested, hugging me.

"I have to be alone," I answered.

"No, you're being crazy."

"Look, you're thinking about this too much. Everything's going to be OK."

+++

My first night at the apartment without Neera was lonely. The night was cold and no matter how many quilts I piled on myself, I could not stop shivering.

I would roll over and smell Neera's perfume on her pillow.

"What have I done?" I thought. "How could I lose her? Neera please come back to me."

In the morning, I woke up, prepared tea for myself, and threw the pan in the kitchen sink already brimming with utensils. I had no intention of going to work, and I got back into bed.

I woke up a few hours later, still tired, and lonely.

+++

With every passing day, I found it increasingly hard to go to my job. I would spend half my day, lying in bed, staring at the ceiling and thinking about my mistakes.

If I had been a better husband to her, maybe she would have not left me even after I kissed Yukti, I would tell myself, repeatedly.

We often have an image of ourselves in our heart, and to preserve it, we lie to ourselves. I had tried doing that but I could not forget, even for a moment, that even though I was used to thinking I am a good person, who happens to be somewhat lost in life, in actuality, I was a failure at being a decent human being. This realisation tormented me daily during my waking hours.

Sharing my troubles with any living soul was not an option.

During moments like these, God comes in handy, but I was a non-believer - whom do I turn to, if the whole world seems incapable of helping me? Loneliness was my only resort.

+++

I received no calls from Neera, no texts. I thought when she calmed down, she would suggest talking or some other way of resolving our problem, but no matter how long I waited, I heard nothing from her.

I would check my phone every ten minutes, daily. The wait was making me uncomfortable and angry.

I paced the room, talking to myself, "How dare she do this to me! All I made was a little mistake. Has she never screwed up? She left me, took my baby. Am I supposed to sit here waiting for her? God!"

The room heater was trying to keep me warm, to no avail. I felt myself shiver.

I took out my phone, and sent her a text:

"Neera, stop being obstinate. We need to talk."

No reply.

I threw my phone at the wall.

+++

I needed someone to talk to. I wanted to vent out my frustration; to yell.

Innaya had always been someone I shared everything with, but on this occasion I could not. I knew her. No matter how much she loved me, she would say that I had wronged Neera. Asking for her support when Neera and I had found out about the pregnancy was easy. I had not done anything wrong per se, ergo Innaya, the righteous, was obviously going to be by my side; but kissing Yukti was like blasphemy in her book. Had I told her, she would have thought of me as a bad human being.

"Why add Innaya to the list of people whom I have disappointed?" I asked myself. "Let her think that Neera left me because of some petty fight. I still need to call someone to talk about this. Mudit, maybe? No. He'd ask for all the details. Not him. Then, who else? It's funny, I know the answer but I just don't want to entertain that notion. Yukti. No, Neera would be pissed if she finds out that I am talking to Yukti. But, only Yukti knows the *exact* state I am in. So maybe I should call her."

I opened the contact list on my phone, scrolled to Yukti's name, and put the phone back in my pocket. Took it out again, and repeated my actions. Finally, on the fifth try, I dialled her number, and she picked up after three rings.

"About time you called me, you asshole!" she said.

"Well, 'hello' to you too."

"Prachur, what the hell do you want?"

"I want to talk."

"I don't," she said, before hanging up.

I dialled again.

"What?" she yelled.

"Yukti, I'm sorry for what happened. I need to talk to someone. Don't hang up."

Click, followed by three beeps.

"Damn it!" I yelled.

I called her again.

"Yukti, I am sorry I made you look like a bad person. I am an idiot. I freaked out, OK? Please, don't be so rude to me."

She sighed.

"Neera left me."

"Good."

"I am lonely," I said, in a child-like voice.

"OK."

"Talk to me, please."

"Nope."

She hung up.

CHAPTER XXV

Karuna, the receptionist at my father's business, smiled at me as I walked into the office.

"You're late, Prachur," she said. "Mrs Bhatia has been looking for you all morning, and she's not happy."

I nodded.

"She's waiting for you in her room. Go right in."

I walked into Mrs Bhatia's office, with no apprehensions. What could she do that would make my life worse than what it already was?

She yelled at me, and told me how dismally I was faring at my job. She pointed out how she could train a langur to do my job, and how that would be easier for her than to handle me.

I stood listening to her drivel. After she was tired of shouting at me, she asked me to get back to my *cubicle of depression.*

What was I doing? Wasting my time, and that of everyone else around me? I was dead-weight for the organisation. I was someone who was there just to hold a position and while away my time.

I left work as soon as the clock struck five, and an empty apartment greeted me. No wife to hug me, no daughter to take up in my arms; only cold air and dark rooms.

I did not switch on any lights. What was the use - who was I supposed to see? My own face in the mirror? The pictures of Neera and me, with Aadhya, on the wall?

Over the time we shared the flat together, Neera and I had made it our home. The remnants of our broken marriage were neatly arranged around the place.

The sofa that we had bought, after bickering about the colour for hours...I could not care less, and Neera wanted me to make up my mind, and when I had blurted that I preferred black, she had asked me to explain, in detail, my reasons.

The small refrigerator in the kitchen, yellow and withering...The drive to Shimla to purchase it...The day all the ice cream had melted.

The wooden closet that I had brought from my room at my parents' house; Neera's clothes inside...her smell; a half-used bottle of her cologne; her *kajal.*

The bed with three pillows — two for me, one for her.

Aadhya's crib, that was mostly unused, for Neera preferred our daughter to sleep next to us.

The unwashed dishes in the kitchen sink.

Memories - fond ones, and the others.

+++

I had never found the illusion of comfort that stems from faith in God as convincing. I saw it as lying to myself, but when Neera left me, my cynicism left too. I wanted to try everything, even if it meant praying. But why pray? If God knows everything, is everywhere, then would *it* not know what my heart desired?

Screw logic, I thought. Let's try something new.

I walked to a temple near the flat on a fine Saturday afternoon. I was feeling exceptionally anxious and the lush greenery that I encountered during my walk comforted me. Thankfully, no one was present at the temple premises to watch me humble myself in front of a stone statue.

"Khush toh bahut hoge tum," I wanted to say, imitating Mr Bachchan's mannerism, but restrained myself.

"Hi, God," I began, with my eyes half-closed. "Long time, yeah?

Sorry about that. I got caught up in stuff, and besides, you know how I think you don't exist? So, if you're listening, and of course, if you exist, there are some things I would like to ask of you. I hope you wouldn't mind. I mean, half the world comes to you when they're in trouble, why not me? OK, here goes: Please give me the strength to endure Neera's absence. Give me wisdom, so I can become a better husband and father. Give Neera all the happiness she desires. And Aadhya, please take care of her. I swear if you give them both back to me, I'll be a better person. I'll never hurt Neera. I will spend more time with them. You're probably laughing right now, aren't you? Well, that's fair. Laugh all you want, but please, give me what I ask of you."

I opened my eyes and the statue of Shiva did not acknowledge me. He was angry with me, or busy, perhaps, attending to matters that actually demanded his attention.

Before I left the temple, I did not forget to make a donation. After all, God only helps those who have the means to pay a small fee for what they want.

+++

Five weeks after Neera walked out of my life, I told my father that I was incapable of working for him. He agreed, reluctantly, and advised me to not think too much. If only I could instil this advice deep into my psyche!

Not that I gave up without a fight. I tried going to work every second day, then every third day, before I stopped altogether. My father tried to motivate me, so did my mother, and Innaya, to no avail.

"Try focussing on your work, Beta," my mother stated on a phone call to me. "It will help you take your mind off Neera. She'll be back. I am going to meet her today. I want to know why she left my son."

"Don't do that, Ma."

"I have to. I am a mother. I'll set her straight."

I only sighed.

The change in my habits was making my parents suffer as well. While I was aware of the ruin that my actions were causing to my family's life, I could not force myself to act as if nothing was wrong.

My mother called me after she visited Neera.

"She won't tell me anything. What is going on, Prachur?"

"Ma, please. Don't interfere in this."

"She told me to ask you what was wrong. She says that you did something. She won't tell me anything more. I told her she's silly and a girl shouldn't leave her home; that she's our daughter now, and Rana Ji's place is not her home anymore. But, she did not come back. I brought Aadhya along for the night."

I did not reply.

"Say something, Prachur. How absurd can you kids be! Marriage is not a joke."

"Ma, forget it."

Apparently, my avoidance of the subject made her contact Mrs Jamwal, who would come to my room and try to cheer me up. Her presence made me miserable and I spared no effort to make this clear to her. Eventually, to my utter relief, she stopped visiting me.

To add to my misery, I did not receive any reply to the request that I had made of Shiva. Neera neither called nor messaged.

Days seemed long, nights even longer.

+++

I heard my phone vibrate. I reached for it hopefully, but it was only Yukti calling me.

"Hi, Neera. I mean, Yukti..." I said. I was half asleep.

"Hello, Prachur. How're you holding up?"

"Fine."

"You did not try to call me after you told me Neera left you."

"I left you messages, Yukti. You didn't reply."

"I was angry with you."

"I know. What do you want?"

"To talk."

"I don't want to talk right now. I'll call you later," I said, before going back to sleep.

+++

Symptoms of depression do not, usually, present with an insight. I started feeling that I had nothing to look forward to; that it will never be better. Never. My future seemed dark and life seemed unending. I should have known that there was something wrong with me, but as I had had some of these thoughts since I was young, I felt they were valid. How could I know?

Now that I had the whole day to myself, the only time that I would leave the apartment would be to drive to Shimla and walk with Aadhya. Apart from that, I would mostly sit on my table, pretending to read.

Words lost their charm. Mark Twain and Charles Dickens failed to amuse me anymore. I either did not eat at all during the day or ate like a hungry bear.

I would stand looking out of the windows observing monkeys and langurs; frolicking, impervious to my situation, to my broken family. Being a sentient animal has its disadvantages. Monkeys need no purpose; they have no marital problems.

"How could Neera do this to me?" I would think often. "She left me. No, I must not lie to myself even if it makes me feel better. She didn't leave me; I lost her. I managed to destroy my own life. That is the only thing I am good at — destroying my life. I have whiled away the last twenty two years, and now I am doomed to spend the next sixty alone — if I am unlucky enough to survive that long. What will Aadhya think of me when she grows up? She'd ask her mother why we live separately, wouldn't she? Of course, she would. What if she asks me? What would I say? "Sweety, your father is a bad person." Is this what I'd have to tell her? I don't ever want to live to see that day. What is my life worth? What am I contributing to the world? I am a failed 'want-to-be' writer, who can't even keep a marriage together. What purpose do I have anyway? I have no reason to exist. If I were to die tomorrow, the world would not stop. Maybe a few people would be a little sad, but does that matter? They'll forget this 'loss' in no time. Aadhya and Neera would be better off without me. Suicide is not cowardly, is it? Life has no purpose and I have no reason to continue this charade. If I choose to end it, maybe Neera will find someone else. Maybe she'll be happier. Anyhow, how would I do it? I don't want to hang myself. That is just so cliché. If I were to cut my wrists and bleed to death, I would make a mess; that is something I would not want to do to this house. I think, taking sleeping pills is the most practical way of doing it. I can take them and slowly drift into slumber and into the abyss. Yes, that seems fine. Not that I'm thinking of doing it right now, but if I have to do it, pills seem the most gentle way. Why shouldn't I go to a chemist today and get this over with? I must list all the reasons I should live for. That seems like a good thing to do. If I failed to do so, maybe I can do it today. We need no reason to die, but we do need a reason to live, right? Yes. OK. So what do I live for? My family? If they find out what I've done, they'll lose respect for me anyway. Aadhya? It's better for a child to grow up with a loving father, but I'm horrendous at my job. It shouldn't matter to Neera and Aadhya if I were to be absent from their lives. Neera would actually become an IAS officer and they'll have plenty of money to live by — I'll be mere dead weight. Neera, she is so intelligent and such a good person! She never mentioned the reason for our break-up to anyone, just to protect me. Even if she's angry, she cares so much for me. And

I lost her. Her! I'm nothing but a stupid kid. I wish I could go back in time. I would change everything. I would never kiss Yukti. I would never mistreat Neera. How worthless am I! I must end this dreary existence. Yes, I must. I will do it soon. First I must say my goodbyes."

+++

Yukti kept calling me, but I was too irritable to talk.

"Yeah?" I said, answering one of her calls.

"Are you OK? You don't reply to my messages. You don't pick up my calls. What's up?"

"Nothing. I'm just a little busy these days."

"Yashika called me yesterday. Called me a 'bitch.'"

"What do you want me to do about that?"

"Just talking."

"I'm not really in a mood to talk."

"Prachur, you've been nothing but an ass to me over the last few weeks."

"Well, you kind of screwed me up."

"I screwed you up? I'm the one who's being called a slut for kissing my friend's husband, and you think you got 'screwed'? Piss off!"

CHAPTER XXVI

My mother had always been concerned about the well-being of her children. Therefore, when I rolled into, what she ascertained was, severe depression, she tried every trick in her book to get me back on track. I would not call her schemes 'ruses', but most of them were quite intricate.

To lift my spirits, she invited Mudit, the weekend I was visiting Shimla, to our home, without informing me. After hearing what had happened, he drove to Shimla.

"I heard that a funny guy is needed in here," he said, bursting into my room.

"Mudit! What are you doing here?" I was lying on my bed.

"I'm here to cheer you up!"

"I don't need to be 'cheered' up."

"Your mother thinks differently."

"There's nothing wrong."

"Get up, let's go out," he said, pushing me to get up.

"I don't want to go anywhere!" I shouted.

He was taken aback and after sitting with me for a while, in silence, he slowly walked to the door and said, "Sharing your worries with me will help, you know."

I did not answer, and he left me alone with my thoughts.

What was I supposed to share with him? The reason why I lost Neera? That I was contemplating suicide? How could he have helped me?

+++

When Mudit failed to make me happy, my mother tried a fresh approach.

"Prachur, can you go and post this for me?" she asked, the following morning, handing me a package. Mudit was with her. "It is for your cousin. She really likes these candies."

"Can't you do it on the way to your college?"

"No, I might get late for work. Take Mudit with you."

I sighed and took the package from her. She obviously wanted me to leave the house, no matter what the pretence. It had been a while since I had seen sunlight, ergo, I took the bait.

With no motivation, I took a shower, and headed outdoors with Mudit. Innaya's car was standing in the driveway, and in it we drove to Vikas Nagar.

People in India have a tendency to queue parallel to a counter, rather than perpendicular to it, so when no lines greeted us at the courier company's office, I felt relieved. Within a few minutes, we were free of the duty assigned by my mother.

As I headed out of the office, I turned to Mudit and asked, "Don't you have a job to go to? How come you're here?"

"I'm here for you, bro," he said.

"And your supervisor was OK with you taking a holiday?"

"I did not tell him. I would tackle that problem when I go back. Your mother called me and sounded very concerned. I couldn't believe you kept your separation from me. I hate when you hide things from me. It makes me feel like you don't trust me or care enough about me."

"Mudit, you don't need to concern yourself with my problems," I replied, irritably. "You should go back to your life."

He nodded, and muttered, "I'll go when I feel like going; maybe when I feel your condition is improving."

His reply made me feel embarrassed. I had been crude with him and he was still concerned about me. How could people be patient? Where could I learn how to be this empathetic?

When we reached the parking lot, my eyes fell upon none other than Yashika. She looked thinner than usual, and the dress she was wearing merely hung on her shoulders. Her eyes had sunken into her face. In all honesty, she looked more horrifying than ever. She was standing alongside a car which was Mr Rana's. We avoided her, and walked carefully to my car. Apparently, we were not inconspicuous enough, because I heard her call after me.

"How're you?" she asked Mudit, with her face turned away from me. "What are you doing here?"

"I'm fine. How about you?" he answered. "I am here on some business."

"Good. Neera's inside that Café," she said, looking at me.

I glanced in the direction she was pointing in, and said, plainly, "OK. That's nice."

"I want to talk to you about something, Prachur," she said, hesitatingly. "This is not a good time, because Neera's waiting for me, but if you can meet me in the evening, that would be swell."

"What could you possibly want to talk to me about?" I asked, nonchalantly.

"Just tell me if you could meet me or not."

"I can..."

"Good, come alone," she said, and turned around to walk into the Café.

"That was weird, wasn't it?" Mudit wondered, aloud.

I shrugged.

+++

In the evening, I waited half an hour sitting at a table in *the Indian*

Coffee House before she showed up.

"What would you like to have?" I droned.

"Nothing. Just coffee, maybe."

We ordered and she sat sipping before I asked, "Why are you in Shimla?"

"I came to see Neera," she replied. "She called me."

I nodded and stared at the table. Silence ensued for a while before she asked, "So, you and Neera broke up?"

"Is this why you invited me? To ask rhetorical questions? I knew coming here was a mistake."

"No. I was making conversation. Look, I know you guys split up, and I know the reason for that as well. How could you do this to her, Prachur? I always thought that you were a useless person, but I never expected you to do something like this. Terrible!"

"Yashika, please keep your opinion to yourself. I don't want to hear these things. I'm leaving, OK?"

"Run away from the truth. That's the only thing you're good at," she snapped.

"Do you have a point to make or did you invite me to tell me about my present situation?"

"I do have a point. I hate you for everything that you are, but the sad truth is that Neera loves you. Even after what you've done, she loves you. Unbelievable, right? It's true, though."

"She doesn't act like she has feelings for me. She treats me like I don't even exist."

"She's pissed off, Prachur, and you deserve that." I did not answer, and she continued, "She was happier with you. I know this much. She's so sad now, I can't even tell. Win her back."

"How?"

"I don't know. Do something yourself, for once. Anyway, I didn't come here to cry with you or to help you get her back. I was here only to tell you about Neera's state. If you want, you can change it."

"I have been trying to talk to her, but she just shuns me. There is nothing I want more than to get my family back together, but I can't change the past; there is nothing I can do now, the damage has been done."

"I've made myself clear. You might make her miserable, but she is way worse than that at the moment. Figure something out."

With these words, she got up and left me alone at the table.

+++

The chat with Yashika barely revived my spirits, and with a heavy heart I drove home and retired to my room. Barely a minute had fleeted by before Mudit walked in through the door, and offered me a cigarette.

I was half way through a Marlboro Light, when he asked me, "So, what did Yashika want?"

"Nothing special."

"You can tell me, you know."

I sighed, "She thinks that there is a glimmer of hope of me getting Neera back. She thinks Neera still loves me. I don't think so, though."

"That's great news! Get her back then. You must take your chances."

"I don't think that there's any way..."

"Stop being so negative. You love her. You told me a million times that she's your life, and now you even have a baby. Are you just going to give them up? The more you delay the more the distance between you will grow."

I knew he was right. Neera and Aadhya were everything to me. I could not possibly give them up for good just yet.

I nodded to indicate that I agreed with what he said.

I must try, I said to myself. You can always delay killing yourself.

There was no way of getting Neera back without sorting my own issues. My parents had been constantly prodding me to approach a psychologist. I had been reluctant because I knew exactly what my troubles were, and thus, I felt no need to share them with a stranger; but, as I stood staring down the valley from the balcony, with Mudit beside me, I was determined to follow a fresh approach.

I texted Ruchir and requested him to recommend a psychologist or a psychiatrist that I could visit. On receiving a reply, he and I engaged in a conversation, and during dinner, I spoke, thusly:

"Ma, Pa, I talked to Ruchir and I think I should see a doctor."

My parents looked at each other, before my mother said, "Glad to hear that, Son." She looked relieved.

"When do you want to do it?" my father asked, after swallowing a mouthful of rice and curd.

"As soon as possible. Ruchir gave me a contact and told me to visit day after tomorrow."

"Good," smiled my mother. "What would you tell the doctor?"

"I'm not going to tell you that, Ma."

"Whatever you feel is best for you, Prachur," my father interjected.

"Can I move back here?" I enquired. "The empty house at Shoghi makes me crazy."

"Of course, my Son," he replied.

"Thanks. I'll get my stuff tomorrow."

Innaya clutched my hand. Mudit looked at me and smiled.

"Let's hope the doctor can help me," I muttered, before beginning to finish my food.

+++

Two days later, I drove to Chotta Shimla to visit Dr Negi, the psychiatrist recommended by Ruchir. Innaya and Mudit were with me and while waiting outside her office in the hospital, I looked around to see other crazy people besides me. Mudit was chattering endlessly and was sniggering occasionally, and this fact made me comfortable -people obviously would think he is the one with the problem.

By and by, Dr Negi invited me into her office. It was a cold and dark room, with barely any amenities. The window overlooked another building with withering paint. I wondered how a mentally ill person was supposed to feel happy here.

She asked me to sit on a wooden stool, while she took her seat. I sat awkwardly looking around the room.

"Dr Ruchir told me that you're having some trouble," she droned.

"Yes, Ma'am. Ruchir Bhaiya thinks that I am depressed."

"OK. Tell me how you feel."

"I feel very irritable all the time. I am angry for no reason. I'm not eating much and I skip meals. And I have some thoughts of failure."

"Any suicidal thoughts?"

"No," I lied.

She nodded and enquired, "How's your personal life?"

Here I went on to tell my story to her, including the lack of purpose and the fights with Neera. Of course, I did not tell her everything, including my separation — patient–doctor confidentiality is nonexistent in India. I could not risk revealing anything to her that could possibly change my family's opinion of me.

At the end of the session, she prescribed me anti-depressants and gave me a tedious lecture on setting my priorities. It was a generic conversation, which I felt would not help me immensely. But I had hope that the medicine would certainly have some effect. Also, she told me that I was supposed to have weekly sessions with her, because apparently, I had "some deep-rooted issues."

Even though the consultation went pleasantly, overall, I could not help feel disappointed; maybe, because I was stupidly expecting her to wave a magic wand.

On reaching home, I was greeted by my ever supportive parents.

I explained to them what I had been told, omitting some of the embarrassing details.

"I will get my wife and my baby back", I resolved, in their presence

Mudit stayed for a week more. Eventually, I managed to persuade him to return to his life. He did so very reluctantly, only after I promised him that I would keep updating him about my progress.

As I slipped into bed, I ignored all the depressing thoughts and tried to imagine Neera and Aadhya back in my home. I dreamt of them that night.

CHAPTER XXVII

I was standing outside Neera's home, on a Sunday evening, gathering courage to ring the doorbell. Earlier in the day, I had called to schedule a walk with Aadhya; Neera had answered the phone and the conversation had ended abruptly, after she gave me permission to come and fetch Aadhya.

Mrs Rana opened the door and invited me in before slumping back on the living room sofa.

Soon enough, Neera arrived with Aadhya in her arms, and passed her to me.

"How're you?" I enquired.

"I'm good," she replied, apathetically. Her eyes had sunken into her face. She had been losing weight. Her hair was dishevelled, and her face appeared pale.

I took my daughter from her.

"Is there any way that you'd consider walking with me?" I asked.

"I don't think that's a good idea," she answered. "I'm kind of busy."

"OK," I sighed, and turned towards the door.

"Take a walk, Neera," Mrs Rana said. "It would be good for you. You've not left the house in a long time now."

"Mama," she began, but Mrs Rana interrupted her.

"Go," she said, sternly. "It would be good for Aadhya to see her parents together."

Neera hung her head down, and walked out of the door, indicating that I must keep up with her. No one spoke and we walked together as

I stole glances at her. I knew I had to start the dialogue.

"How's your preparation going on?" I questioned.

"Fine."

"You look beautiful." She did not reply. Silence followed before I blurted out, "I love you, Neera."

"You know what? I should just spend some time alone and go back. Is that fine with you?"

"No, please, I want to enjoy your company," I pleaded. "I won't say anything if that's what you want."

And I kept my promise for the rest of our outing. When we arrived back at her parents' home, she took Aadhya from my arms.

"It'd be fine if you took Aadhya home with you, but she needs to be fed," she stated.

"I know."

Without bidding me a warm goodbye, she walked into the house.

+++

"Yukti?" I said on the phone.

She did not say anything, but I could hear her breath.

"I'm sorry, I was an idiot. I shouldn't have treated you that way. I'm going through some personal stuff right now, and I took it out on you. You're an amazing friend. Don't hate me, please."

Silence.

I ranted on, "I know you don't want to talk. It's fine. I just wanted to apologise. Whenever you feel you want to talk to me, feel free to call. I'll be waiting."

"Bye," she replied, dryly.

+++

The following day, I was diligently at Neera's doorstep again, and she understood that my intentions were to make our outings a daily practise. Without saying a word, she walked out with me.

Change is either gradual or abrupt, the latter usually being part of fictional tales. Practically speaking, there was no way for me to show Neera in one gesture that I was a changed person; but if I met her every day and waited, I was sure that she would see that I was evolving. That was the only way for me to get my wife back - better myself for her, and let her notice.

I did not want to force her to live with me. I wanted a wife, a partner, for the rest of my life and that could only be a possibility if she were to return back happily and of her own accord.

+++

I started keeping a daily journal of our walks, and would often read them, while lying on the bed, to feel that I was making progress with her. Never before in my life had I kept a diary or a record of my days, but since I lacked substantial human interaction during my depression, pouring my heart out to a computer seemed very comforting.

JULY 3

I was at her house at six. The sun had nearly set, but the sky was not dark yet. Aadhya looked healthy and happy. Neera looked beautiful. I wanted to tell her so, but was afraid of her reaction. We walked for an hour. She wouldn't even look at me.

"I'm trying to quit smoking," I said. "And drinking as well."

She looked at me in disbelief, rolled her eyes, and said, "Yeah, sure." Her tone was ironical. Of course, she didn't believe me. She had every reason not to.

"I'm telling you the truth," I replied. "I'm not saying that I will quit. I'm trying my best. I haven't smoked since the morning."

"If you do manage to quit, it'd be good for you," she replied. She sounded disinterested.

Strangely, I slouched back home with a calm mind. Maybe I am feeling hopeful, for the first time in days. Are the anti-depressants working? Na, it's too early for that.

Also, Yukti still hasn't called me. Man, she is pissed!

+++

Neera and I walked together daily, and after about a week, time came for my second session with Dr Negi.

The appointment was scheduled for early morning. My eyes were heavy with sleep as I drove to the hospital. The clean and fresh morning air reinvigorated me by the time I reached my destination.

I was the lone patient waiting outside her office. I walked around, reading the posters on the walls detailing various mental illnesses prevalent among Indians. By and by, I heard her footsteps. I turned around, she smiled at me and gestured that I wait for a few minutes.

Eventually, she called me into her office. I went in and occupied the wooden stool.

"You need to talk to me, Prachur," she said, after a while. Her gaze was fixated on me. "I can't help you if you don't say anything. Describe what you feel. Maybe describe some event that affected you particularly since our last meeting, or even before that."

"I don't feel happy, I guess," I sighed. "I don't know how else to describe what I'm feeling. I feel my life has no purpose. I am not contented with anything. It gets worse every day."

"And why do you think you don't feel contented? Is it what you feel personally or do people around you make you feel so?" she asked.

"No, no one makes me feel like this. I feel it myself."

She nodded. "And have you explored why you feel discontented? Do you lack something in your life? Don't you like what you do for a living?"

"I have tried to find answers to these questions, ma'am. I don't know what I lack in my life. I have a supporting family, a loving wife, and all the comforts in the world. As I told you during our last session, I work for my father. It is not a job that I wanted, I had to take it, so I won't say that I like what I do for a living."

"Have you any interests - something you can pursue instead of what you're doing at the moment?"

"I enjoy writing, a little," I hesitated. "Although I understand that it is not a viable option because success in it is improbable. My main problem is that I always wonder why I should pursue anything at all! I mean, if I start writing, what good would that do? I can't change the world, or affect the universe with my actions, anyway."

"I think you're looking outward too much. Before you wonder how your actions affect the universe, and what your place in this world is, you have to ask yourself what *you* want to do."

Maybe I looked unsure of her advice, so she added, "Or you can look at it this way: You have tried one approach for the last twenty years or so, right? You say that you never felt contented. Why not try a new one now?"

I nodded and said, "I don't know - maybe I am just afraid of turning 35 and being still dependent on my parents. What if I pursue writing and I never get any commercial success? In my heart I feel that this shouldn't matter. I mean, money isn't everything; but at the end of the day, I do need to buy food, right?"

"That's a legitimate view, Prachur, but sometimes in life you must take chances. If you enjoy something - writing, for example - don't you think you'll feel more gratified by pursuing it rather than going after practicality? Your family certainly has the means to support you. Also, you're expecting everything to be a hundred per cent certain, and that is just not possible. You can't control everything. The harder you try to do so, the worse things are going to seem."

"So I should just close my eyes to reality?" I asked, lazily.

"What you see in your future is not reality. It is your speculation. You may be right or wrong; but that you'll find out only when you grow up. Learn to be patient - you cannot expect things to change in a heartbeat. Maybe you should try pursuing writing and see if you feel happier than you do right now."

I agreed, half-heartedly, and said that I would consider her advice.

The session ended soon after, but not before I got a sermon on how precious life is. Telling her about my suicidal tendencies was a mistake...

+++

JULY 12

I feel that I'm growing more comfortable with Neera during our walks, but she is still acting distant. Had some funny moments today. Would write one down to remember:

"You know what I was thinking?" I began, cheerfully. "These walks are like you and I dating again; like I'm trying to start a relationship with a woman with a kid."

She did not say anything, but her smile emboldened me.

"Let's act like that, what do you say?" I continued. "Stranger, tell me something about yourself."

"Prachur, let's not do this," she replied, drearily.

"Please, tell me - how come a girl as pretty as you is single?"

"Because some guys have no idea what they have and end up losing it," she snapped.

"One must be a moron to lose someone like you."

"Yeah, my ex-husband was. An idiot, really."

"Ex? Really? Wow! Anyway, maybe he's sorry. Have you even tried talking to him about it?"

She did not reply and our excursion ended soon. I felt happy after the walk.

I'll get her to melt.

+++

I was sitting at my laptop, typing an entry in my journal. Distant sirens, of fire engines rushing to douse a forest fire and the tapping of the keys on the keyboard were the only discernible sounds.

I got out of my chair, and looked through the window. The night was pitch dark. The moon was hidden behind the clouds and the city was asleep.

Why did I want to pursue arts? My session with Dr Negi made me ask myself.

Was it for self-contentment or recognition? If it was for the former, failure should not have made me give up what I enjoyed doing. Ever since I got the letter of rejection from *Panorama*, I had been avoiding writing.

If I was doing it for recognition, I knew it was ultimately futile, primarily owing to the bitter reality of death. What good is fame after you have been cremated?

I am not a person who enjoys burning the midnight oil, so to say. I was awake because sleep eluded me. I looked at the clock on my laptop screen. It was half past three. I rubbed my eyes, and resumed typing:

JULY 15

Thought about Dr Negi's advice. It makes sense. Maybe I should take a chance. What if I fail? Life's more about the journey, right? I enjoy writing, no doubt. If I fail, maybe I can assume that I was too far ahead for my time. Hehe. Writing does seem like the logical way for me.

As for my walk with Neera - today too, I went to her parents' house, faithfully at six. I still haven't told her that I am getting help from a shrink. Maybe I am afraid that she'll think I'm a nut job.

She was gabbier today and asked me, "Innu di told me that you're not going to work. Is that true?"

"Yeah. I stopped going some time ago," I replied. "Actually, I'm thinking of going into full-time writing."

"That's very good," she said, with an assuring gleam. "That's what you're meant to do."

I nodded and our gazes met, but she instantly broke it and asked, "Will you continue writing poetry?"

"A little, yes. But primarily, I think I'll try finishing my book."

"I am happy for you, Prachur," she said.

It was a good day.

A few minutes later, I was snugly tucked into bed. I thought about Neera and Aadhya, and went to sleep with a smile on my face.

+++

The following morning, I received a text from Yukti.

It said:

"Are you free tonight?"

"Yeah, why?" I replied, promptly.

"We could Skype...."

"Sure!"

CHAPTER XXVIII

On the 20th of July I had my third session with Dr Negi. She asked me about my personal life. I told her about Neera and my breakup.

"Can I count on your discretion?" I asked, sitting up on my chair.

"Of course, Prachur."

"Nothing leaves this room, right?"

"Nothing," she assured.

I took a deep breath, and said, "So, Neera and I have this friend Yukti, and - I won't go into details - I kissed her. When I told Neera about it, she left me. Now she lives with her parents."

"Oh, so you two are not living together anymore?" she enquired. "You never mentioned this before."

I nodded my head, slowly.

"And how do you feel about it?" she asked.

"I feel sad. I feel like I have lost my happiness. I don't blame her. She did the right thing. I don't think I deserve her."

"Do you know why you did what you did?"

I hesitated, "Honestly, I don't. It just happened. It's my mistake. I did something irrational and stupid. Maybe I was a little confused. Neera and I had been drifting apart lately, and seeing Yukti after so long..."

"What do you like about this girl, this Yukti?"

"I like how funny she is, and how carefree her life is. She is brilliant, but she is not one of those nerdy types, you know? When we were in college, she would never nag me, or impose her will on me."

Dr Negi squinted, and asked, "And, these are the qualities that you think Neera lacks?"

"Yeah, I guess. I mean Yukti and Neera are two very different people. They were quite close in college. Now they just hate each other."

She nodded. "Just out of curiosity, are you still in contact with Yukti?"

"Yes, Ma'am." I blurted before she had time to ask me a follow up question, "Neera doesn't know."

She shook her head.

"I know it's a stupid thing to do, but I don't want to lose Yukti as a friend. She's very sweet and funny."

"Prachur, this could be detrimental to your progress with Neera."

"I know. Still, I...I don't want to lose either of them."

"I think you should be honest with Neera about this."

"No! God no! After what I did, Neera won't even look at me the same way as before. If I tell her about Yukti, she'll kill me."

"You broke her trust, Prachur. Trust is very important in a relationship. She obviously feels betrayed. Rather than hiding things from her, you should be trying to win her trust back."

"I'm trying to win her trust back, but it's very difficult. We go out for walks every evening. I am trying to make her see that I am a changed person; that she can trust me, you know?"

"Do you even want to win her back?"

"Of course I do," I retorted. "Neera's very valuable to me."

"If that's the case, why did you do what you did? Maybe you just think that you want her back."

I was tongue-tied.

"Prachur, you told me that Neera and you have been together for very long. Maybe, you wanted to get out of the relationship. Maybe that's why you kissed Yukti. Have you ever thought about that? You need to figure out what *you* want. Don't go out bringing her back into your life, only to break up with her again. I want you to go home and think about this."

I ruffled my hair and sighed. "What a mess!"

"Would Neera be willing to attend sessions with me? I think couple counselling could help you both."

"Help as in, to get us back together?"

"No, Prachur. Help as in, to guide you both to figure out what you want. If you want to move on without each other, I would never tell you to continue and make each other miserable."

I nodded and muttered, "I could ask her to attend the next session."

As soon as the meeting ended, I drove back home, and collapsed on the bed.

An hour later, I got a text from Yukti.

"How's everything?" it said.

"Meh. Not good. How're things with you?"

We chatted for a while, before she asked me, "What are you going to do, Prachur? Are you going to try to get Neera back?"

"Yeah....I guess."

"You're crazy."

I did not reply and my phone buzzed again.

A text from her read, "Should I come to Shimla to meet you?"

"No."

"Why?"

I remembered her lying atop me. Felt her warm tongue, her tender lips.

"No reason. Just don't want things to get worse."

✦✦✦

JULY 21

I skipped my walk with Neera and Aadhya today, and decided

to tell Neera about my sessions with Dr Negi. I hope she agrees to accompany me there.

Also, I have been thinking about what Dr Negi said about Neera. I guess I want her back in my life. She and I had planned so many things together. Maybe I felt trapped. She decided so many things for me, for my future.

Yukti would've never done this. She would give me freedom, but Neera's the mother of my child...

JULY 22

The day was washed out with rain. All afternoon, I sat in the room, staring out of the window, hoping for the drizzle to stop. When it did, I rushed to Neera, and despite the road being turned into a swamp, she agreed to go out. Since we felt that the rain might resume, we did not take Aadhya with us.

The trees were laden with water.

"There's something I haven't told you," I said, after I gathered some courage. "I am seeing a psychiatrist on a weekly basis. She thinks I am depressed. She prescribed me anti-depressants, although I don't know if I need them so much. My walks with you are therapy enough."

"That's surprising to hear. I'm sorry."

"You messed me up," I joked, which she found inappropriate.

"Is it very bad?" she asked. "What did the doctor say?"

"Na, I'm fine. She told me that I'll be better in a few months, possibly even good as new. I just need to focus; to try to enjoy the present and redefine what satisfaction means to me. As far as the last two weeks are concerned, I am trying to get one part of my life back." She looked at me, and I continued, "Dr Negi, that's the name of the psychiatrist, feels that you and I could benefit from a few sessions — couple's therapy, you know? Would you be OK with joining me for the next session? She's a nice person. You'll like her."

Neera walked, meditating the proposal. When I was getting ready to leave for my home, after bidding Aadhya goodbye, she said, "I'll join you. But I only promise to be there for one session. If I don't like it, I won't attend anymore."

"Sure," I replied.

JULY 29

I don't know how to feel about today's session with Dr Negi. Neera was not very cheerful and when she described what she felt after my betrayal, I wanted to kill myself.

"I don't know who I can trust anymore," she cried in front of Dr Negi. "I trusted him the most in my life — more than myself, my parents. But he did something like this...he destroyed me...The worst part is that I still love him. I can't move on and I can't live like this. My life is over..."

Dr Negi looked at me without any emotions on her face, as is her job, but everything said, she's a human - she was obviously thinking what an abysmal person I was.

I couldn't do anything but apologise.

Nothing I said made Neera look at me during the session. She was either staring at Dr Negi or out of the window.

"One chance, that's all I need. I would do anything you want. I would change. I am trying. Please. Don't leave me," I sobbed but she wasn't moved.

Dr Negi asked Neera to describe her life after our separation. I had been oblivious to her state but when she described her deplorable days to Dr Negi, my eyes welled up.

She elaborated how she had not slept soundly since that fateful night, and how she had lost her drive to eat. Our daughter was the only being who gave her a reason to live. She was not studying for her exams, either.

How could I make her suffer like this? I had made a mistake, I should be the one to suffer, not her. Depression was not punishment enough. How could God be this unfair?

I should make myself suffer more, I decided during the session.

At home, I lit up a cigarette, without any intention to smoke it - I wanted to stay true to my promise to Neera. After lighting it, I put it out on my left forearm.

How very convenient for me that I prefer long-sleeve shirts to tee shirts. Hiding the burn marks is not a problem.

+++

A few days passed and I heard nothing from Neera. One morning, as I stood sipping black coffee looking out of the window of my room, I received a call from Yashika.

"What the hell, man!" she exclaimed. "I told you to get Neera back and make her happy, not get a divorce."

"Divorce? What are you talking about?" I asked, bewildered.

"Neera's giving you a divorce."

"What? No, she's not."

"Well, I'm sorry this is news for you, you dumb ass, but she is."

There was no way Neera was going to leave me. Not on paper at least, I thought.

"I have to call her," I said.

"No, don't. She'll know that I told you."

"Don't worry about it. She won't know it was you."

Before she could answer, I hung up.

+++

Neera answered my call.

"What the hell is this I am hearing about you trying to get a divorce?"

“Prachur, I don’t want to talk about this,” she droned.

“Neera, what is wrong with you? I thought you’ve been walking with me every day because you wanted to get our marriage back on track.”

“Firstly, I don’t want to talk to you about what I want to do with my life. If I feel that we should get a divorce, I would get it. Secondly, how did you come to know about this?”

“I have my sources.”

“Yeah, whatever. Anyway, it wasn’t me. My dad consulted a lawyer, to make it official.”

“Official? Make our separation official?”

“Yeah.”

“You’re OK with it?”

“I don’t know. He just talked to a lawyer. I haven’t signed anything.”

“Is he doing this of his own accord?”

“As I said, I don’t want to talk about this. I’ll do what I see fit. Bye.”

+++

“How dare he!” I was talking to myself, walking up and down the stairs. “When we wanted to marry, he didn’t support us, now he is all caring. Bloody ass-wipe! I hope he dies. Retard. I have to go and talk to him. He should know what I feel about him. He can’t just interfere in other people’s business. Tomorrow, I will go to his office and tell him to mind his own business.”

+++

“You won’t believe what Neera’s father just did,” I said calling Yukti.

She patiently heard my story, and finally said, “Well, if you and Neera can’t be together, you should get a divorce. Why be sad with each other?”

"I don't want to lose Neera. I'd die."

"Well, I'll be there for you," she laughed. "You won't die alone."

"Stop kidding around, Yukti. I will rip that idiot's head off tomorrow, when I go to his office."

"Hmmm," she said.

CHAPTER XXIX

I drove to Mr Rana's office, jumping red lights and yelling at people. Finding a space to park was a challenge, but I had a singular purpose in mind - to make Mr Rana admit that he was wrong to interfere in my marriage. I slammed the door shut, and crossed the road, without caring about the traffic.

The Secretariat in Shimla is a beautifully designed building sadly put to such deplorable use. I went in through the security without any hassles. I expected to be stopped and heavily questioned, but I was not.

The problem with government employees in India, be it a peon or a DM, is that they all think they run the whole system. "Where are you going? Whom do you want to meet? Do you have permission to see her?" they ask. None of them has time to do any work but poke their nose into other people's problems.

Having no intention to answer any of these questions, I wandered to Mr Rana's office, avoiding anybody's gaze. I asked his PA whether he was in, and when asked who I was, I told him, "His son-in-law."

The intercom buzzed and Mr Rana asked his PA to let me in. The bald man stared at me with suspecting eyes, as I walked in to his boss' office.

Mr Rana was fuming. I closed the door behind me and took a seat, without an offer.

"I knew you were a manipulative guy, but this is something I felt you'll never do. Show up at my office, tell my PA that you're my son-in-law, how could I refuse letting you in?"

"Well, Uncle, the problem is that you care about other people's opinion a lot. If you didn't, you could have sent me back."

He snarled, "What are you here for?"

"Did you go to a divorce lawyer yesterday?"

"I did."

"Who the hell do you think you are, trying to control your daughter's life?"

"She is miserable with you, you swine. I'll do what I want to. Is that all you wanted to ask?"

"What kind of a father are you, trying to break up your daughter's marriage? She has a child with me, you know that, right?"

Mr Rana snorted. "I am her father, I know what's good for her. She did not listen to me once, now look at her. She is living with her parents, crying the whole day, trying to look after a child at an age she should be studying to make something of herself. She will destroy her life with you, plain and simple. You're not good for her. Ever since you were a kid, she has compromised for you. You think you deserve her? You don't. She is far too good for you. I don't know what happened between the two of you, but I know very well that you wounded my daughter in a way that she may never recover. She did nothing but give and give. You never understood her value. Never. I couldn't believe when she told me after the results of IIT-JEE were in that she wanted to leave her seat at IIT Delhi to study with you. Stupid girl! But what could I do? She's my daughter; she is everything to me. So, I relented. Then, you two went on to give birth to that baby. Have you ever realised that you are holding her back? That you're stopping her from achieving what she really deserves? Neera's a brilliant girl. Our country needs people like her. If you ever cared about her, ever loved her, you'll let her be happy. Let her go."

As he spoke, a murderous rage overcame me. I started wondering how I could kill him and walk out of the office without raising any suspicion; but then, in a jiffy, something struck my mind and I calmed down.

I realised that his sole motive was to assure his daughter's well-being. He had no other intentions. The sad reality that I was the only bad guy in the room dawned on me. He only cared about Neera's happiness, even if it meant a separation from me. On the other hand, I was the one who hurt Neera with my actions. I said that I loved her, that I cared about her, but I made her leave me. I was the worst thing anyone could be — a hypocrite. She left her family for me, went through the pain of being a mother for me, and I, what did I do? Only betrayed her trust! Despicable!

"You want to be a better person for Neera, Prachur?" I asked myself. "You want her back? Then don't hurt people that she cares about. To grow up into an adult, you must act like one. Doesn't matter what he says, all you should care about is Neera's happiness. Neera loves him, so you must too. This is your chance to make things right. Your chance to redeem yourself!"

I sighed and ruffled my hair.

He was staring at me, waiting for me to reply.

I tried to speak, but words never left me. I cleared my throat, got up and walked to the door.

"I'm sorry for barging in like this," I said, slowly.

I drove back home, in silence.

It was over. I knew that probably I would lose Neera soon.

+++

Yashika called me in the evening and asked me about my progress with Neera. I told her about my conversation with Neera's father.

When I finished, she asked, "And you just left like that?"

"Yeah, I did."

"You're more useless than I thought. You should have at least said something."

"He was right, Yashika. I'm not good enough for Neera. I mean, what do I have in my life? I don't have a future. No purpose. Nada."

"Yeah, I agree with him on that point, but, that silly girl loves you. She won't be happy without you."

"She will be. I know her. She finds happiness in every situation. She'll be fine. Give her some time."

"No she won't be. Prachur, you don't understand what she feels for you. You're stupid. Very stupid."

I did not say anything so she queried, "It's not like you don't have anything to do. You write, don't you?"

"Yeah, but it's not like I can do that for real. I mean, full time."

"Yup, but Neera always admired your passion for it. She won't shut up about how much she loves your poems. Even these days, she still talks about them."

"She does?"

"Yup."

I smiled.

She continued, "And wasn't there some story that you used to tell about pursuing art; Something that you read? What was the name of that guy? Sene…something."

"Seneca."

"Yeah, him. What was that story again?"

"He tells of a craftsman who was asked why he bothered to work on his art, when it would reach so few people. So he replies, 'Quarter Life Crisis for me; so is one; so is none.'"

"Yup, take some lesson from that, idiot. Who cares if you can write full time? Do it whenever you have the time. Who cares how many people buy your work? Maybe no one will. Maybe some will. Maybe you'll be revered as the greatest writer of all time. Who knows? At the end, who cares? You do it because you like it, right? Only working on your art to earn money would be corrupting it, won't it? Also, since when have you started caring about what people think? You've always been this guy people thought was weird. So what does it matter if you fail?"

"Yeah..."

"You can always work for your father. You have an option to fall back on. Give yourself a chance, Prachur."

"I can try."

"'Do or do not, there is no try', wise words from a green little thing, Prachur."

"You like Star Wars? I didn't know that."

"You don't know much about me, do you? Anyway. I love Neera. You love Neera. Rana Uncle loves Neera. We all have that in common. I think we can find a way to call truce, don't you?"

"I do," I laughed.

"I have to go now. I don't have all day."

"Thanks, Yashika. You don't know what this call means to me."

"No problem," she said. "And one last thing, buck up. We all make mistakes. You'll get her back one day. Just be patient, all right?"

+++

During my college years, I had always felt that Yashika despised me; but here she was, helping me get my wife back.

All my life I had thought of Rana Uncle as a bad person, as an overprotective father; but now I saw him as someone trying to do what is right according to him. I could not hate him just because he thought me unworthy of his daughter, could I? He had every right to feel that way.

Why is everything so unpredictable? People, life — you can never be certain.

Maybe, I *was* trying to control my surroundings. Maybe, Dr Negi was right. This realisation meant that maybe, I was growing up.

Maybe, I was finally becoming an adult.

Maybe a few would be enough...

✦✦✦

We have been inculcated with so strict a definition of success that we often forget that certain things ought to be done for the sake of solace and not for mere survival - in a society lusting only for commodities - or to achieve eternal fame. Practicality is just another word for mediocrity. We should take a few chances, sometimes.

I got out of the chair that I had been occupying for a good two hours, walked to my laptop, and opened the file that contained my book.

"CHAPTER III," it said.

I took a deep breath and started typing until sleep overcame me.

✦✦✦

Mental illnesses have a stigma surrounding them. "Those who go to a psychiatrist are crazy," people believe. Not that I am excluding myself from this set; before I was designated a 'crazy' I might have held the same view.

It is funny to see people hiding their mental illnesses as if they were contagious. When I was diagnosed with depression, my parents were supportive no doubt, but they never talked about it in public. For the rest of the world, I was fit, ready to take on the world. My father would insist that I buy my medicine from an out of the way drug store. He just had my best interests in mind, so I obliged at first, but finally gave up and started buying them at our regular chemist.

Whenever I would joke and call myself a '*maansik rogi*' - a mental patient - my parents would cringe. I was never ashamed of my impediment, because for the most part, I did not choose it.

Something in my brain went haywire. What could I have done? My family did have a history of depression, my uncles on both sides had suffered from it. So, it was technically not my fault.

I sat in Dr Negi's office discussing the same with her.

"But, you're holding up well," she said.

"Yeah, I am. I have come to terms with the fact that I have gone gaga."

"Joking about it makes it easier for you to accept, doesn't it?"

"Yeah, kind of. But it's not that it is a coping mechanism or something. I have actually accepted it, in all seriousness."

"And what about your writing?"

"I am pursuing it. I have started working on the third chapter of the book that I told you I couldn't finish."

"And?"

"Wrote some three hundred words yesterday. It's not much, but you know, the first few are the hardest."

"Do you think you can feel contented with it?"

"Yeah, I think. Somehow I was thinking too much of the success part, you know? I don't know who put that notion in me. Maybe from books, or movies, I don't know. Anyway, I think I shouldn't care how many people read my book, as long as Neera does. I am hoping for no laurels, no money; neither am I sceptical of failure. I'll write, and then whatever happens, I will accept. Like a stoic would say, I am indifferent to the result. I want the 'middle station of life', the one Robinson Crusoe's father describes to him, you know? That's what I want — just a slow moving life with my wife."

CHAPTER XXX

"Neera still won't budge," I said, on a phone call with Yukti. "I called her this morning. She made it clear that she wants nothing more from me than what we have right now. At least she's not ignoring me anymore. And you know what the worst thing is? She's so enthusiastic about reading what I write, she asks about it every time we speak. I have hurt her so much, still she cares about my passion. I feel awful."

"Ah haan," she replied, without any enthusiasm.

"What?"

"Nothing."

"You sound irritated."

"I don't want to talk about her."

"Oh..."

"Does she know that you talk to me?" she enquired.

"No, of course not. I could never tell her."

She sighed and asked, "Why is that you do it then?"

"I like talking to you," I answered. "It's very difficult sharing these things with my family and Mudit."

"And can't you understand it's difficult for me to hear this?"

"Come on, Yukti. We're friends."

"What if I want more?"

"More, like what? A relationship? I am married and have a kid, remember?"

"I don't care about that. I don't think you'll be happy with Neera."

"I think I will be."

She hung up.

+++

The next day, I got a text from Neera:

"You went to my father's office?"

"I did. Like three days ago," I replied.

"My father just told me in passing. What did you talk about?"

"Nothing special. We finally agreed on something. I'm not good enough for you. Can we talk about something else? Please."

"Have you written anything?" she replied.

"Not yet. Like I told you, I am working on my book."

"Would love to read it."

"Will send it to you as soon as I finish the third chapter."

"Waiting for it :)"

"Neera, are you serious about getting a divorce?"

No reply.

Defeated, I began working on my book.

I did not care how silly the idea of the book was, or whether it would be published. I just wanted Neera to read it. I did not want her acceptance or her praise. I just wanted her to see that I was still that guy she met in the third grade.

Three hours later, I was still writing. Finally, when I finished the first draft of the third chapter, I sent it to Neera by e-mail.

I stood up, stretched, and decided to get a few stationery items.

On my way out, I met my parents. They were sitting in the living room, watching TV.

"Prachur," my father said. "Where are you headed?"

"To Kasumpati market, Papa. I need some printer cartridges and paper."

He nodded.

"Papa, I was thinking. Can I come back to work for you?"

"Of course, Prachur."

"Thanks!"

"How're things with Neera?" my mother asked.

"Good," I replied.

"Is she coming back home anytime?" she wanted to know.

"I don't know."

"I went to talk to her yesterday and see Aadhya," she said. "I told her that I was too rough with her. It wasn't fair of me, but I am your mother. She understood. What a thoughtful girl!"

"That she is, Ma."

"She looks horrible. Prachur, I don't know whose fault it was, but you need to do something. Make everything right."

"I will, Ma."

"You're young, Beta," my father articulated. "Life seemed easy to you until now, eh? Remember we're always here to help you."

"I am aware of that," I smiled.

Innaya entered the room, munching a pear. She noticed that I was talking to our parents, so of course, she felt a need to interject.

"What's up, bro?" she grinned. "Heading out to Neera's home?"

"No."

"When is my sister coming back?"

"Soon."

"Today?"

I shook my head and moved towards the door.

"Do you mind if I come with you?" she asked.

"I do mind, actually," I replied, but she followed me anyway.

"Remember the times she made you happy, Prachur," Innaya said, during our car ride. "She is a wonderful girl and most importantly, she loves you. I can't believe it, but she does. Maybe she's screwed up in the head."

"I know she loves me."

"You had a lot of fights with her..." she began.

I interrupted, "I *used* to feel she expected too much from me. She wanted me to 'make it big', you know? She still does. It's just that she doesn't understand that I don't have it in me to be as great as she wants me to be. I am not as good as she thinks I am. Back then, I think I just relented under pressure. Maybe I blamed her for everything wrong in my life. I don't know...but, that was some time ago. Now, things are different. I just want her back. I can figure out the other parts of my life with time."

Innaya started laughing.

"What?" I asked, bewildered.

"Nothing. It's a little funny. Everyone, and I mean everyone wants a person like Neera in their life: Someone who believes in you, someone who loves you, someone who stands by you, no matter what. You happen to have found what everyone desires and you couldn't see her value. I know you hated that she pushed you to work hard. After all, you *are* lazy. Tell me, what does she get by it? Nothing. All she wants is for you to reach your true potential. She believes in you. Every time I talk to her she tells me how talented she thinks you are, and how you'll do something very big in your life. Don't be stupid, dummy. Don't lose her. I don't know what the reason for your separation is. Whatever it is, fix it. Fix it before it's too late."

I nodded, and requested a hug from her.

On returning, I spent my afternoon thinking about what my parents and Innaya had said to me. No matter how many times I told myself that Neera had every right to leave me, and that I must accept her decision, I still hoped to get her back.

In the evening, just before my walk with Neera, I saw that I had got a text from her.

It said, "Loved the chapter! Want to discuss. Can't wait for our walk."

I had to be fair with Yukti. I could not keep talking to her, and lie to Neera about it. I took my phone and wrote a text to Yukti:

"Neera's my future. I love her. If you want to continue as friends, we can, but I'll have to ask Neera first."

"Good luck with her. Don't ever try to contact me."

+++

When I showed up at Neera's door for our walk, I saw Mr Rana walking around the balcony of the second floor of his house, with Aadhya. I smiled. He had to accept Aadhya, she was as cute as babies come.

When Neera and I went out for our walk, Aadhya was in my arms. Dressed in a sea green baby suit, she looked adorable. She would stare at the wide world with curious eyes, while occasionally looking at me and Neera. She had no idea how important those excursions were for her father, and I sincerely hoped that she would never find out.

Neera told me her thoughts about the chapter. She expanded on the parts she thought were funny, and gave me her suggestions. How good a man could she make out of me!

"You know what tomorrow is, right?" I enquired, when we were done talking about the story.

"Yeah," she replied, plainly.

"Do you want to go out for dinner maybe?"

"No, Prachur."

"How can you not want to go out on our anniversary? I think I have been more than a perfect partner to you!" I joked. "I deserve this."

She smiled.

"Let's go, Neera, please," I requested. "Just you and me. I swear you'll be back home by eleven. I won't keep you after your curfew."

"I don't know."

"I am not asking you to go with me to patch things up. Let's go as friends. I have accepted that we might have to end this relationship someday. Please, go out with me tomorrow."

"OK," was her answer. "But not to a romantic place."

"Yeah. There shall be no candles in the restaurant. Just the smell of rotting cow dung, I promise."

+++

The next evening, on 11 August, Neera and I drove to a restaurant on the Shimla-Chandigarh highway. It was not an expensive place but the ambiance was romantic - so technically I did not keep my promise to her. Thankfully, Neera and I had always adored the place, so she did not resist.

We sat in a well-lit room, at a wooden table draped with a white table cloth between us. I could see a chandelier behind her, which did not bother the couple sitting under it. If it were me, I would be looking up the whole night. The air was serene and the chatter was minimal. Lovers preferred this place, mostly because of its location. It overlooked a valley and during the daytime, you could see a village below, bustling with life.

I sat admiring her. Dressed in a red one piece, she looked stunning. She had got her hair straightened. I could not help but stare at her *mangalsutra*, the symbol of our bond. She had not taken it off - did that mean she still thought of herself as my wife?

"Do you want to attend one more session with Dr Negi?" I asked, sipping whiskey from my glass.

"Maybe. I am not sure. The last one made me very sad."

I nodded slowly. I wanted to approach the subject of the two of us getting back together, but it had to be done subtly.

"I know," said I. "But, I think it was good for us."

She shook her head.

"What?" I asked. "Don't you think Dr Negi can help us?"

"I don't know how she can help *us*? Maybe she can help you."

"I meant she could help resolve our issues."

"I don't think our issues can be resolved," she replied, plainly, looking away from me. "You've hurt me plenty."

"I'm sorry, Neera. I never meant to hurt you. Don't you have feelings for me anymore? Do you think there is any hope for us to be together?" She kept silent and I continued, "I get a feeling that you don't want to talk about us ever being together again - I'm not going to force you to do anything you don't want. I just want to tell you that I'm very sorry for what I did and I'm sorry for destroying our marriage. You don't need to take me back - I don't deserve you, I am aware of that. I hated to see you cry at the session with Dr Negi."

She started and I paused. I tried to meet her gaze, but to no avail. Carefully, I added, "I only want you to know that I still love you and that I always will. If you want to move on, you can. I will not interfere in your life. If you choose to end this marriage, I won't bother you after we separate. I will just try to be a better father to Aadhya."

She said nothing, but her demeanour did not abruptly change, like it used to whenever I brought up the topic of our separation during our walks. She kept looking into her glass of wine. This I took as a positive sign of a healing relationship.

"I don't think I can forgive you for what you've done, Prachur," she replied, after a while.

"You don't have to forgive me. All I ask from you is a second chance to prove that I can be a better husband. Neera, we have such a long history, with so many beautiful moments. I know I have been a jerk to you in a lot of instances during our time together, but please let me have an opportunity to show you that I am a changed man. Come home with me. You don't need to act like nothing happened between us, you can be angry with me. You can hate me. Just let me have some time to earn your love back. Please."

"I don't know," she mumbled.

"I don't like staying away from you and my daughter. Think about it, please. I won't press this matter anymore. I will respect whatever you choose to do."

"Prachur, how can I endure being in the same house with you? Looking at you will remind me of everything you did. I would feel miserable."

What was I to say to that?

"My family would appreciate if you do it, though," I suggested.

She did not answer.

"Let's talk about something else," I blurted, realising that I was losing her in the conversation. "Is it true that you're not studying for your IAS examination?"

"Yes."

"Why?"

"Why do you think?" she snapped.

"Because you're lazy," I laughed. Wrong joke at the wrong time - my speciality, indeed.

"I never imagined we would be in a situation like this ever," she said, grimly. "Things were perfect before. Maybe I should not have forced you to have a baby with me. I forced you to take up too many responsibilities."

"No, that was not the problem, Neera. I made a mistake. A big mistake, I know. It had nothing to do with your pregnancy, and everything to do with my immaturity. You were a perfect wife to me, but nevertheless I felt trapped. I could not appreciate what I had. Marrying you and having a baby were the best things I have done in my life. It doesn't matter if we never get back together, I will always cherish our past. Thanks for letting me have those moments. You were the only human being who made me love something other than myself. I really hope that you find happiness, even if that means that we lead different lives. I mean this."

"Let me ask you something," she began. "*Why* should we not get divorced?"

I was startled by her question. After struggling for a few moments to find the right words, I stammered, "To be honest, I need you. I need you more than I need anything else in this life. You and Aadhya are everything to me. Now I feel I have nothing to live for, you know."

"Those are just words, Prachur. If we actually meant anything to you, you would never have destroyed our family in the first place."

I fell silent, gulped down the remaining whiskey in my glass, and ordered another.

"Anyway, is it true, that you have 'nothing to live for'? Dr Negi mentioned something about suicidal tendencies. I heard that, even though you tried to hush her up," she said, concernedly.

I wanted to lie. I had no desire to make her come back to me, because of pity; but, after thinking for a while, I decided to be truthful to her.

"It might have been true, to a certain extent. Such thoughts are common in depression, you know?"

Her face was streaked with worry. "How could you hide this from me? How could you think like this? Did you ever think about your daughter?"

"I know those thoughts were wrong, Neera," I interrupted. "I am trying to ignore them now, and presently, I have no intention of going through anything like that."

"'Presently'? So you *were* thinking of that. Oh, Prachur!" she wailed.

"At one time, I was. I am stupid, I am sure we have established that plenty of times. The important point is that I am better now."

"But, how could you even think of something..."

"Look, you know me. You know my thoughts about life. You are aware that I deeply feel that we need a reason to live, that every day we must answer the question 'why should I not put an end to this drama today?' When we were together, I was living to spend one more day with you, but when we separated, I lost that reason. So I could not explain to myself why I must go on living, you know? I have failed as a husband, a father, and a writer. So, yes, I contemplated killing myself. And if you ask me, I have every right to choose when to end my life. But, as it turns out, I have a mental illness, and I wasn't thinking rationally - I can only see my future as a dark void, which is only half the picture. Anyway, after a few conversations with Dr Negi, I decided to give life another shot, to try my luck once more at writing. To try to get you and my baby back — that's why I am here."

She was fuming. The waiter came to our table to ask if we would like to refresh our drinks. Neera's sharp look made him walk away instantly.

"If you had done that, Prachur, I would have never forgiven you," she snapped.

"I know," I answered. My words were barely audible. I was fearful of her tone.

"No, you don't," she replied, clenching her fists. "You think you understand what you mean to me, to your family, but you don't. You never did. You are right. You are stupid, Prachur. You don't understand what love means, and that's why you did what you did with Yukti, and that's why you thought that it's OK to kill yourself!"

Her volume was ascending with every word. I looked around to see how far the other diners were. Sadly, they were very close, and I could see one grumpy looking old man staring at us, with his spoon in his mouth.

"Neera, please, can't we just enjoy our dinner?" I enquired.

"No, Prachur. I want to talk about this. Were you even going to tell me, or Innu di, or your parents before you did it, or would we have known after?"

"I did not plan..." I began, innocently, not realising that it was a rhetorical question. Do not judge me, I was out of my wits.

"You're selfish, Prachur. Very selfish." She got up and stormed out of the restaurant.

After I paid the bill, I ran after her, but not before I could say to the old gentleman in my vicinity, "You should take that spoon out of your mouth. It has been in there so long that it might melt, you know?"

+++

"Neera wait, listen to me," I ran, shouting after her. I could barely make her out, except when cars passed by. The stars were the sole witnesses to the spectacle that was about to take place.

After I caught up with her, I grasped her hand.

"Please, wait," I panted.

"What for?" she yelped. "Let me go!"

"Go where? It's so dark. Let's get back to our car, please."

"If I said 'no', would you kill yourself?" she snapped.

"No," I answered. "Neera, it's so dark out here. I'm sure that there are like five leopards watching us. I don't want to be someone else's dinner, especially when I did not get to finish mine."

"Go away, you!" she said, trying to loosen my grip on her arm.

Following a struggle, I managed to lead her back to our car. I let her go, and she stood, leaning against the bonnet.

After she calmed herself down by yelling profanities at me, and pushing me away whenever I tried to get closer to her, I drew a long breath, and decided to pour my heart out to her.

"I am a weak person, OK? I'm sorry!" I said. "I saw a little hiccup in my life and I wanted to kill myself, but now, I understand my mistake. Isn't that what's important? Look, I love you Neera. You were my life. How could you expect me to not react when you left me? I know I have a daughter and I should be more responsible, but I felt lonely. Forgive me, OK?"

"Don't ever think about it," she murmured.

"I won't. Ever. I promise."

She hugged me. We sobbed, wrapped around each other.

I spoke, after we broke our embrace, "Neera, you are my reason to live. You are the reason I wrote so many poems, you know? When we were in school, I loved how appreciative you were of them, and that's why I tried to write as many as possible, so that you'd read them and think of me as a creative and interesting person. You were the reason I studied to get into our college. You were the reason I slogged through it for four years. You are the very reason for my existence, Neera. I want to tell you this, not because I want you to come back to me, but because my heart would explode right now, if I did not say all this. I don't want your pity. I don't want you to try to fix our marriage, just because you're afraid I will kill myself. I want *you*. I need you. I am a man unworthy of you, but I *must* have you. *You*. Here look, I wrote something about this."

Frantically, I went through my phone's mailbox, and read out something I had written for her.

I began:

When you look at me,
with those big deep eyes,
My breath runs fast,
I know no one else will suffice.

I want to shower you with,
all the love that I reserve,
I strive to be better each day,
to be the man you deserve.

I hate that you are leaving,
leaving me dead inside,
I will never feel the same way,
in here only you reside.

"Prachur..." she began.

"It's not complete yet. I am working on it, you see. But, the crux of it is that I want to be a better man for you. Please come back to me, Neera."

She stared into my eyes. Her breathing was erratic, but her face was pallid. Her lips looked soft as ever. I leaned in and kissed her. She did not resist.

Finally, she shoved me away, and said, "Take me home, please. My parents' home, not yours."

+++

The following morning, Dr Negi was busy when I called her to schedule an emergency appointment, but she budged after I told her that I was feeling overly anxious.

"What happened?" she asked.

I narrated the story of how Neera and I had kissed.

"I don't know what to do now. She's not answering my calls or texts. I visited her house this morning, but she did not meet me."

"Prachur, she's obviously confused with what happened. You need to give her time. Don't go pushing her into doing something that she doesn't want."

"I am feeling so anxious. I couldn't sit still this morning. I called her five minutes after getting up. When she didn't answer my call, I got up and drove to her home."

"I can change the dosage of your medicine. What are you taking right now, 40mg? I can bump you up to 60, if you want. That should help you with your anxiety."

"Yeah, that sounds nice."

She scribbled something on my prescription.

"What exactly do you expect will come out of this, Prachur?" she enquired.

"We kissed. It had to mean something, right?"

She shrugged. "Could mean a lot of things."

"Yes, of course. What am I supposed to do?"

"Patience, Prachur. That's what you need — both in your relationship and your writing."

I nodded.

+++

AUGUST 15

Neera hasn't walked with me since the dinner on our anniversary. Today, she refused for the fourth time. I think I offended her. It was too much to ask of her to move in with me. The kiss was just a crazy idea. Why am I so impulsive?

Tomorrow, I will go to her house again and try to convince (beg) her to at least walk with me.

+++

On the sixteenth day of August, I walked to her house and again, she avoided walking with me. When I entered the living room of her house, on returning back after a walk with Aadhya, she asked me to take a seat beside her on the couch.

"Prachur, I have been thinking about what you said. I am not going to forgive you, maybe ever; but, as for your proposal of coming back, I can come to sleep over at your home tonight, with Aadhya, if you want. Just tonight. At least, your family will get to meet her. I can do this much for your family and you."

"That's perfect!" I answered, jubilantly.

"It's only a night."

"Yes, I understand. Only one night, every day."

"No," she smiled. "Just tonight." She added, "You can't sleep with me, though."

"Whatever you want, babe. Whatever! But what if I am a super good husband today? Will you consider increasing the length of your stay."

"Maybe. Maybe, I will give you another chance; but mind you, if you slip once then, I will be gone. Don't hurt me again, Prachur. I will die if you do."

"I will never do anything so horrendous again, Darling."

"Good," she mumbled.

I hugged her but she pushed me away because we heard the main door unlock and her mother walked in.

+++

My parents were ecstatic on Neera's return, and they refrained from asking any questions.

The first night that she spent with me was tough. I had to sleep on a makeshift bed on the floor, but I found solace in the fact that my wife and my daughter were in the same room as me.

Finally, morning arrived and I diligently picked up my laptop and began typing the first paragraph of a new chapter of my new book.

"Do you plan on sending the first three chapters to publishers?" she asked, brushing her hair.

"I don't know. I am not writing to get published anymore. How can I have my brainchild judged by anyone? Screw those pretentious people at *Panorama*. I can work, save money, and publish my work myself."

"I am happy for you," she said, kissing my head.

The rest of the day went peacefully with Neera engaging in her study and my parents and Innaya not letting Aadhya leave their sight for more than a few seconds.

I managed to write a few pages — a sign that my journey had

started, but there was still a long way to go. Leastways, I had the love of my life accompanying me.

A few hours later, I looked out of the window and a partially clouded evening sky greeted me. Venus had shown up and was waiting for the stars to join her.

"Would you stay another night?" I asked Neera.

"Maybe," she replied.

One more day, I rejoiced!

Though this predicament, according to Neera, was temporary, I felt that happiness was here to stay.

CHAPTER XXXI

The month of December was very harsh. There had been no snow in Shimla, and the clouds were adamant. Dr Negi's office was even colder than the first time I visited it.

On one side of the room, a heater was on.

"So Prachur, how're things with Neera?" Dr Negi asked. "I believe it has been four months since Neera started living with you. Let me remember, it had been three months on your last visit. So yeah, four months, right?"

"Yes, Ma'am. It's been five months now. I won't say that things between us have completely healed. Our relationship has not been abysmal, but neither is it hunky-dory. The very mention of Yukti's name makes things very heated, you know? Neera says many times that she hasn't forgiven me, and truly, I have to have a murky perception of reality to not see that the balance in our relationship has shifted."

"Are you living with your parents?"

"No, we shifted to our apartment in Shoghi two weeks ago. I think we need some independence."

She nodded. "What about Yukti?"

"She hasn't tried to contact me after I told her that Neera had come back to live with me. I feel that I lost a valuable friend, but at least, I didn't lose my wife. "

"We lose some things, we gain others. That's life."

"Yeah, Ma'am."

"Are you still writing regularly?"

"Yes Ma'am. I have started working with my father again, so I write in my free time. I guess I wanted to feel like I am doing something material. I am about to finish my first novel. It's in the editing phase. I am getting some people to read my draft and give their comments."

"And what, after this?"

"Well, Mudit, a close friend from college, suggested that I write a book about Neera and me. So I'll be working on a memoir, probably."

"Good, I am happy for you Prachur. You've really improved over the time I have known you. And don't you worry about Neera. Healing takes time."

"Yes, ma'am. I have time - my whole life with her. I am going to win her back someday. I just hope I don't mess things up, even more. I hope that I can be a better father, husband, brother and son. I hope to evolve. I hope..."

She smiled. "We can continue your medication for another six months and then go from there."

"I'm feeling very calm these days, Ma'am. I don't think I would ever want to get off these pills."

"Well, you'll be able to feel better without them soon. Don't you worry."

"Thank you," I added. "I wouldn't be as happy as I am today if not for you. I have a long way to go, before I feel normal, but I'm learning to be patient."

"You're welcome," she replied, before she got up to pat me on my arm.

With a calm heart, I drove back to my home to my wife and my angel.

+++

I never told Neera that I was talking to Yukti during our separation, but in my defence, she did not ask me. She will, like my other readers, find out when she reads this draft. I hope she will take it in the right spirit, although I seriously doubt that.

Mr Rana has been constantly visiting our home, and things are merry on this account. We are now a family and Neera feels contented; at least that is what she portrays.

As for my companions, Mudit is working at the same job and proving consistently to be an *average* worker. Riayat is working, happily, for his father. Pranay has been quite busy and hitherto we have not spoken to each other in the last six or seven months. Time goes on and we forget our past friends - this fact never bothered me, although Neera is upset on this account. Anyway, Yashika's behaviour has been growing amiable towards me every day, and if we continue at this pace, two or three decades from now, we might even refer to each other as "friends."

Yukti has not spoken to me since.

Before I finish, I must state that I have altered some facts of this story; reality is bland, the narrator of a story, that is founded in reality, must season it adequately.

+++

"As you sit writing this, are you contented?" the reader might ask. The answer is that I do not know.

Over time I have realised that probably I am forever doomed to search for a meaning in my life, but this fact does not imply that I cannot enjoy the journey. I might die without contributing anything substantial, but I am not God - this is enough for a mortal.

+++

THE END

Acknowledgements

I will like to express my gratitude to everyone who helped make this book a reality.

My parents for supporting me all my life.

My sister, Apra, for being my first reader, my closest friend, and a constant nag, prodding me to keep working.

Mrs Vandana Bhagra for reading and editing the drafts, and helping me shape the story.

Mrs Liji Narayan for editing the final drafts and polishing the story with her suggestions.

Pushkal Katara for taking the time to read the initial draft and give me his feedback.

Mr Sudershan Sharma for the illustrations.

Mr and Mrs Katara for their support.

Mrs Rajitha Prakash and everyone else at pblishing.com for guiding me through the publication process.

Crowd-funders

(NAMES LISTED ALPHABETICALLY)

- Akshay Ranga
- Amit Kashyap
- Apra Attri
- Avanish Rai
- Dr. K.K. Mangal
- Dr. Kiran Azad
- Dr. Shailen Guleria
- Dr. Tanuja
- Dr. Ravikanta Negi
- Esha Singh
- Harsha Aggarwal
- Ishita Thakur
- Karuna Negi
- Meenakshi Bhatia
- Mukta Choudhary
- Naina Negi
- Parul Sharma
- Parveen Bansal
- Priyanka Bhatia
- Pushkal Katara
- Rajani Kumari
- Rajeev Katara
- Rakshit Seth
- Rohan Agarwal
- Sahil Oberoi
- Suleman Zaidi
- Vikram Kirti
- Vishal Gupta

ABOUT THE AUTHOR

ANSHUK is a twenty-six year old aspiring author with a postgraduate degree in Aerospace Engineering from the Technical University of Catalonia, Spain. Inspired by the works of Mark Twain, Charles Dickens, George Eliot, George Orwell, and Seneca, he hopes to find his place in the world of literature as a professional writer.